PRAISE FOR
IN THE SERPENT'S COILS BY TIFFANY TRENT

"A luscious read."

—Shannon Hale,
author of Newbery Honor Book, *Princess Academy*

"*In the Serpent's Coils* is a moody, atmospheric story, full of ghosts and dark imagery, magic and mystery, which will keep readers guessing right up until the last page."

—**Realms of Fantasy**

"Spooky and compelling, *In the Serpent's Coils* feels both authentic and surreal. At turns dark, inventive, and exciting, it's definitely the start of an exceptional series."

—**Cherie Priest, author of *Four and Twenty Blackbirds***

"*In the Serpent's Coils* is a rich, earthy, engrossing novel that heralds Tiffany Trent as one of the best dark fantasy writers of our time. I was completely mesmerized by her tale, and deeply gratified in the end. Bravo!"

—**David Farland,
The New York Times best-selling fantasy author**

"Seriously, you look up from the novel and expect to see fog around your ankles and a taloned hand reaching for your neck . . ."
—**Sarah Beth Durst, author of *Into the Wild***

"Equal parts spine-tingling and intoxicating, this is one historical fantasy I can't wait to reread."
—**Jennifer Lynn Barnes, author of *Golden* and *Tattoo***

"Fueled by mystery, fantasy, history, faeries and fear, *In the Serpent's Coils* catches its audience with the perfect blend of magic and realism."

—**Lisa Oldoski, young adult librarian**

In the Serpent's Coils

By Venom's Sweet Sting

Between Golden Jaws
March 2008

Maiden of the Wolf
May 2008

Queen of the Masquerade
August 2008

Oracle of the Morrigan
November 2008

The Marsh King's Daughter
March 2009

Snake Dancer
May 2009

Redemption
November 2009

Ouroborus Undone
Spring 2010

HALLOWMERE™

Volume Two

By Venom's sweet Sting

TIFFANY TRENT

MIRRORSTONE™

Hallowmere™
By Venom's Sweet Sting

©2007 Wizards of the Coast, Inc.

Cover design by Trish Yochum
Cover Art © Jörg Steffens/zefa/image100/Corbis
First Printing: December 2007

Library of Congress Cataloging-in-Publication Data

Trent, Tiffany, 1973-
    By venom's sweet sting / Tiffany Trent.
        p. cm. -- (Hallowmere ; v. 2)
    "Mirrorstone."
    Summary: In 1866, after her boarding school is destroyed, Corrine and two of her classmates travel to Scotland to retrieve the stolen rathstone from the Unhallowed, but when tensions arise among the girls, Corrine is uncertain in whom to put her trust.
    ISBN 978-0-7869-4230-5
    [1. Magic--Fiction. 2. Fairies--Fiction. 3. Orphans--Fiction. 4. Scotland--History--19th century--Fiction. 5. Fantasy.] I. Title.
    PZ7.T314By 2007
    [Fic]--dc22

                                                                              2007022002

---

9 8 7 6 5 4 3 2 1

ISBN: 978-0-7869-4230-5
620-95863740-001-EN

U.S., CANADA
ASIA, PACIFIC, & LATIN AMERICA
Wizards of the Coast, Inc.
P.O. Box 707
Renton, WA 98057-0707
+1-800-324-6496

EUROPEAN HEADQUARTERS
Hasbro UK Ltd
Caswell Way
Newport, Gwent NP9 0YH
GREAT BRITAIN
Save this address for your records.

Visit our Web site at www.mirrorstonebooks.com

To my bonnie Scottish lasses —

*Tiger, Cally, Amber, Amanda, Gail,
and Felix*

PROLOGUE

May 1373

My Dearest Brother:

It has been long since your last letter. We hope for news of you, but perhaps at this moment, that is too much to expect. We know you will hunt down the witch and this time, perhaps, with the help of our Friend and the Father, you will succeed.

At your suggestion, we have sent Mary Rose away to London. We hope, as you do, that she will not be followed there, that she will continue to grow in her love of the Church and prosper in the eyes of God. We have continued to keep her parentage from her, though as you warned, she often resists our attempts to quell her. Her tongue exceeds her prudence at times, but the binding on her holds true. She will never know herself, and in her ignorance, may she find the peace that eludes those of us who serve our dear Friend.

Yours in Hope,
Gregorius

ONE

Christmas Eve, 1865

CORRINE LISTENED BY THE NEWEL POST AS THE VOICES upstairs rose and fell—Miss Brown and Uncle William were arguing. Since they'd arrived at Uncle William's estate two days earlier, the tension between the adults had mounted like an afternoon thunderstorm. Before it had all been furious whispers, intimations, glares behind napkins. But today, the storm broke. Father Joe had gone out on an errand and all the servants were occupied with the Christmas Eve supper in the kitchen. No one would catch Corrine eavesdropping.

"Come, Corrine," Christina called, "the popcorn is finally ready and Mara has brought the cranberries. It's time to decorate the tree!"

Ilona grabbed Corrine's arm and tried to tug her into the drawing room, but Corrine resisted. "No, we need to find out what they're talking about."

Ilona released Corrine's arm and grinned. "She's right, Christina. Besides, it should be more fun to listen in. Maybe we'll figure out more of what they're up to. I don't know what to do with all those fruits and nuts, anyway."

Christina rolled her eyes and cast a last glance toward the parlor before allowing Corrine and Ilona to draw her along.

They crept up the stairs carefully. Corrine trailed her fingertips over the wainscoting. As they crested the landing, the voices arrowed out through the transom above Uncle William's study door.

Uncle William said, "You don't understand, Thea. If you take those girls to Scotland, you are not just endangering your reputation. You endanger their very lives! I know the destruction of Falston wasn't your fault, but you must think of the consequences!"

"What are you saying, William? That I am thoughtless? That I am not fully cognizant of the danger? Believe me, I know it all too well!"

Christina's dark eyes gleamed. She smothered a giggle behind her hand. Corrine ignored her and listened more closely.

"Then why do you persist in this course?" William asked. "Is it because *Father Joseph* says you must?"

"Do not bring him into this, William."

"Why? Because you would not have me speak scathingly of your beloved priest?"

"William!"

The three girls exchanged glances. Ilona gave Corrine a knowing wink. Before their school had been destroyed, they had wondered if the headmistress and chaplain were secretly in love.

"I'm tempted to call him in here to account for himself," Uncle William said.

"He has no accounting to do." A rustle of skirts suggested that Miss Brown had shifted her position in the room.

"He most certainly does! He has gone against the rulings of the Council time and time again. He has endangered you. He has even deliberately endangered young, helpless girls! And look at the result!" Miss Brown made a noise of protest, but Corrine's uncle, ever the relentless lawyer, continued. "I have half a mind not to allow my niece on this expedition. I am not convinced that an offensive approach is the best solution."

"But William, you can't deny her," Miss Brown said, finally managing to interject. "You know . . ."

Miss Brown lowered her voice. Corrine strained to hear. This was always how it was—they talked about her but never talked *to* her. Despite all she'd been through, they still didn't trust her enough to include her. Corrine still was forced to discover their plans for her through scraps of overheard conversation.

For a while she heard only murmurs, then: "She bears the bloodmark. You know she is the one he seeks. And you also know that you cannot protect her; my studies have shown that the women of your line are far more powerful than the men."

"But she doesn't know how to use the power!"

"All the more reason to let her be schooled!" Miss Brown said.

"And you feel you must take her to the old haunts of the Unhallowed to do it?"

"What choice is there? The entrance to the rath here is closed. Rory took Falston's rathstone with him to Scotland. We must get it back! Besides, I've already cabled Sir James," Miss Brown said. "He's sending one of his people to escort us to his estate . . ."

Behind Corrine there was a step and a breath at the top of the stairs. She and her friends turned.

"Miss Corrine, I know you girls ain't listening at your uncle's study door!" Betsy, her uncle's maid, said. Her voice was loud enough to alert Miss Brown and Uncle William that they were being spied upon.

Betsy stood with her hands on her sharp hips, daring Corrine to lie. "Now go on! Get that tree decorated!" She flapped her apron at them.

Without answering her, Corrine, Ilona, and Christina ran downstairs to Corrine's room before Uncle William could come out on the landing to shout at them for their impertinence, nearly toppling Father Joe as he came up the stairs. Christina giggled as she passed him, but Corrine glared at her feet, annoyed that they'd been caught before she understood exactly what Miss Brown was trying to say.

Ilona shut the door behind them and they all jumped into the middle of the creaky bed. They burrowed together under the down coverlet to smother their giggling, as well as to keep out the December chill.

"It is true," Christina said, her voice nearly slurring into her native French in excitement. "Miss Brown and Father Joe—"

"And your Uncle William—" Ilona interrupted.

"In a love triangle." Christina continued. "How romantic!"

Having just been the recent victim of a disastrous love triangle herself, Corrine was not so sure it sounded all that romantic. "I don't think—" she began.

But Ilona said, her voice think with her Hungarian accent, "Oh, it's plain as day. Your uncle's in love with Miss Brown!"

"Oh, yes," Corrine said, drawing the covers tighter. "I knew that, even before I came to Falston." The photograph of Miss Brown, so lovingly taken, so carefully placed on her uncle's desk, had proven that. But that wasn't the thing most at stake now.

"You did?" Christina said. She gripped Corrine's knee, redirecting her attention. "And you never told us?"

"Well . . . There were things that seemed more important."

"How did you know?" Ilona asked.

"He had her tintype on his desk. It looked like it was taken a long time ago. She was wearing a ball gown, and . . . she smiled. I think perhaps my uncle took the photograph himself."

Christina sighed. "So he has loved her for a long time secretly?"

"I suppose so," Corrine said. What had Miss Brown meant about her studies into her family line? What did she mean about the women being more powerful than the men? And why did Uncle William dismiss this?

Corrine tried not to relive the events that had brought her to this strange conversation. Two nights ago, she had explained to her friends what had really happened at Falston, inasmuch as she understood it. Somehow, she had attracted the attention of the Unhallowed Prince, who led the vampiric Unhallowed Fey. The Prince's bloody-handed Captain had followed her to Falston, where she had been tricked into believing that the Falston witches were an evil threat. The Prince and his minions had managed to convince her to steal not one, but *two* of the precious rathstones that allowed entrance into the Fey worlds. And every one of her actions had led to the destruction of Miss Brown's Falston Reformatory School for Young Ladies, the ice-rimed ruins of which they had left behind in Culpeper.

"Mon Dieu," Christina cried, "it is hot!" With the three of them, it had become stuffy under the coverlet. She fell back on the bed, throwing the blanket onto the other two, who were subsequently forced to wriggle out from under it.

Corrine emerged from the blanket to find Christina on her side, her head propped on her hand. Her sober expression was more becoming of a French diplomat's daughter than her earlier giggling. After Christina had accused her of deliberately getting their secret society into trouble at school, Corrine had worried that they'd never be friends again. But with the destruction of Falston, Christina had seen the truth—that Corrine had been a pawn in a plot that involved supernatural forces beyond any of their imaginations. Corrine was relieved that Christina trusted her now.

"But Corrine," Christina asked, "what did she mean about a bloodmark?"

"And 'she is the one he seeks,' 'she has power'? What does that mean?" Ilona asked. At Corrine's glance, Ilona combed her fingers through her hair nervously. It was slowly growing out, but was still too short in the back to put up.

Corrine sighed. "I don't know much," she said. "But if I tell you, you have to promise not to talk about it in front of them. I think they're still afraid you might say something to your parents."

Neither of them had ever expressed the least interest in betraying her or the Council's secrets to their families after the destruction of Falston, but Corrine worried that perhaps she wasn't being careful enough. Goodness knew, she hardly believed all of this herself sometimes.

"We won't," Christina whispered.

"They saw something in my eye right after I woke up—a bloodmark, they called it." Corrine continued.

Ilona peered at her left eye, the one with the misshapen pupil. "Do you mean that silver mark there?"

"Yes. It was red at first, but I noticed in the mirror yesterday that it had turned silver. Like a scar."

Ilona stared. "Mmm . . . yes, I see." Her scrutiny discomfited Corrine, so she shifted her gaze to the floral still life which hung over the bed.

"Does it give you some kind of power?" Christina asked, releasing the coverlet's pale roses.

"No," Corrine said. "At least not that I know of. Not that they'll tell me." Miss Brown had said she possessed some kind of power. But what?

"But we should expect further visits from the . . . Unhallowed?" Ilona tripped over the last word, still unfamiliar with the term.

"In all likelihood. I think, for some reason, after I gave the second rathstone to . . . to Rory,"—she could still barely bring herself to say his name—"the Council thought the Unhallowed were finished with Falston, that somehow they would leave us in peace."

"But they were wrong," Ilona said.

Corrine closed her eyes, hearing the hooves of the ghost horses as they burst through Falston's gates. Again, the three veiled women bent over her.

"Yes," she said, opening her eyes and looking at her friend. "Very wrong."

"And now it seems your uncle does not want you to go into further danger," Christina said.

Corrine prickled with surprise. Her uncle had seemed distant and angry with her much of the time she had spent recuperating from the swamp fever in his former home. She understood his manner a little better now. He guarded tremendous secrets, secrets that she was only just beginning to discover.

"Does seem that way," Corrine said. Yet, he had sent her into danger last time, knowing full well the one who followed her and what could happen if the bloody-handed Captain caught her. Had he really believed Falston's iron gates and the protection of its rathstone were that powerful?

"What will you do?" Christina asked.

"About what?"

"If he won't let you go to Scotland . . ."

Corrine thought. The Captain could follow her anywhere; the Prince knew how to visit her in her dreams. Though she had seen neither of them while awake or in her dreams since leaving Falston, she was sure the respite wouldn't last.

"What will we do without you?"

Corrine had been concerned that her friends might be separated from her after the incident at Falston, but their parents had shown no interest in having their daughters returned to them.

"Will he send us to our parents?" Ilona growled, echoing her thoughts.

Corrine shook her head. "I think he'll let me go," she said. "I think he'll let all of us go. Miss Brown will convince him, I'm certain of it."

"But will he be as able to convince her to marry him?" Ilona said.

Before Corrine could answer, a feather pillow hit her squarely across the mouth.

Later that afternoon, the girls sat together in the drawing room by the fire. The naked Christmas tree waited in the corner while Christina sat on the piano bench, threading a string of cranberries and popcorn onto a garland.

"This will never be finished in time," Ilona said, holding up its pitiful end.

Corrine cut snowflakes from paper with her sewing scissors. Ilona looked helplessly at the bowl of fruit and nuts on the table.

"We must try," Christina said. "At home . . ." Christina trailed off, biting her lip.

"What?" Corrine said. "What would you do?"

Christina looked as if she wanted to cry, but instead she ducked her head and pushed cranberries onto the string as if her life depended on it. An envelope had arrived that morning from her father and it had contained money but little else. Such coldness had hurt her more deeply than she would ever say.

"Come now," Corrine said. She dropped her snowflake and scissors and went to Christina's side. She put her hand on Christina's arm. "Tell us what your Christmas was like. I'm sure it was grand." Corrine thought of Christmases past—her old woolen stocking hanging alone by the fire, the few boughs of greenery scattered throughout the house, her mother and Nora singing, the surprise snows in Maryland . . . All probably nothing compared to the glamour Christina must have enjoyed with her family in France.

"Yes," Christina said, glancing upward. "At our Paris house, we would go to the midnight mass and come back to *Le Réveillon*. And we would have oysters and *bûche de Noël* and . . ."

Christina fell silent as Siobhan, Falston's former laundry maid, entered the drawing room with a basket of pinecones. She set them near the bowl of fruit Ilona still contemplated. "Miss Brown said as you might want these she collected too," Siobhan said. She glanced at Corrine with nervous questions in her eyes that Corrine knew would remain unspoken. Siobhan was still fragile, likelier to startle than to smile.

The sound of carriage wheels drove them to the window. Siobhan trailed a little behind them.

A young man climbed out of the carriage, looking quite the worse for wear. His dark hair stuck out from under his hat at stiff angles, and his wool suit, though serviceable, was ragged. His face was tight, careworn, as though he hadn't slept well in a good while. Corrine noticed that unlike most men, he was clean-shaven. In fact, his face almost looked as smooth as a woman's. Perhaps it meant he was young, but his ill health made him appear older, so much so that Corrine wasn't sure of his actual age.

Siobhan hissed and hurried out of the room without another word.

Corrine turned back to watch the man just as the driver handed him his valise, the only piece of luggage he seemed to possess. The man bent in a fit of coughing and spat into the bushes as the driver climbed back into his seat and clucked at the horses.

Betsy came then, opening the door before the man could even knock. Corrine shrank from the window and huddled with Ilona and Christina, watching as Betsy showed the man up the stairs toward Uncle William's study. Corrine caught a hazel glance and a wolfish half-smile before he was gone.

The girls looked at one another.

"Who was that?" Ilona mouthed.

Corrine shrugged. Uncle William had clients and colleagues who visited him all the time, though it did seem odd that one of them would come on Christmas Eve. She went to her snow-flakes, scattered in a pile across the Queen Anne table.

Not long after the girls had put the final touches on the Christmas tree, Betsy called them to supper. Gilt frames, crystal, and silverware glimmered in the lamplight and candle flames. A white horse reared in the shadows of an oil paint-ing over the teak-and-mahogany-inlaid buffet. Corrine's spine tingled as she moved toward the table.

Uncle William sat at the head with the strange man sitting close to him. Miss Brown sat on his right while Father Joe was farther down on the left. Three seats had been left for the girls. Christina was seated closest to Uncle William. Of the girls he had recently been forced to take in, Uncle William seemed to prefer the French ambassador's daughter most. Corrine wasn't surprised, though she couldn't help but feel a little jealous. She took the seat farthest from him, next to Father Joe.

The strange young man rose and bowed as the girls entered. Corrine could see that he'd changed his travel-worn suit for kilt, jacket, and tartan, though she had no idea how they had fit in his small valise.

"This is Euan MacDougal," Uncle William said, as the girls settled themselves into their chairs. "He is the gillie—the gamekeeper—for Sir James Campbell on his estates in Scotland. And a fine fencing master, so I hear."

Mr. MacDougal's lips quirked at the last comment. "Ladies." His voice was breathy and dark, with none of Rory's affected brogue. His gaze swept across them. He barely glanced at Christina as he resumed his seat. Corrine was impressed. She was accustomed to everyone—particularly men—staring at Christina.

"Did you have a fair journey, Mr. MacDougal?" Father Joe asked.

Mr. MacDougal blanched, almost as though the thought of travel nauseated him. He coughed and said, "I'm afraid I'm a bit worse for the wear, Father. I've a yenning for the old Highland soil. The high seas don't take too kindly to me."

Father Joe nodded as he settled his napkin in his lap. "I understand," he said.

Mr. MacDougal peered at him. The wolfish half-smile she'd seen earlier curved his lips. "I believe you do at that."

"We're sorry to have taken you away from your home," Miss Brown said.

A draft of cold air brushed Corrine's shoulders, like someone watching her from beyond the window.

"It's no trouble, no trouble at all. Sir James thought a bit of the sea air would do me good, cure this lung fever. Guess he didn't reckon on all the bad weather."

Miss Brown nodded, looking at him with concern.

"I am sorry to hear your school was burned down," Mr. MacDougal said to Miss Brown. "Sir James spoke of it. A great fire in the midst of winter . . ." He clucked sympathetically.

Miss Brown looked at him and smiled hesitantly. "Thank you, Mr. MacDougal." Corrine guessed what her fellow Council members thought. How much did he know? What had Sir James told him? Corrine wondered if her uncle had known Mr. MacDougal when he had known Sir James. The gamekeeper's age was impossible to tell—he could be a few years older than herself, or he could be as old as her uncle, for all Corrine could gather.

"You'll be starting a new school in Scotland then?" Mr. MacDougal asked.

Corrine couldn't exchange glances with Christina and Ilona, but out of the corner of her eye she saw their heads turn toward Uncle William.

Uncle William cleared his throat. Miss Brown lifted her chin as she looked at him. "We hope to," she said.

"We are still discussing it," Uncle William said. He locked eyes with Miss Brown.

"'Twould be a pity were you to change your mind, Mr. McPhee," Mr. MacDougal said. "We've been making the estate fit for the presence of the young ladies. And I've come a long way to escort nothing but my tartan and kilt home again."

Uncle William's expression hardened. "We shall see." His tone was disapproving. Unwilling to meet his gaze, Corrine stared at her glass of cordial, which glowed in the light like a ruby heart.

Before Uncle William could say more, Mara, Falston's other servant, arrived with the oyster stew steaming in a tureen that looked large enough to drown a small child. Tall as Mara was, her knobby arms scarcely seemed capable of bearing such weight, but she set the tureen on the table as gracefully as if it were a feather pillow. Raphael, the little boy who had helped tend Uncle William's gardens at the old house, brought a basket of freshly baked rolls. Uncle William's maid, Betsy, carried in pickled vegetables and a salver of butter.

Christina clapped her hands at the sight of the steaming tureen. "Oysters!" She exclaimed something else in French, and Uncle William smiled, inclining his head. "At least we can attempt to make the evening pleasurable for you, my dear," he said.

14

Mara ladled the stew into each bowl with an expert flick of the wrist that kept the stew from spattering across the fine linens. Corrine sniffed the milky sea-breath of stewed oysters appreciatively.

Father Joe said grace, giving special thanks for the coming miracle of Christmas. While he did so, Corrine looked around the table at Miss Brown's careful composure, Uncle William's sulking face, and Father Joe's solemn expression. Mr. MacDougal stared at his bowl, green with nausea. Oysters clearly weren't his favorite dish.

Ilona leaned out to wink at her, and Corrine grinned, but bowed her head again when Father Joe put his hand in a light warning on Corrine's arm. When grace was over, they fell to eating, and the silence between the clinking spoons and butter knives was nearly fatal. Corrine's discomfiting feeling of being watched intensified.

Finally, Corrine could stand it no more. She turned as discreetly as possible and nearly choked on an oyster as it slid down her throat. The darkness outside the window wavered, pulsing in an aortic rhythm. The lamplight tricked out eight gleaming eyes staring from atop the throbbing body. What had seemed like a mess of dead vines over the windowpane resolved into blunt, oscillating jaws. As she watched, the jaws parted and a tube emerged—a long, venom-filled saber.

"Corrine?" Uncle William said.

She whipped around, overturning her glass. As the ruby cordial spilled across the table, Mr. MacDougal caught her eye. He shook his head slightly, but whether he was affronted by her clumsiness or just amused, Corrine was unsure.

No one else seemed to notice the creature plastered against the window. Father Joe was busy fending off the tide of cordial while Miss Brown rose and came around the table, hurrying to sop it up with her napkin. Corrine stood away from her chair, drenched in scarlet. She ventured a glance back toward the window, but the thing was gone.

She searched Mr. MacDougal's expression, but his eyes were fixed on the table.

"Corrine!" Uncle William said again, exasperated.

"It's . . . I'm very sorry, sir," she said. She considered saying more about what she'd seen, but uncertain as she was of Mr. MacDougal, she decided to maintain her silence.

Uncle William humphed and opened his mouth to mete out her punishment, but Miss Brown headed him off. "Why don't you go to your room and change?" she said, steering Corrine toward the door. "You can meet us for roasted chestnuts in the parlor after."

Corrine nodded and hurried out of the dining room, too embarrassed to look at anyone. Spilling things or having something spilled on her had happened more times than she could count in the last few months. She had ruined one pinafore, and it looked like now she might have ruined her best one. Uncle William was probably tallying the cost of her clumsiness even now.

She went to her room and changed out of her sodden pinafore and dress. She shrugged into an old dress and pinafore, patting the patched pockets in disgust at the thought of having to wear it in front of Mr. MacDougal. Had he seen the creature? For a moment, she thought he had, and for an even tinier moment, she thought she'd seen alarm spark in his eyes.

But then she wasn't so sure. Who was he? It seemed that he knew something about them, but how much he was in Sir James's confidence she couldn't tell. And the others weren't freely discussing anything at the table that might seem untoward. They normally kept Council business quiet anyway, but Corrine wondered if their silence tonight was indicative of mistrust.

She considered not returning, but Mr. MacDougal had made her curious. She waited until she heard their voices in the hall moving toward the parlor. She came just behind them as they entered, skittering over to Ilona and crowding onto the sofa next to her. No one said anything about her reappearance, and Miss Brown was nowhere to be seen. Christina was already at the piano, running her hands along the keys reverently.

"Play something," Uncle William said. "A carol to lift our spirits."

Father Joe nodded as he poured chestnuts into a roasting pan.

Christina smiled and pulled out the bench. Flushing a little, she faltered into "God Rest Ye Merry Gentlemen." Mr. MacDougal took a small flute from his jacket pocket and accompanied Christina. The fire wreathed him in shadows, and the song melted into a primeval music, its melody entwined with a world of ancient trees and deep moss where the sun forever kept winter at bay. Soon, Corrine couldn't hear the piano anymore. She drowsed against Ilona's shoulder.

Father Joe rattled chestnuts in the roasting pan so loudly that she startled awake.

"Well done," Uncle William said, as the carol ended.

Christina nodded courteously while Mr. MacDougal bowed.

"Another?" Mr. MacDougal asked.

"The chestnuts are ready!" Father Joe announced, a little too loudly.

Father Joe held the hot roasting pan out in front of him like a weapon. Miss Brown appeared from the hall, flushed and holding a large mixing bowl. "I couldn't find Mara or Siobhan," she said, frowning. "This will have to do."

She set the bowl down on the coffee table while Father Joe tipped the steaming chestnuts into the bowl.

"Another carol?" Miss Brown asked. "I only heard the last from a distance."

Mr. MacDougal and Christina exchanged glances. Mr. MacDougal's hand went to his chest and he coughed slightly. Corrine took a handful of warm chestnuts and held them to her cheeks before beginning to peel them.

"Are you well enough, Mr. MacDougal?" Christina said. "Shall we try 'Silent Night'?"

He nodded. But before her hands quite touched the keys, he said, "But let's try another tune, if you don't mind. 'The Holly and the Ivy'—do you know it?" And he smiled at Corrine. Or Ilona. Corrine wasn't sure.

Christina's hands fell on the keys in the ancient tune, and the flute soon followed her. Corrine felt the same sort of lethargy creeping over her, only this time she thought she heard the hedge outside shuffling around the house in a queer sort of dance. The Christmas tree filled with living light that turned in time to the music.

The light grew until it blinded her.

Three familiar dark figures moved through the whiteness, three women veiled in black walking up a mountain of snow. They carried something between them, whether a straw man or a corpse Corrine couldn't guess. The vision swooped closer. She felt the biting wind against her cheeks, ice freezing her tongue. Then she saw the closed eyes, the brown curls obscuring the stubbly cheeks. A single drop of blood fell from her father's mouth, staining the snow red.

Corrine realized she was staring into the fire, the last notes of the carol fading from Mr. MacDougal's flute. She squeezed Ilona's hand, trying not to make another scene.

Uncle William said, "Right. Well, I believe it's time for the ladies to retire. Perhaps you gentlemen would care to join me in the study for brandy and cigars?"

Both Mr. MacDougal and Father Joe shook their heads.

"I'm fair tuckered, I am," Mr. MacDougal said, as he replaced the flute in the breast of his jacket.

"And I had best not," Father Joe said, glancing at Miss Brown,

"Off you go, then, girls," Miss Brown said.

Mr. MacDougal raised his hand to them as he bid them good night. A tarnished silver ring darkened his right ring finger. "Happy Christmas," he said.

Ilona stiffened and stepped toward the hall.

"*Joyeux Noël*," Christina said, blushing a little as Mr. MacDougal smiled at her.

Then, the three of them lit candles and scurried out of the room and down the hall.

As the girls said good night, Ilona looked at Corrine over the flicker of her candle.

"What?" Corrine asked, opening her bedroom door.

"Just . . ." In the few months Corrine had known her, Ilona had always had difficulty discussing the supernatural. It seemed to hurt her too much.

"Tell me," Corrine said.

"Just that, when Mr. MacDougal raised his hand just now, your eye—the scarred one—it flashed in response. Like lightning answering lightning."

~ Two ~

January 3, 1866

CHRISTMAS PASSED WITHOUT MUCH FANFARE AND NEW Year's even less. Corrine received a few necessary items for gifts—a new pinafore, a pen set, some new boots—from Uncle William. Christina's doting mother sent over a carved rosewood box full of items for Christina's toilette. Christina held up the ivory-handled mirror to hide her tears. Ilona got nothing except a few handkerchiefs Corrine had hurriedly embroidered for her and a scarf Christina had knitted. The dark fall of Ilona's hair had obscured her expression as she picked at the edges of the handkerchiefs on her lap. This had been Corrine's first Christmas without her parents. It was painful, but she couldn't imagine how much more painful it was to be neglected like Ilona.

Corrine thought about this again as she stirred her morning coffee at the breakfast table. She longed, as she had at Falston, for Father Joe and Miss Brown to be the parents of her make-shift sisterhood with Ilona and Christina. But as the days went by, she was more certain that this would never be so.

This morning, Miss Brown bit her lip as Uncle William joined them in his stiff black court suit. Father Joe cleared his throat as if to speak, but Uncle William held up one hand as he shook out his napkin with the other. Mr. MacDougal had gone on some errand yesterday and hadn't yet returned.

"It's no use," Uncle William said. "I've made up my mind. Corrine will stay here with me." He picked up a piece of toast and scraped a thick pad of butter across it with the butter knife.

"But . . ." Miss Brown began.

Father Joe set down his coffee cup so strongly that Corrine feared he'd broken the saucer beneath it. "That's preposterous, William! She can't stay here. You cannot protect her. All will be well if you allow me to do as I suggest."

"As you suggest? As *you* suggest?" The butter knife clattered back onto the butter tray. "Corrine," Uncle William said, "do you know what your school priest has 'suggested'?" His winged brows drew down threateningly.

"William," Miss Brown murmured. "The girls . . ."

"Confound it, Thea!" His voice rose like a gathering storm as he stood. "Into my study, then. But I haven't time for more of this. I have a case today."

Miss Brown nodded. "Ilona, Christina—please wait in your rooms until I come for you," she said. She dabbed at her mouth with her napkin and stood, offering her hand to Corrine. Christina and Ilona cast a quick backward glance as they hurried to their rooms. Miss Brown and Corrine followed the men out of the dining room and up the stairs to Uncle William's study.

Silence fell heavy as snow as they settled themselves in Uncle William's study. Corrine mourned the fried egg growing cold on her plate downstairs.

"Corrine," Miss Brown said finally, "you know we want to protect you."

Corrine nodded.

"And you know," Father Joe said, "that sometimes in order to protect you, we must do unpleasant things."

Corrine nodded again. Her glance flitted to Uncle William, who stared outside, his fingers splayed across his desk as though he were steadying himself against gale-force winds. Then, his eyes snapped back to hers.

"They want to exhume your mother," Uncle William said, before either Father Joe or Miss Brown could speak further.

"Exhume?" Corrine said.

"Dig up her grave," her uncle said.

Corrine was not sure she'd heard him properly. "Whatever for?" she asked.

"Because they have no sense of shame, no sense of propriety!" Uncle William began, but Father Joe undercut him with a sharp, quiet tone.

"To protect you. Your mother wore an iron cross, did she not?"

"Yes."

Father Joe removed his spectacles and began polishing them on his cassock, his habit when he was nervous or angry. "That cross was her only protection from the Unhallowed. If she hadn't worn it and kept it safe, it's likely she would have suffered the same torments you do, Corrine. That cross has some of the strongest magic our Council possesses. Elaphe himself was present when the abbot of the Kirk of St. Fillan forged it, and it was given to the descendants of Brighde when the abbot died. There is no other."

Corrine remembered the dark thing lurking on the dining room window on Christmas Eve. There hadn't been an opportunity to say anything about it to anyone. Up until today, Mr. MacDougal had always been around and she was still unsure of how much he knew of Council business. Perhaps now . . .

"All of this history is fascinating," Uncle William said before she could speak. "But the fact remains that you plan to dig up my sister's corpse and steal from it like a common grave robber!"

"Are you more disturbed by the commonness of the act or the act itself, William?"

Uncle William bristled.

"Joseph," Miss Brown murmured.

"You are talking about exhuming my sister!" Uncle William shouted. "I should think that would be disturbing enough!"

"William, we don't want to do this," Miss Brown said. "But if it will protect Corrine . . ."

All eyes turned to her. She dropped her gaze from Father Joe's.

"No," she said quietly.

"What did you say, Corrine?" Father Joe said. She looked up and felt the unnerving power she always felt around him.

"No," she said. "It simply can't be done."

"But, Corrine," Miss Brown said, shifting forward on the divan where she sat. Her skirts whispered against the brocade. "The cross is very powerful. It could be the only thing that will truly keep you safe in Scotland. We know the Prince is very strong now, more than he has been in centuries. It would be a shame not to use this resource against him."

"My mother's body is not a resource!" Corrine said. "If you take the cross and give it to me, I will throw it into the bottom of the ocean, so help me God." Her words rang with an authority she didn't quite feel.

Father Joe stared at her. "An oath has been sworn," he said. "By the Law of Elaphe, we can do nothing to alter it."

Uncle William relaxed ever so slightly against his desk. He sighed and said, "Corrine, you really don't have to go. You may stay here with me, if you wish."

The offer surprised her, but the tiredness in his voice didn't.

It mortified her that after all that had happened, after all the secrets and lies, her uncle still saw her only as a burden, a painful reminder of the sister he had lost.

"No, Uncle William. I'll go." She looked at Father Joe and Miss Brown. "There are things I need to set right."

A rapid knock came before the door opened. Mr. MacDougal stepped in, his face glowing as though he'd been in a sharp wind. And though he wore the same suit he'd arrived in, he wasn't the faded man who'd stepped out of the coach on Christmas Eve. He stood taller, his frame muscular and alluring. He was so handsome in that instant that Corrine's face burned and she looked away.

"Yes, what?" Uncle William said. "Clearly, a door is no use in this house."

Mr. MacDougal's wolfish grin appeared briefly as he sauntered across the room, pulled a packet of papers from his coat pocket, and laid them on the divan beside Miss Brown.

"Tickets for your Atlantic passage," he said. "Sir James sends them with his compliments." He bowed slightly and a faint blush spread across Miss Brown's cheeks.

"Well," Uncle William said, looking down and straightening the already neat piles of paper on his desk. "It appears the matter is settled." Corrine noticed that the only remaining framed portrait was the damaged one of her mother. The tintype of Miss Brown in her ball finery was nowhere to be seen.

"Yes, sir," Mr. MacDougal said. "We shouldn't delay getting down to the docks. There's word of closing the European shipping lanes soon. Heavy weather brewing in the North Atlantic. The *Great Eastern* may be the last passenger ship to leave for a good long while."

Uncle William nodded, but Corrine guessed he felt that his hand was being forced. "Thea, I trust you have the preparations in hand?"

"Yes, William," Miss Brown said. Her tone was sad, as though what she wanted to say would remain forever unspoken.

"Good. Then I'll leave you to it," William said. He left without saying good-bye, refusing to look at Father Joe.

Mr. MacDougal leaned against a library shelf, idly touching the spines of the books. Corrine would almost have sworn they leaned into his fingertips, as if longing for his caress.

"When should we be ready to leave, Mr. MacDougal?" Father Joe said.

"As soon as ever you may. The seas only grow rougher with time," Mr. MacDougal said. He avoided Corrine's eyes. She thought again of the dark thing at the window and how she was fairly certain that he had seen it.

Then he left. The books and room faded again into stillness.

"Well," Father Joe said. He looked a little like a dog startled from a dream.

"I'll have Mara and Siobhan begin preparations," Miss Brown said, rising from the divan. "Ilona and Christina will go with me to the market for any necessities for the journey. Corrine, please stay here and work with Father Joe. There is Council business for you to attend to."

Corrine nodded. She tried to pretend that she was disappointed, but she didn't much care for shopping. Christina would be drawn to the dress boutiques; Corrine pictured how she would hold the silk dresses against her creamy skin, silently protesting the injustices of her banishment from fashionable society. For herself, Corrine knew her plain features couldn't be much improved by a bonnet or a silk pelisse, so such things seldom interested her.

Miss Brown rose from the divan.

"Thea," Father Joe said.

But Miss Brown shook her head, her lips pressed firmly together. Whatever was between them would have to wait. Then, with a whisper of skirts, she too was gone.

Father Joe turned to Corrine, but not quickly enough to hide his desolate expression. Corrine realized for the first time how terribly lonely he must be. As she had often thought at Falston, she was sure that he was much more than a priest with a deep interest in the occult.

Father Joe ran through the trees, a young man dressed in rags. A silver bell sang on a silver collar as he ran.

"Where are you, my pet?" a voice said. It was a woman's voice—rich and generous, full of liquor and honey.

He kept running, and the moon white hounds coursed on his heels. Then, she was there, the amber-eyed witch astride her demon horse. Muscle and sinew gleamed through transparent flesh under her thorn-spurred heels.

"You cannot run from me forever!"

"Corrine!"

Corrine shook the vision from her eyes. Father Joe was standing over her, his eyes full of thunder.

"I was speaking to you," he said.

"I'm sorry, Father."

"We need you to work on copying these letters. These are the only other copies we have, since those at Falston were destroyed."

Corrine nodded. He settled her at the desk, showing her the packet of letters, ink, nibs, a blank journal. The stained portrait of her mother sulked at her from its corner.

"You needn't copy the originals," he said. "Just the translation." He touched the edges of the packet as though giving them a benediction.

Corrine swallowed and stared at the letters. "Miss de Mornay said my penmanship wasn't very good," she said in a small voice. She remembered the day Miss de Mornay had locked her in Falston's library, the way she had looked askance at the essay Corrine had written with her spell-blistered hand. She tried not to see the teacher shatter again into glittering ice fragments at the school gates.

Father Joe put his hand on her arm and the memory dissipated. "It will be fine, Corrine. You needn't worry. Now, I must leave you."

He was almost to the door before she could bring herself to ask, "Father, do the Unhallowed have spies?"

"Spies?" He stalked back to the desk. "What have you seen?"

She described the dark thing over the window on Christmas Eve.

"From your description, I'd hazard you saw a daoi. Shadowbeings the Unhallowed once used to spy on mortals until their power was broken by Elaphe. They haven't been able to use them until now."

Corrine could hear echoes of his thoughts. *Until they were given so many rathstones.*

"Your uncle should set better wards. All will be well, Corrine. We'll leave soon. Sir James guards much of the Council's magic. He should keep us safe there."

Corrine nodded.

"In the meantime, if you see anything else like this, anything strange at all, inform me immediately. It's too late to set wards now, but Mara might have been able to do something, had she known."

"Yes, Father." Corrine looked down at the blank journal.

"We must begin your training, as well," Father Joe said. "We cannot always rely on Mara."

"My training?" Corrine blanched. When all this had started, all she had wanted was for it to end, to be able to go back to the life she knew. Going to Scotland and trying to face the

Unhallowed was frightening enough without learning their magic too.

"You've sworn a vow against the one thing that would have protected you—your mother's iron cross. The only alternative left is to learn the magic and use it to defend yourself. Otherwise . . ."

"Otherwise?"

"You will fall victim to the schemes of the Unhallowed." Father Joe went to the window and looked out as nonchalantly as if he were giving a history lesson. "They'll begin in small ways—give you something you admire, bargain for things you are impatient to possess. They'll enter your dreams and whisper things into your mind—images, hopes, fears. They may even steal your possessions and use them to control you." He turned from the window and looked at her pointedly, as if to remind her that much of this had already happened.

"And then?" she prompted.

He turned from the window. "You are theirs. Body and soul. To do their bidding. To be their feast."

His voice cracked on the last word, and Corrine saw him again, running through the forest with the silver collar around his neck. She could only guess at what he had endured at the hands of the Unhallowed, and she wasn't sure she wanted to know more. But she also knew that she didn't want to become like him—forever hiding from shadows in the dark, forever alone, forever fighting a war it seemed he couldn't win.

"I don't . . ."

"Don't swear!" he said, holding his hands out in a warding gesture. "If you bind yourself against the magic, there is no chance at all. No chance at all, do you understand?"

Corrine nodded.

He came to her and knelt near her chair, taking her hands in his. Her palms vibrated with the undercurrent of power.

"Tell me what you fear, Corrine. We will help you in any way we can."

Becoming like you, being alone. She couldn't say it. "If I learn all this, will I still be able to have an ordinary life?"

"An ordinary life?"

She blushed. "A . . . a husband and children and . . . and horses." She felt like a five year old. She thought of her mother—always startling at shadows, always hiding secret sorrows. Had this all been the reason? Had she been worried that even the iron cross couldn't protect her or her daughter?

Father Joe sighed and clasped her hands even more tightly. "I pray that you will, Corrine. I shall do all I can to make it so."

Not as comforting as she'd hoped, but it was a start. She took a deep breath. "All right, then."

Father Joe released her hands and stood. "Good girl," he said. "We'll start on the ship, if we can. For now, just try to begin noticing your breath. Notice what it feels like as it moves in and out of your body. Try to hold it for five counts in and five out. Try to let your thoughts flow away on your breath. Magic originates with intention. And intention can only be developed through the power of concentration. Try to develop that quality in all you do. Let's try it once or twice right now to get the idea."

Corrine nodded and tried to do as he asked, breathing slowly for five counts in and five counts out.

"Good, good," Father Joe said. "You're concentrating just on your breath, right?"

Corrine nodded again, her eyes closed, her mind actually racing with all the unanswered questions she knew Father Joe would only sigh over and polish his spectacles.

"For now, just focus on your breath. And work on copying

these letters into the journal." He laid his hand on her shoulder briefly before he left.

Corrine inhaled the smell of books and newly polished wood. She held it there and counted to five one last time as she exhaled, opening her eyes. She flipped ahead to a letter she'd never read before, thinking about her breath and hoping Father Joe was right.

[Trans. note: estimated early August 1357.]

To Sister Brighde, Isle of the Female Saints, from Brother Angus, Kirk of St. Fillan, greetings.

My beloved—

I am torn in my soul for you, who have gone into the silence where I cannot follow. I write these words and wait, hoping that you will not secrete yourself from me forever, that the duty you give now to Christ will not somehow lessen that which you owe me.

What you saw at Midsummer frightened you. The courier tells me that you distrust me, that you will not receive my letters. Perhaps you go into the silence hoping you can escape him. Perhaps you hope to escape thoughts of me. But there is no escape from what is between us now. Even if you left the Isle and went to another convent, I would still find you. We are one. Before you fled that night, you pledged yourself to me. Nothing now can break that pledge.

The Fey were witness to this oath, and they will enforce it. Do not suffer needlessly, my love. All will be resolved if you will come to me by All Hallow's Eve. You need fear nothing, if you can but do this small thing.

Yours Eternally,
Angus

Weak afternoon light crept across the window. The house and the winter wind spoke fretfully in the gloom, while Corrine's pen scratched across the parchment. Many of the letters were those she'd already read in Falston. They had been hidden everywhere, remnants of a darker, older story, wherein the Unhallowed had used the illicit love affair between a monk and nun to further their plot against mortals. She sighed as she set down the last letter she remembered reading before leaving Falston, a letter in which Angus begs Brighde to cast aside her life of devotion to God and join him in devotion to the Fey. Her hands ached. The distant sounds of servants clattering around for afternoon tea drifted up the stairs. She stood and went to the window, rubbing her ink-stained fingers in a vain attempt to disperse the black patches on her skin.

Below her, Alexandria's shipping port nestled in the curve of the great Potomac River. Her uncle had said that the port was not as prosperous as it had been before the War, and that most large shipping and passenger liners now docked miles away in

Baltimore. A building she guessed had once been the old slave market was empty and disheveled, its courtyards occupied by tinkers and peddlers. But carriages and people bustled up and down the streets, busy with making New Year's calls. Corrine watched a young lady with golden curls on the arm of a well-dressed gentleman with a pinprick of envy. She could only long for such freedom to walk in the twilight, unencumbered by the danger of the Unhallowed.

She felt him before she saw him—the dreaded Captain who had followed her from her uncle's old home north of Washington D.C. down to Falston in Culpeper. The Captain who had taken so many girls from Falston, kidnapped them for the Unhallowed. And now he was here in Alexandria. He stood on the street, his dark cloak shedding shadows as he raised his hand in greeting to her. The failing sun darkened his blood-stained palm to black. Corrine's knees quivered and nausea clenched her stomach. People moved around him as though he didn't exist. They couldn't see him, couldn't feel the danger that shivered all around them, that struck her in the gut as palpably as a fist.

She had hoped with the destruction of Falston that the Captain would leave her in peace. But here he was. She had hoped in vain. And there was no mother now to protect her, no ghost with her iron cross standing between Corrine and what waited outside. She snapped the heavy drape shut over the window.

The front door opened and voices ascended the stairs. She turned just in time to see Christina and Ilona tumble through the study door. Miss Brown trailed in with a frown that would have scalded a cat.

"Corrine, Corrine!" Christina bustled up to her, roses blooming in her cheeks from the winter wind. "You cannot guess who we saw!"

Corrine slipped her hand in her pinafore, seeking the cover of the serpent-bound book for reassurance. It shrank a little, like the rathstones had, as though it knew it should hide.

"Who?" Corrine asked, though she was sure she already knew. If she had seen the Captain, other bad news couldn't be far behind.

"Guess," Christina said, her brunette curls bouncing about her shoulders.

Corrine thought of several possibilities, but the one she thought of most stuck in her mouth. *Rory.*

She looked at Miss Brown, who arranged her shawl over her shoulders, still frowning.

"I don't know," Corrine said finally. "Tell me."

Ilona pushed her hair behind her ears, and the dark gleam in her eyes made Corrine sure her deepest fear was true.

"Melanie," Ilona said.

THREE

January 3, 1866

"ALL RIGHT, GIRLS, TIME TO PACK YOUR THINGS," MISS Brown said. "We'll leave before dawn tomorrow. And send Mara up here, if you see her."

Father Joe came into the study just as Corrine and her friends left. Worried murmurs trailed her as she wandered down the stairs.

Of all the people Corrine had hoped would stay gone, Melanie Smith, her nemesis at Falston, ran a close second to the Captain. From her first day at Falston until Melanie's disappearance, the former Southern belle had taunted, pinched, and otherwise harassed Corrine unmercifully. Melanie, along with Miss de Mornay, had served the Captain in the Unhallowed plot to destroy Falston. Melanie had vowed revenge on Corrine just before her disappearance, but Corrine had hoped that her vision—a vision in which Melanie was chased by ghost hounds—had meant that Melanie would meet her fate at the hands of her Unhallowed allies.

And now Christina, Ilona, and Miss Brown had seen her wandering the markets of Alexandria. Just after Corrine had seen the Captain.

"What did she look like?" Corrine asked as they all piled

into her room. Mara was busy packing folded laundry into Corrine's new carpetbag. "Miss Brown wants you," Corrine said to Mara. "They saw Melanie in the market."

Mara nodded, her eyes narrowing, and hurried from the room.

"She looked quite well-off, actually," Christina said. "She was wearing a peacock blue silk dress, with a splendid lace shawl. Even her shoes matched! And she was on the arm of a wealthy-looking gentleman."

"Did she recognize you at all? Did she say anything?"

Christina shook her head. "I don't know if she saw us. Miss Brown whisked us away as soon as Ilona spotted her."

Corrine nodded. "It's good you didn't speak to her. She's very dangerous." Corrine told them about how Melanie had aligned herself with the Unhallowed and had sworn revenge against her for wrecking her plans. Then she said, "I saw the Captain just before you returned. I'm glad we're leaving tomorrow." She just hoped the Captain would leave them alone through the night. But she didn't want to say it out loud.

Ilona and Christina went quiet. Neither of them had ever seen him. There had been a time when they hadn't wanted to believe her. They were still dubious, but ever since they'd experienced the Unhallowed attack on Falston, Ilona and Christina were much more easily convinced.

"What did he do?" Ilona asked.

"Nothing." Corrine finished stuffing the laundry in her carpetbag. "He just wants me to know that he's here, that he's come for me. Or one of you."

"No," Ilona said. "He won't have us." Her dark eyes shimmered. "Any of us."

"Remember who we are," Christina said. She held her hand out, urging Ilona and Corrine to do likewise.

"Victory, memory, hope, perseverance." Their old Society motto at Falston.

Ilona and Corrine joined her in the last lines. "We shall never forget. We shall never forgive. We shall prosper."

Such small hope, she thought. She knew how much danger they were going into, how fruitless their attempts had been to find Rory, who had taken Falston's rathstone from her. She couldn't help but wonder what had become of him, if the curse Mara had set on him had worked. She feared how strong the Prince's hold would be in his homeland; she feared things she couldn't even begin to imagine. But she had to believe there was hope. She had to believe there was some worth in trying to right the mistakes she had made at Falston.

"Yes," she said, as she released their hands. "Yes, we must believe it."

January 4, 1866

The early morning came far too quickly. Corrine had spent a mostly sleepless night, watching for shadows outside her curtained window. She guessed that everyone else had shared the experience; Mara had probably been up all night keeping the Unhallowed at bay with her dark magic.

"Corrine!" Miss Brown called and knocked before she opened the door. "The carriages are here!" Miss Brown wore a handsome new traveling suit, a burgundy wool three-tiered skirt and matching close-fitting jacket over a black lace chemisette. Even her bonnet matched, trimmed in burgundy and black lace. The headmistress pulled on black kid gloves as she stood in the doorway.

Corrine felt utterly plain beside her. She was surprised when Miss Brown blushed.

"A last gift from your uncle," Miss Brown said, gesturing at the dress.

"It's lovely, Miss Brown," Corrine said.

"Come now," Miss Brown said. "Gather what you need and let's be off."

Corrine surveyed everything quickly, but was certain she had all that she needed until they were onboard the ship. Mr. MacDougal and the driver came after her carpetbag. Mr. Mac-Dougal nodded at her as they passed, his gaze lingering only a moment.

The walls of Uncle William's house melted, replaced by a dim hall, an empty throne eclipsed by golden rain . . .

Miss Brown gripped her arm and steered her toward the door.

As Corrine stepped outside, the cold pressed against her like a wolf with bared teeth, the predawn light only barely peeking above the horizon. She remembered leaving her uncle's former house just months ago. The rain and thunder then had been nothing compared to his disapproval and the fear of the red-handed man following her. Now, the danger was the same, but she hoped with friends that the journey would somehow be more bearable. Christina handed her a fur muff, then Corrine snuggled down between her and Ilona. Miss Brown covered them with a wool blanket, tucking its edges tightly around them, and then laid another rug across their knees.

"It won't do to have you catch cold," Miss Brown said, as she seated herself on the opposite bench facing the girls. Siobhan and Mara entered last. Siobhan hovered uncomfortably until Miss Brown indicated that she sit down. Mara sat straight as an iron poker, looking at some infinite point behind Corrine's head. The whites of her eyes gleamed like shells. Father Joe and Mr. MacDougal settled into the second coach.

Uncle William stood in the door of the carriage, just as he had months ago. Only this time, it was cold, not rain, that poured in around him. Corrine noticed that he avoided Miss Brown's eyes.

"Godspeed," he said, "though I cannot help but feel this venture is foolhardy. It may prove far more costly than you guess."

"We must try, William," Miss Brown said.

He didn't answer her directly. Instead, his brows drew down over his hard eyes, and he said to Corrine, "Be careful! You're flying straight from the frying pan into the fire, as far as I'm concerned. The Prince will be stronger on his native soil and you have very little protection. Don't give in to him as easily as you did here."

Corrine swallowed and looked down. No one had said an incriminating word against her, but she had to admit that she often felt the sting of their rebuking glances, particularly Mara's.

"I'll be careful," she said.

Uncle William nodded, and his swift, dark glance encompassed them all. "Then I wish you good fortune. May Elaphe protect you," he said, glancing at Miss Brown.

"Good-bye, Uncle," Corrine said. She felt a strange little tug in her heart for him, living alone, always left behind to keep up appearances.

"*Au revoir,*" Christina said softly. Corrine felt Ilona nod on her other side.

Uncle William stepped down from the carriage, and the inside of the coach plunged into cold gloom as the coach lurched forward.

Several roadhouses, two carriage changes, and thirteen hours later, the coaches entered Baltimore. Corrine looked out through the swaying window flaps, her eyelids stiff from hours of vainly chasing sleep. She started. The city was on fire, the tall flames leaping like dancers from building to building.

"Ilona!" She nudged the Hungarian girl awake, who grumbled at her and uncurled her hands from under her chin, wrists snapping.

"Look outside!" Corrine said. The fire was so loud she almost couldn't hear herself speak, and yet . . . there was no smell of burning or smoke.

"What? Why?" Ilona pushed the leather flap out to see.

There was nothing but twilight—a weak, red sun disappearing beyond the roofs of row houses. Corrine sat back, perplexed.

Ilona frowned at her and dropped the flap. She curled her hands under her chin again and leaned against the side of the carriage without speaking further.

"A vision?" Miss Brown said. Next to her, Siobhan looked at her sidelong, but didn't say anything.

"The city was in flames," Corrine said.

"They're coming more often, aren't they?" Miss Brown said.

Corrine nodded, digging her fingers deeper into the fur.

"Father Joe talked to you?"

Corrine nodded again.

Miss Brown leaned forward. "You will learn, won't you? You foreswore the iron cross. The only thing left is to allow Father Joe to train you. Otherwise . . ." Miss Brown shook her head.

Unbidden, Mara spoke. "You belong to them," she said. Her eyes shifted to Corrine, cold and dark as always. "Their slave. Forever."

Corrine didn't say anything. She was afraid of magic, afraid of the disastrous mistakes she might make because of it. But she was willing to try. Miss Brown still sought her expression in the gloom. Corrine wondered why she cared so deeply. What was her stake in all of this? How did she become involved in the Council? She had no magic that Corrine knew of. Or did she?

To reassure her, Corrine said, "I'll try."

She thought suddenly of Madame DuBois, her former French teacher and a member of the Council of Elaphe. She had left for the holiday before Falston's destruction, but she had often hinted that Corrine was more important than she could possibly guess. Where was Madame DuBois now? And what business did she have with the Council? Despite being its newest member, Corrine felt she didn't know nearly enough about the Council, much less her role in it.

The carriages finally rolled to the docks. The women's carriage driver climbed down and shouted to someone to come unload their bags. Father Joe opened the door, looking surprisingly spry for having ridden nearly fourteen hours in a carriage.

He helped Miss Brown and the girls stumble out into the twilight. The chill leached color from everything; even the sooty pigeons that waddled along the docks seemed snowy-white.

Corrine had never seen more than the paddle steamers that sometimes churned up the Elk River in Maryland. The *Great Eastern* was so long that Corrine couldn't make its name out on the hull; it seemed to go on forever, a self-contained city too vast for the dock to hold. It hugged its paddle wheels to its sides like folded wings. Its six masts obscured the sun. Steam meandered from its five stacks, gulls shrieking around them like lost souls.

"It was first called *Leviathan*," Father Joe said. "Apparently with good reason. It seems to be the ship that swallowed her maker's life."

40

"How so?" Ilona asked. Ever curious about things mechanical, she stepped closer to Father Joe.

"She was designed by Isambard Kingdom Brunel to be the largest, most luxurious ship in the world. But she suffered a few mishaps not long after she was first launched. It's rumored that one of her riveters was trapped between her iron hulls, and that his ghost caused all the mischief in revenge. Brunel himself died not long after taking his photo on her newly finished deck."

Corrine blanched. The last thing she wanted now was to be besieged by another ghost. "And we're taking this ship across the ocean?"

Father Joe glanced at her. "I understand your concern after all you encountered at Falston, but she's likely the only ship that can withstand the weather at this time of year. Mr. MacDougal vouches for her. Let us hope she's become a well-intentioned beast, unlike her Biblical counterpart."

Corrine nodded. She watched Mr. MacDougal and the dockhand carry Christina's trunk to the loading platform. He had a grim look on his face, as if he'd just been served another plate of oysters. Corrine wondered if he was put out by the thought of ocean travel or the weight of the baggage.

"Come along, girls," Miss Brown said, herding them toward the growing passenger line.

Corrine glanced at Ilona and saw that her friend was grinning practically from ear to ear. The tall girl was already in love with the mechanical monster.

Corrine stumbled as she walked up the gangway. Ilona steadied her on her left side, while Christina walked slowly on her right. Corrine looked back only for a moment, thinking of the city on fire and the *Great Eastern*'s history. A pinched, hard face looked up at her from the crowd, holding her eyes with a familiar imperious glare.

"Melanie!" Corrine said.

"Where?" Christina asked.

"There!" Corrine said, slipping her right hand out of her muff to point.

"I do not see her," Ilona said.

Melanie lifted something to her lips and smiled, then threw it toward the slit of water visible between dock and ship. The thing twinkled like ice in the sun as it fell end over end. A skinny white hand lifted out of the water to receive the trinket, then disappeared beneath the oily water.

Corrine rubbed her eyes. It occurred to her briefly that lack of sleep had perhaps weakened her brain as the swamp fever had in late summer. She scanned the growing crowd, the bit of harbor where the hand had appeared, but Melanie was gone.

"Come, Corrine," Ilona said.

Corrine hesitated for a moment longer, curling one hand around the railing. "I don't think . . ." She looked up at the ship waiting to swallow them in its toothless maw and then back to the teeming docks. "I don't think we should do this."

"What?" Ilona said.

Miss Brown, two people ahead in line, came back to them as irritated passengers swarmed around Corrine and her friends. Mr. MacDougal and Father Joe were farther ahead. Mr. MacDougal turned as though he'd heard Corrine speak. He was pale but his gaze was sharp as shattered glass.

"Is there a problem, ladies?" Miss Brown's eyelids wrinkled with lost sleep.

"It's just . . . I don't think we should go . . ." Corrine said, trailing off with lack of confidence. She swallowed against the knot rising in her throat.

"Have you seen something?" Miss Brown said.

"Melanie."

Miss Brown looked about, but the crowd surged and pushed them all forward. "I don't see her. We'll have a look when we're settled. It's the best we can do." And she gathered her skirts and forged ahead of them.

Ilona and Christina slid their arms through hers and helped Corrine onto the ship. Their sympathetic glances vanished when they stepped onto the *Great Eastern*'s slow-rolling grandeur. Corrine looked back, but Melanie was indeed gone. And the hand that had risen out of the harbor's murk was definitely nowhere to be seen.

In the second-class women's quarters, Christina, Ilona, and Siobhan settled into one cabin, while Miss Brown, Mara, and Corrine were in another. Father Joe and Mr. MacDougal were sent to the men's quarters.

Miss Brown stowed her carpetbag in the locker by the door, removing her bonnet and gloves and placing them atop her bag. Corrine stood beside the iron bunk bed, feeling awkward and trying hard to avoid the iron's cold sting. She wished she had been placed in a cabin with Christina and Ilona instead. Mara ignored them both.

"Let's all rest for a while, girls," Miss Brown said, as she shut the locker.

Mara nodded stiffly and lay down, covering herself with a wool blanket. Corrine climbed to the top bunk wearily, listening to the iron squeal of the bedsprings and the thick rustle of skirts and crinoline as Miss Brown lay down below.

Corrine looked down at the shadow of Mara in her bunk, the whites of her eyes gleaming in the dusk. She thought again of the white hand rising from the waters of the harbor and shuddered into sleep.

In the distance, someone wept. Corrine heard the sobs from the outskirts of the city where she sat in the dust, the drifting feathers of milkweed redirected by her shallow breaths. She'd been stone, locked in marble for centuries until that distant sorrow had somehow freed her. She stood and drifted toward the sound.

The city was absolutely dead. If she explored, she knew she'd only find gnawed bones and gold teeth, nothing of life or substance. And that, she guessed, was why the one at the heart of the city's vast labyrinth grieved.

When she found him, he was sitting on his throne of brittle thorns, trapped by a pool of his own tears. The little boy looked up at her, his face streaked with black blood.

"You were meant to be with me," he said.

He looked familiar. The way his sinewy fingers, too old for his small frame, clutched the arms of the throne reminded her of someone else.

And then she saw the one she remembered—the Unhallowed Prince— hiding in the shadows of the boy's body, his stone heart beating out its stolen rhythms. The bitter memory of how she had given him that heart, how she had been tricked, washed into her dream-mind.

No, she said.

The boy vanished, but the Prince remained. He stood from his throne and extended his hand to her. She couldn't see his face.

Silly child, he said, I know where you are.

She sat up and hit her head hard on the ceiling.

Miss Brown was gone and Mara was awake. Her eyes were wide and unfocused, as though she was in a trance. "He was in your dreams, wasn't he?"

Corrine rubbed her crown and met Mara's gaze.

"I saw him there," Mara said. "In your mind."

"How?"

"How do you see things?"

Corrine blanched. Though apparently Corrine could do magic just as Mara could, she still was afraid to trust the girl. The Council members knew that she had visions, but she'd never shared the depth or breadth of them with anyone, and certainly not with Mara.

Mara waited, her black gaze inscrutable.

"I just . . . see them. They come into my head like . . ."

"Pictures? Or just feelings?"

Corrine remembered how the visions of one of the disappeared girls at Falston had come to her—as a cold, creeping terror that drew her into a moon-filled forest, usually the result of touching something the girl had touched.

"Both," she said

"You need to get control of that," Mara said. "If you don't learn how to work with the visions, they'll overcome you."

"How do I do it?" she asked.

"You have to strengthen your mind. Father Joe can teach you."

The door latch stuttered and both girls turned as Miss Brown stepped into the room. A chill breeze blew in after her.

"I hope you both had a nice nap," she said.

Mara and Corrine glanced at each other.

"I'm happy to report that we found no sign of Melanie anywhere, and no sign of the Unhallowed. Come to dinner," she said.

Corrine and Mara followed Miss Brown out of the cabin, and two doors down to where Ilona, Christina, and Siobhan were staying. As her friends emerged, yawning, unexpected relief flooded Corrine. She'd been afraid something would happen to them, now that they were no longer at Uncle William's under what little protection he could offer. She thought of the daoi spying on her from the dining room window, and once again she was forced to acknowledge that nowhere was safe anymore. It seemed only a matter of time before danger caught them in its teeth, but for now it was good to know her friends were safe.

The sound of the sea churned through a gap in one of the ship's corridors, but Corrine was glad no one insisted on investigating. The ship's movement made her slightly queasy, and the thought of so many miles of cold ocean beneath her feet made her long for land. Everyone followed Miss Brown to the galley—a long, low room with a narrow table bolted to the floor.

Corrine caught Christina's disdainful glance at the room, the other passengers in their drab, respectable clothes. "Papa always travels first class," she said. "You should see it, Corrine—usually there is a grand ballroom with stained-glass windows, sometimes mahogany mantels and parquet floors . . . It's beautiful!"

Corrine managed a smile at her enthusiasm, even as she felt intimidated by the thought of such wealth. Corrine had no idea how wealthy Sir James was, but no matter how much money he had, first class for three girls, two servants, and three unmarried adults would have been an extravagant expense. But she knew it galled Christina to live below her station, and she wondered again what Christina must have done to end up at Falston. Christina herself had remained mum, and no one else ever spoke of it. Corrine was afraid to ask.

Father Joe and Mr. MacDougal joined them, talking animatedly about the size of the ship. A glance passed between Father Joe and Miss Brown; Corrine guessed he'd still been searching for Melanie. They might not believe her, but she also *knew* she'd seen Melanie, waiting below in the crowd, and Miss Brown had seen her just yesterday. Why was Melanie stalking them? What had she given the thing in the sea?

Mr. MacDougal caught her eye then. He smiled at her, a smile that seemed genuine. "'Tis a big ship," he said. "The finest on the water, don't you think?" Despite his smile, he looked a little green and Corrine wondered if he suffered from seasickness.

"Yes," she said. She looked down at the worn wood of her chair. At first, she hadn't thought him very handsome, thinking still of Rory's blue eyes and black, curling hair, his crooked grin. But Mr. MacDougal was handsome in a different way—less boyish—though still close to her age, she thought—with a rugged wildness that made meeting his eyes difficult. It was like trying to make conversation with a wolf or an eagle. She didn't know what else to say. Why would he bother talking with her when charming Christina sat across from them?

Corrine settled into her bolted-down chair and hunched uncomfortably toward the table. As she ate the lukewarm food in front of her, she mused over why the Unhallowed hadn't taken Melanie away, as they had all the other girls they'd kidnapped. Or had they? Jeanette's ghost had called to her and shown her the terrible story of her abduction. But what if Jeanette wasn't a ghost?

Something loomed on the edges of her vision. She fumbled with her spoon, and it careened off the table and across the floor as the ship heaved slightly. Mara looked at her, but then the vision took hold.

Christina was falling from a great height, trailing veils and scarves and strands of pearls behind her. Someone was waiting for Christina at the end of her fall, someone who had promised to catch her. And he did, though the fall toppled both of them over into the moonlit grass. When they untangled themselves, Corrine saw his face.

"Rory," she said out loud.

Mr. MacDougal's look pierced her to the bone.

Miss Brown gripped her hand hard, almost pinching the skin between her fingers. "Not here," the headmistress said under her breath. "Not now."

"I can't help it," Corrine said, gritting her teeth. She could see Rory bending to kiss Christina, while the castle tower from which she had jumped threw its shadow across them. At the same time, she felt the other passengers staring at her. Siobhan shuddered and crossed herself.

Mr. MacDougal put his hand over her other hand to steady her. The vision faded, though she could still feel the edges of it tickling her consciousness.

"Eat," Miss Brown said. She gave Corrine a clean spoon.

Corrine pushed down into the murky bowl, unsure whether the tremors she felt came from the ship or banished vision.

After dinner, Mr. MacDougal excused himself. Miss Brown and Father Joe escorted the girls back to their cabins.

"We'll resume your studies tomorrow," Miss Brown said. "I see no reason not to, since there's little else to do while on board. Father Joe and I will discuss our lesson plans this evening."

"You are not to leave your rooms under any circumstances while we're gone," Father Joe said. He pinned each of them with a severe glance that didn't brook objection. "We don't yet know the dangers on board."

Each of them nodded, Christina looking far more solemn than Corrine thought the situation merited. And each of them—saving perhaps Siobhan and Mara, who could not afford loss of their employment—had already planned to defy Father Joe's orders.

"Sleep well," Miss Brown said.

Corrine saw the glint in Ilona's eyes as she went into her cabin. She only had to wait long enough to be sure Miss Brown and Father Joe were truly gone.

As she shut and latched the door, Mara interrupted her thoughts by asking for a bit of her hair. Little silver sewing scissors perched on the maid's thumb and forefinger.

"Why?" Corrine said, shrinking into her bunk.

"A little working might keep the dreams away until you're better trained," she said.

"What do you have in mind?"

"You'll see," Mara said. "Just let me cut a piece."

Corrine put a hand to her hair. It was very much in want of a wash, but there had been no time before leaving Uncle William's. She imagined Mara asking this of Christina and the horror and shock that would ensue.

"Well . . . all right," she said. "But, maybe . . . can you cut where no one would notice?"

Mara half-smiled, but it was a cold grin. "Yes'm."

She crossed the narrow space between their bunks and reached behind Corrine's head with her free hand. Corrine had never been this close to Mara that she could remember, close enough to smell the grease she put on her hair and the strange herbal scent that clung to her skin. Corrine felt the tug and snip, and then watched Mara come away with a long strand of brownish hair.

"What will you do with it?"

"I'm still thinking," Mara said. There was a bit of a snap in her voice, as though she'd prefer not to be questioned about her magic.

"I'm going to visit Christina and Ilona," she said.

"Miss Brown won't like that," Mara said.

"They said it was safe," Corrine said. Surely they were safer the farther they got from land. And no one had seen Melanie on the ship. Maybe she'd never even been on the docks. These days, it was hard to tell visions from reality.

Mara didn't say anything, but unbound some of her own hair from its tight knot.

As she snipped some of it and began chanting, Corrine slipped out of the cabin door.

~ Four ~

January 4, 1866

CHRISTINA AND ILONA HAD BEEN WAITING FOR CORRINE to come to them.

"Where have you been?" Christina asked.

"We were thinking we'd have to go all by ourselves," Ilona said.

Corrine smiled.

Siobhan sat on her bunk, her hands twisting nervously in her apron.

"Siobhan?"

The maid glanced at her and frowned.

"What's wrong?" Corrine said. Since the devastation of Falston, Siobhan had been silent much of the time, her nervousness betrayed by her ever-wringing hands.

"This ship, that man," the maid muttered. "They're no good. No good at all."

Corrine went and sat beside her. She tried to take her hand, but Siobhan refused.

"What do you mean? Who?"

Siobhan had, in the past, often foreseen what the Unhallowed were doing or had done. She could somehow see through all the entrapments of the Fey, though Corrine was still not sure how she did it.

Siobhan wouldn't look at her, but rocked back and forth on her bunk. "Can't you hear it?" she whispered.

"What?" Corrine said.

She heard a sigh of indignation from Christina, who had little patience for such things.

"The knocking," Siobhan whispered. "It never stops. That man . . ." She began to sob and rock harder.

Corrine put her arms around her and held her. "Stop," she said. "Don't think about it anymore."

Siobhan remained stiff, until finally Corrine released her. "Perhaps if you come with us . . ." She began.

Another sigh from Christina.

"Come," Ilona said. "If you don't hurry, Miss Brown will return and we'll miss our chance."

Siobhan just shook her head. She dashed at her eyes with one hand, burying the other again in her apron. "He'll find you, miss. *He knows where you are.*"

Corrine shivered just a little. Would she turn into someone like Siobhan if the visions continued to control her? Nearly mad with fear of the Unhallowed? Yet Siobhan usually saw the truth. Corrine wavered.

"Come," Ilona said again. Corrine considered the choices— explore the great ship or sit nearby while Mara wove dark magic with her hair.

Corrine rose. She patted Siobhan on her arm, but knew it was a useless gesture. Siobhan dug her hands deeper into her apron. "Not my fault," the maid whispered to the wall.

Christina slid the bolt away as quietly as she could and peered outside. The girls crept slowly out of the cabin and down the corridor, straining to hear footsteps above the whistling wind and snarling ocean. The ship listed, throwing them together against the wall. As they untangled themselves, the motion of the boat coupled with the vibrations of the paddle wheels sent nausea creeping through Corrine's stomach. They climbed down onto the paddle wheel deck and she grasped the railing, seeking a breath of fresh air. The salt wind soothed her ailing stomach. She looked three stories down to the ocean. The gaslights on deck made weak circles on the foam. She imagined a man falling from the grand promenade above, the horror of being swallowed by the white torrent of the depths at her feet. The nausea tried to return, and she almost looked away, but something caught her eye.

A human torso rolled and tumbled in the darkness. For a moment, she thought her fancy had been a vision, until she saw the torso move and a long, glistening tail erupt from the waves.

"Look!" she said.

The mermaid turned on her back and looked up. Her face and body were bloated and white as a corpse's; bits of her skin peeled off in long strands that hung around her like tattered bandages. She smiled up as Corrine vomited over the side. Row upon row of razor-sharp teeth gleamed. Then she was gone, the flick of her tail lost in the black ocean.

Ilona held Corrine to keep her from falling, while Christina, looking away, handed her a handkerchief.

"What do you see?" Ilona asked.

Corrine wiped at her mouth, disgusted by the lingering taste of bile.

"It was ... something dead, I think." Corrine's visions frightened her friends, and she had seen how Christina looked at Siobhan. She didn't want them to think she was going insane too. She patted at her lips once more, then sheepishly put the handkerchief in her pinafore pocket.

"Faugh," Christina said. "No wonder you were ill." She patted Corrine on the back absently. "The Grand Salon will make you feel better," she said.

"The Grand Salon?" Corrine felt her plainness deeply—her windblown, greasy hair, her strange eye. She looked down at her pinafore to see if she'd stained it. It looked rumpled and dingy, but not too much the worse for wear. Still.

Christina could see that she was about to protest. "I am an ambassador's daughter. I will manage this. As long as you are with me, have no fear." She tossed her chestnut curls and winked at Corrine.

Corrine smiled, but didn't feel anything that resembled confidence.

Father Joe had said the *Great Eastern* was the largest ship on Earth, and Corrine believed it as they crossed deck after deck, barely avoiding tumbling into other passengers as the ship rocked on the swells. When at last they arrived at the first-class section, Christina took the lead.

She charmed the concierge who guarded the Salon entrance, claiming that they had left their boarding tickets in their cabin, and would he really force them to walk all that way to get a silly thing like that? He ushered them in without so much as a raised eyebrow.

"How do you do that?" Corrine asked as they passed the cloakroom.

"I know my place," Christina said, and kept walking with her head held high.

Ilona gestured at her head and to Christina to signal Christina's craziness. Corrine smiled.

As they emerged into the center of the Grand Salon, however, she forgot all about her friends. The maroon carpet spread in a luxurious river toward the velvet-covered couches. Columns painted white and gilded with gold and silver vaulted upward toward the great, iron-latticed dome of the skylights. A balcony circled the upper half of the booming hall; a few couples walked the promenade and admired the view from above. Frescoes of children frolicking in the waves lined the walls, and great mirrors two stories tall shielded the iron stacks from view as they rose through the decks. Corrine was entranced by how the mirrors magnified the grandeur of the room.

Something pale danced in one of the mirrors. Corrine went closer to inspect, while Christina and Ilona moved deeper into the Salon. The mirror reflected the balcony, the men and women admiring the delicate gilt work, the silvery columns. But another form shifted and wavered there, resolving into a man in top hat and waistcoat. Corrine stepped back as he pulled a stopwatch from his waistcoat pocket. She saw the letters IKB before he flipped it open and looked at the time in a gesture so reminiscent of her uncle that it made her shiver. Then he looked up at her and said, "The time is coming." His words cut at her like shards of glass. She stepped back, looking about to see if anyone had noticed.

Christina and Ilona were halfway down the gallery now, arm in arm and ignoring the view as though they'd seen it many times and were bored by it. Otherwise, men and women strolled by unhurried, unaware of the ghost wavering in the mirror.

She glanced at him once more. He looked up and smiled, a smile almost as full of teeth as the mermaid's. She backed further away and turned to follow Christina and Ilona before he could say anything more.

She didn't know if her legs were trembling from the slight vibrations of the ship or the prickling of memory. Just a few months ago, she had stood on the riverbank at Kelly's Ford, petrified by the ghost of Confederate artillery officer John Pelham. He had called her fairy girl, but she had never known what he meant or what he wanted. Rory had saved her then, dissipating the ghost and destroying the two-headed serpent that had also tried to attack her. Now, she was unsure whether Rory had been trying to save her or give her to the Unhallowed, especially since John Pelham had returned, leading the ghostly cavalry charge that had destroyed Falston. But that didn't solve the problem of this new ghost or why she was seeing him. Or what he wanted. It boded ill, she was sure.

She caught up to her friends, who were about to enter the Ladies' Salon, a smaller chamber off the main promenade. Nearby, a mustached bartender waited behind a green marble-topped bar.

"Ladies, what will you have this evening?" he asked. He stared a little at Corrine's scarred eye, his smile overly wide.

Christina said, "Three hot cocoas, please."

The bartender nodded and set three mugs on the bar. As he mixed cocoa powder with sugar and hot milk, he said, "To which room should I charge these, miss?"

Without missing a beat, Christina said, "Room 105."

Corrine stared at her. Before she could open her mouth to say anything, Ilona squeezed her hand in warning.

They each picked up their mugs and headed toward the smaller salon.

"Christina, I can't believe you . . ."

But whatever she was about to say died on her lips. Melanie smiled at them from a damask-covered divan.

"Welcome, ladies."

Melanie Smith rose. Her golden curls snaked out from under her plumed bonnet. She wore silk of an improbable blue, which gathered at her waist and fell in ruffles to her matching slippers. Corrine saw no trace of the thinness or rags she had seen at dusk in the crowd.

She walked toward the three of them. Corrine braced herself, wondering if Melanie would call forth an army of ghosts or Unhallowed here in the midst of such a crowd.

Someone—a gray shadow—slipped by Corrine then, and she realized as he stood in front of her that the shadow was

Mr. MacDougal. Some of the ladies in the room gasped at the impropriety of a man entering their chamber.

Something about Mr. MacDougal looked different but Corrine didn't know how to describe it. He seemed taller, more vibrant, certainly not the wan, almost green man who'd picked quietly at his food at dinner. She felt again how his hand had come down over hers in the galley, stopping the vision before it could fully take hold. She looked back to Melanie and gasped.

As though a veneer had been peeled away, Corrine saw the mermaid lurking in Melanie's shape. She smelled the corruption of her flesh—an odor of shellfish too long exposed to the sun. The mermaid smiled, her triple row of teeth gleaming like little knives in her mouth. Her eyes were all pupils—black as the depths and as expressionless. Pocked with suckers like the tentacles of an octopus, the mermaid's tongue glided over her rubbery lips.

Corrine put her hand against her rumbling stomach, trying to hold her mug of hot cocoa steady with her other hand.

"Corrine," Mr. MacDougal said, "this lady wasn't bothering you, was she?"

It was all Corrine could do to shake her head. She knew Ilona and Christina couldn't see the mermaid hiding behind Melanie's image. Corrine saw again the ravening face on the docks in her mind, the shining thing arcing end over end, only to be caught by a skinny white hand emerging from the Baltimore Harbor. *She must have given the mermaid some kind of spell, something to make the mermaid look like her so the mermaid could walk among us.* The thought that any Unhallowed might be able to do so made her fingers tremble. Warm cocoa spilled across the back of her hand.

The mermaid wearing Melanie's face looked at Mr. MacDougal. "The time is coming," she said, echoing the shark-toothed ghost.

Then she left the room, tiny drops of water falling from the hem of her dress.

Mr. MacDougal turned to them, fading back into himself. "I'll be escorting you ladies back to your cabins now," he said. His tone was stern and loud enough that the other women in the room, who were still gawking at his presence, could hear it.

But all Corrine could think of, as she set down her untasted mug of cocoa and blotted at her damp hand with Christina's handkerchief, was that she had been right. She followed Mr. MacDougal and her friends from the Salon. *He sees what I see. Who is he?*

~ Five ~

January 5, 1866

"OF ALL THE FOOLHARDY THINGS YOU COULD HAVE DONE,"
Miss Brown said. She shook her head and paced back across
the tiny cabin. Neither she nor Father Joe had said anything
about it last night when Mr. MacDougal had brought them
back to their cabins. Corrine guessed that they had been too
angry. The girls had been told to go to sleep and expect their
punishment in the morning. Christina and Ilona had already
been spoken to and had been barred from leaving their cabin.
Now, it was down to Corrine.

"But we found that the Unhallowed are on the ship too,"
Corrine said. She had already told Miss Brown and Father
Joe about the mermaid masquerading as Melanie. Somehow, though, she couldn't quite bear to tell them about Mr.
MacDougal. She wanted to confront him herself. The fact
that he could see the same supernatural things she could
might mean he was just another young man the Unhallowed
were manipulating, but Corrine wasn't sure. After all, he
worked for Sir James and the Council trusted Sir James
implicitly.

"Yes, perhaps, but she also knows for certain that you're
here now."

"Didn't she already know that?" Corrine asked. "I saw the mermaid in the water before I saw her in the Salon. I know she saw me."

Mara shook her head. Corrine noticed the circle of woven hair perched on her knee, an interweaving of dark and darker.

Miss Brown stared at her. "You are on the verge of impertinence, young lady." Miss Brown stopped her pacing and fixed Corrine with an exasperated glare. "Really, Corrine, do we have to hog-tie you in this cabin? Every time I think we've reached an understanding about the dangers, you do something even more dangerous than before."

Blame melted on Corrine's tongue like a block of sugar. It offered her a sweet way out, but she wasn't about to use it. She wanted to say that Christina was to blame, that Christina had urged her on, that Christina had even charged hot chocolate to someone else's rooms. But she kept her silence. Her mother had warned her against tattling and those warnings weren't easily overcome.

Father Joe entered then, bringing a cold breeze that knifed through the cabin.

"I can't find her anywhere," he said. "Melanie's name is of course not listed on the passenger manifest. I wasn't allowed to search the Grand Salon." He shot a glance at Corrine that made her want to sink through the iron floor.

Miss Brown sat on the bunk next to Mara, her brows knitting as she fiddled with the buttons of her sleeve. "What are we to do?" she asked, looking finally at Father Joe.

"The only thing we can do." He looked again at Corrine. "Keep out of her way."

"Is there no spell or root that can be laid against her? I've little knowledge of Unhallowed who make their domain in the waters," Miss Brown said.

"Mara can lay a few small protection spells," Father Joe said, looking at the circlet of hair that perched on Mara's knee. "But to fight a mermaid . . ." He shook his head. "You know I haven't the power for it."

"But the ship is iron. How can she bear it?" Miss Brown said.

Mara had a distant look in her eyes. "She can't very well right now. That was why she needed Melanie's form to walk in while on board. Once the ship is under water, well, that's a different story."

"Under water?" Miss Brown said. Her eyes darkened almost to indigo.

"She'll try to take the ship," Father Joe said matter-of-factly. "It's the only way she can become a queen. The bigger the ship, the more souls attached to it, the more power she'll have in the marine raths."

Corrine bit her lip, gauging whether what she wanted to say should be said. She had hidden much from them in the past, and it had cost them all dearly, Miss Brown perhaps most of all.

"I saw a ghost too," she said. "In the mirror of the Grand Salon."

"Tell us," Father Joe said.

She told them of how she had seen him in the mirror. Of how he had smiled at her with a shark's grin. Of how both he and the mermaid had said "The time is coming."

"Then she will move soon," Father Joe said. "The Unhallowed have two more stones, and the Prince is using one of them to charge his magic, though at what cost to him, I've no idea." Corrine thought of the dream with the pool of blood, the leaking cavity of his chest. *I know.* "They know now that we are coming. They will try to stop us if they can. Perhaps this is their way."

"But how can she take a ship down herself?" Miss Brown said. "Is she not weakened by using Melanie's form?"

"There's more than one way to skin a cat," Mara said. "They can use mortals, and they know how to raise the dead now to serve them."

"And just how do they know that?" Miss Brown snapped.

Was that chagrin on Mara's face? Usually, the girl's features were so still and proud—almost arrogant—that Corrine couldn't imagine her ever being embarrassed. There was a past here, of which Corrine remained entirely ignorant. Had Mara done something that allowed the Unhallowed to raise the dead? And what had that to do with the mermaid plotting against them now?

"Thea," Father Joe said.

Miss Brown sighed. "Forgive me, all. I am tired and when I am tired, my temper gets the better of me."

"If that's the most we can expect, then we feel fortunate," Father Joe said, smiling. His gaze lingered a little too long before he recovered himself and said, "Well, we must just do our best to be cautious. Mara, you can begin trying to locate her; perhaps we can trap her in Melanie's form in some way and keep her from using her power. Meanwhile, Corrine and I must begin her training. It's critical that she learn to protect herself."

Corrine nodded, but was unsure that she agreed.

"You've kept this knowledge from the other girls?" Father Joe asked.

"Yes, Father," Corrine said.

"Good. There's no need to unnecessarily alarm them. I often wonder whether we should send them away from this madness. What would their parents think?"

Corrine began counting her breaths in her head. She got to five before Father Joe's spectacles came off and he started polishing them on his cassock.

Mara spoke before Miss Brown could. "Don't send them away," she said. Her voice was gritty with vision. Corrine felt it, even if she couldn't see whatever Mara saw. "Not yet. They still have a part to play."

Corrine shivered. She remembered yesterday's vision of Christina falling from a great height. She could only guess at what her friends' roles might be, but the possibilities didn't seem pleasant.

"You've seen it?" Father Joe said.

"I feel it," Mara said. "Can't you?"

Father Joe didn't answer Mara, but gave a last polish to his spectacles and replaced them instead.

Mara picked up the woven necklace and brought it to Corrine. Without ceremony, she put it over Corrine's head, her cold fingers poking it under Corrine's collar so that it settled in a scratchy circle against her skin.

"I don't know how much good it'll do, but it may keep the visions down for a bit," Mara said.

Father Joe reached for the door. "Well then, that's that. I shall return later to begin your training, Corrine. I hope you've been working on your breathing. In the meantime, keep working on copying those letters. They're important. And remember, if you and the others wish to explore the ship, do tell us. We will be happy to escort you."

Corrine nodded. But he'd missed the point of exploring entirely.

Miss Brown took the girls into the second-class passenger salon near their cabins to study. She worked first with all the girls on French and on algebra, a subject Corrine admired for its steadiness. There was always a solution. She only had to find it. When the girls broke off to do homework, Miss Brown suggested Corrine go to a nearby table and work on copying the letters.

Corrine gathered up her things and went to the empty table. A few passengers milled about, reading or talking quietly on sofas bolted to the floors. She opened the writing case Uncle William had given her for Christmas, praying as she uncapped the ink bottle that the ship didn't roll badly and cause her to spill ink everywhere.

A strange undercurrent of sound began under the mechanical humming of the ship and the dull roar of the ocean outside. *Tink. Tink. Tink-tink-tink.* It reminded her of coins falling on a hard metal floor. Or someone striking a pipe lightly with a wrench. She listened to see if it had a rhythm, tilting her head as though somehow it would bring the sound within better range of her hearing.

"Corrine," Miss Brown whispered. "Enough daydreaming."

Corrine blushed and shuffled the letters. Trying to shut the incessant noise out of her mind, she picked up where she'd left off.

[Translation note: (Beginning and end missing] [estimated late September 1357]

. . . Then the creature raised its hand to me, and I could see the Mark of the Serpent upon it. The Serpent is the Enemy of the Fey, even as he is ours. The Prince tells me of one of their elders, who liked to wear the shape of a golden serpent and call himself the ruler of all Fey. He said this golden serpent took something precious from his people, something he called Hallowmere. I cannot

understand whether this is an object, a person, or a place. They are reluctant to speak of it.

This branded creature seemed different from the Fey I know. It was like a wizened, brown old man. It tried to talk to me—much hissing and growling it made—but the Captain came to protect me. He set his red hand upon the thing's head and as I watched, the little man melted into a shining pool. The Prince was very angry when he heard of this and called his guard for a Hunt . . .

The golden serpent mentioned here, she knew, was Elaphe. But she didn't understand how Elaphe had "taken" Hallowmere from the Fey. She thought of the two-headed copperhead Rory had killed at Kelly's Ford, just after the ghost of John Pelham had come after her. When she'd awoken from her faint, she'd seen Rory covered in a shimmering substance. Was it the blood of the Hallowed that Angus referred to here? Had Rory killed a Hallowed creature who had actually been trying to help her? What did it mean when one of the Hallowed was killed? How were they connected to Hallowmere? She remembered Miss Brown and Father Joe's angry suspicions at Kelly's Ford. They'd never said anything to accuse her. The thought that she may have inadvertently caused the death of a Hallowed being, especially when she knew so little about them, made her sick with fear.

Corrine wiped at her pen with a scrap sheet of paper and replaced it in her writing case. She felt her gorge rising and pushed away from the table.

Miss Brown glanced over her shoulder.

"Miss Brown, I need to . . . I have to . . ."

Miss Brown nodded, concerned. "Just go out by the rail where I can see you. It'll be all right."

With her hand to her mouth, Corrine nodded and ran out of the door.

She only just made it to the railing, and as she vomited into the far, gray sea, she couldn't tell whether her face burned from her efforts or embarrassment. The great ship was rolling so precipitously that she curled one arm around the worn wooden railing to steady herself.

A hand came to rest between her shoulder blades as she pulled her handkerchief from her pocket. She held the kerchief to her mouth, feeling her blush deepen as she looked up at Mr. MacDougal.

"You're not taking to the ship too well, are you?" he asked.

She shook her head. He steadied her shoulder and elbow as she released the railing.

"Truth to tell, me neither," he said. His eyes were inscrutable, almost gray in the deepening storm, but there was a sense of relief in them, as though he was glad to share his weakness with someone.

"Shall I escort you back to your cabin then?" he asked. "Perhaps lying down for a bit would do you good?"

Corrine considered. Her stomach protested at the thought of staring at the faded letters against the ship's rolling.

"Yes. Just let me ask Miss Brown."

"Certainly."

He helped her slide the door open into the salon and waited while she made sure Miss Brown didn't mind.

"I'm a little hesitant," Miss Brown said in a low voice, glancing at Mr. MacDougal as he stood by the door. "But I can't very well leave them here alone, either." The headmistress looked at Christina and Ilona who were deeply engaged in their textbooks over in the corner.

Corrine shut her mouth grimly against the bile that rose in her throat.

Miss Brown patted her arm then and said, "Well, it isn't that far. And Sir James wouldn't have sent Mr. MacDougal if he wasn't to be trusted. Mind that you go straight to your cabin. I'll bring the letters and your writing case back when I return with the girls. Father Joe will have to begin your lessons tomorrow."

Corrine held in her sigh of relief and nodded. She knew it might be seen as improper that she walked alone with a man, but he was surely much older than her, wasn't he? She looked at him as he gazed at a painting nailed to the paneled wall. The tilt of his head and the set of his shoulders made him appear younger than he had seemed before.

Miss Brown began gathering up Corrine's things at the writing table as Corrine went back to Mr. MacDougal.

"All's well?" he said.

"Yes."

He slid the door open for her and took her arm after he had closed it behind him. He pulled his fingers back quickly from the metal, as though he'd received a shock. He looked a little pale, now that they were out in the fitful wind and light.

" 'Tis the iron that does this to us," he said, as he took her arm.

She tried not to gape at him. "Whatever do you mean?" she asked. She thought of pulling away from him, but her stomach seized and she clamped her free arm over it.

"You know what I'm speaking of," he said.

She looked at him while the ship rolled slowly away from her feet. His touch infiltrated her coat sleeve, seeking her skin like a vine embracing a tree. It was oddly comforting and familiar.

"You've known I am different since we met. We are the same, you and I. But the pity is that you still don't know what

66

you are." There was something in his eyes, something that she couldn't quite understand.

She stiffened in his grip. "Mr. MacDougal, I hardly know what you're talking about."

He half-smiled at her. "Call me Euan." She swallowed. His eyes bored into her, knowingly, almost predatory. "You know all too well what I mean," he said.

"What am I, then?" she asked.

"The time is coming," he said sadly. She recognized the words of both the mermaid and the ghost with a chill.

"What do you mean?" she asked, trying to pull away. "Why are you saying that?"

But he held her with the strength of oaks, the certainty of rowan.

"I came here to protect you. Danger is close. Do you not feel it?"

She could barely speak. She looked up and down the corridor, calculating the distances back to the salon or to her cabin.

His grip loosened. He looked wounded by her fear of him. "I will not harm you ever," he said. "Trust that." He turned her and helped her down the corridor, his face grim and shadowed. Corrine moved with him, unhappy that her suppositions about him had proven all too true.

When they came to her cabin, he stopped her before she could open the door. Her body felt cold and defenseless as he released her and stepped away.

"I beg you to keep your silence about what I've said. The Council doesn't look favorably on what it can't control."

"But—" she began.

He held a hand so close to her lips she could feel its unnatural heat.

"I've had many opportunities," he said. "And I've taken none of them. Does that alone not prove my goodwill?"

She stared. She didn't know what to say.

"In you go," he said, swinging the door open.

As she stepped inside, the metallic ringing in her head grew louder.

~ Six ~

January 8, 1866

CORRINE'S QUEASINESS CAME BY FITS AND STARTS FOR THE
next few days, peaking and falling with the ship as it strove
against the ever-toughening waves. By the third day of being
confined mostly to quarters, Corrine was sick with boredom.
Her head ached with the constant metallic tinking, but when
she asked Mara about it, the maid looked at her as if she'd
gone mad. During the day, Mara stayed with Siobhan in the
other cabin, whether to give Corrine her privacy or to avoid her,
Corrine wasn't sure. The others checked on her periodically.
Christina groused about the cold, while Ilona boasted happily
of managing to stay on her feet on the grand promenade when
everyone else was sent reeling by the *Great Eastern*'s tossing.
Father Joe was impatient for Corrine to feel up to training, but
ceased his fretting at a word from Miss Brown.

Euan hadn't appeared since he'd escorted her to her quarters.
She wondered if perhaps she'd misheard him; perhaps, despite
Mara's woven spell, she had walked for a moment into a dream.
Still, she kept her silence about him. She reminded herself that
she hadn't promised him anything, yet his plea to remain in
her confidence resonated with her. She still didn't know what
he meant about her or the Council. How did he know? Was he

working with the Council or against them? Sometimes, she had difficulty entirely trusting the Council, as many times as they'd withheld information from her. She wasn't going to feel too badly about withholding some of her own.

She was slipping back into blissful, dreamless sleep, when Father Joe knocked and entered, bearing a few books on his arm.

"I hope you're well enough to begin your studies today, Corrine. Between you and Euan, our crew is in quite a rotten state."

Corrine pulled herself up, trying to avoid hitting her head on the bunk above her. Miss Brown had graciously allowed her to have the bottom bunk during her illness.

"He's ill too?" Corrine said. *'Tis the iron that does this to us . . .*

Father Joe nodded. "Seasickness or something like that. Seldom ever seems to sleep, that lad. I hear him come and go at all hours. I suppose you can sympathize," he said, trying not to look at the bucket Mara had placed on a hook by Corrine's bunk.

Corrine nodded.

Father Joe sat on Mara's bed and settled the books next to him. He frowned a little at the dim gaslight, then drew one of the books from the stack beside her.

"Are you ready to begin?" he asked.

"Yes," she said. *Anything to relieve the boredom and this clanging in my head.*

Father Joe opened the book on his lap. "The first thing you should know is that there are many forms of magic. Mara practices one kind. I practice another. And there are probably still other types that the Council has yet to discover."

Corrine nodded.

"Magic is the only way we can fight the Unhallowed," Father Joe said.

"Why?"

"Because they are magical beings. And the only thing they respond to, the only way we have of stopping them, is with magic."

"And iron," Corrine said.

"But even iron is becoming less effective than it was," Father Joe said.

She had to concede the truth of that. One thought of the mermaid confronting her with Melanie's face in the Grand Salon was evidence enough.

"And they expect us to fight with iron," Father Joe continued. "If we fight with their weapons, we have a much greater chance of keeping them from Hallowmere."

The inscription in the serpent-bound book had mentioned that name, as had Angus's letters. The Unhallowed had called themselves the "Lords of Hallowmere," in addition to the label "Lords of the Earth." Corrine knew that Hallowmere was important, but she still wasn't sure why. "What is Hallowmere exactly?" she asked.

"Hallowmere is very important to the Fey, both Hallowed and Unhallowed. It's the reason for all this unpleasantness."

"But *what* is it?" Corrine reached under her pillow for the serpent-bound book. She felt the serpents shift as she pulled it under the covers beside her.

"It's where the Fey go to die."

"I don't understand."

In three breaths, Father Joe removed his spectacles and polished them on his cassock.

"Hallowmere is a pool or well of magical energy. It's the source of magic, really. In the old times, before the Fey separated into two races, the Fey went there to die and be reborn. Hallowmere renewed them, but the Fey that went into it would return forever altered."

"Altered?"

"Their memories, their feelings, even their very bodies, were changed. A sprite might return a nereid. A hob might return as a phooka. Never could any Fey escape Hallowmere unchanged. This was their fate, just as death and resurrection are—should be—ours. Every Hallowe'en, those who sought renewal came to Hallowmere."

He idly flipped the pages of the book he held.

"But," he continued, "there were those who did not wish to give themselves over to Hallowmere, those who wanted to keep their lives and memories. There was a powerful Fey witch who didn't want to lose her power. She was a shield-maiden to the Morrigan, the great, bloody goddess of Irish battle. It was the Morrigan who taught her that the blood of humans could prolong her life and make it unnecessary for her to enter Hallowmere."

Corrine nodded. One of the serpents gently latched its teeth into her finger. She slid her hand away, startled.

Father Joe didn't notice, so caught up was he in telling the story. "So, she rebelled. And she convinced the Fey Prince to join her. Thus were born the Hallowed and the Unhallowed— those who go to Hallowmere and those who do not."

"Then what do the Unhallowed want with Hallowmere?" she asked.

Father Joe's shadow tilted behind him on the wall. Something eclipsed the edges of his shadow, something muddy and red, bound with a thin line of silver.

"What they have always wanted," Father Joe, said, frowning. "Power. Hallowmere contains all the magic of all the worlds. Much is hidden in it that we mortals can only guess at; much could be manifested from it for those with the power to do so."

Corrine traced the edge of the book, avoiding the serpents' heads. "What happens if the Unhallowed reach Hallowmere?"

"The human world is finished."

Corrine's fingers stopped, clutching the spine of the book. She took a sharp breath. "The human world . . . What are you saying?"

"The Prince will finally have what he has always sought," Father Joe said. "Complete dominion over humanity, an inexhaustible food supply."

The image of the mermaid smiling came unbidden to her mind and Corrine thought she might be ill again.

"But never fear," Father Joe said. "Elaphe has made it so that the Unhallowed cannot come to Hallowmere. Once, the Fey clans gathered and placed their clan stones, the rathstones, in a circle. All the stones together opened the gates to Hallowmere. But when Elaphe sent his power into the stones, he caused them to be hidden from the Unhallowed. And then he sent his human disciple, Iamblicus, to scatter them throughout the earth and the raths."

A horrible thought occurred to Corrine. "But doesn't that mean that *no one* can go to Hallowmere anymore?"

"Yes. Exactly," Father Joe said. "Thus, the Hallowed are weakened every day. Unable to renew themselves, many have gone dormant. Some have fallen ill and died, lost forever. And every time one of the Hallowed dies, the magic of this world is lessened, tainted and twisted by that death."

Corrine's face flamed. She knew they were both thinking of the same thing—the two-headed copperhead who had been killed trying to protect her. That place by the river had died as though no spring could ever revive it. At the time, she had thought the copperhead was an evil servant of the Falston witches. She had thought Rory was saving her. Much to her sorrow, she knew differently now.

But Father Joe didn't take her to task for it. He said, "The Unhallowed have been weakened too. For long, we held all the rathstones or knew where they were. The Prince was trapped in his rath, trying unsuccessfully to lure some hapless mortal into helping him escape through dreams."

Corrine swallowed. The iron bunk loomed over her. "And I've done that now, haven't I?"

"I'm afraid so. But quite honestly, it was bound to happen. Our enemies are relentless. The trick now is to find ways to overcome them. And those ways are best served through magic."

"I don't understand why I'm important, though," Corrine said. *Besides being the one gullible enough to fall for their tricks.*

Father Joe's gaze wavered. There was the barest flicker of an eyelash to indicate he knew more than he was telling. *Tink. Tink, tinkety-tink, tink, tink.* Corrine pressed her hands to her head in exasperation.

"Look, Corrine," Father Joe said. "There are many reasons why you've become important. That you have visions, that you can now see the Unhallowed, are reason enough. But you also gave them two rathstones, and the fact that they still watch and follow you, all this should make you want to protect yourself however you can. Heaven forefend, but there may come a time when Mara or I cannot protect you. What will you do then?"

Corrine thought of her mother's ghost protecting her from the Unhallowed during the last days of Falston. She had never been able to tell anyone about it, and she found she still couldn't. It wasn't as if she wanted to keep it from the Council; no, Corrine just couldn't bear to think what that effort at protection had cost her mother's spirit. Somehow, she knew that her mother wouldn't be able to help her again if something happened—even her mother's spirit was beyond reach.

Thinking of her mother made her remember the Captain, the way he had made sure she had seen him the other night.

And the daoi salivating at the dining room window . . . She shuddered to think of it.

She reached out to receive the book Father Joe held out to her.

"First, you should understand what we're working toward here," he said. "The higher magics, those that could best protect you, can only be performed by perfecting what the ancients called an alchemy of mind. That is, you create the proper state in your mind to channel the higher powers. Without this alchemy, disaster can result."

It sounded as though he had experienced such disasters far too often.

"So, we will begin with a study of the cardinal directions," he continued. "It's always best to begin with the east—the direction of intellect, the dawn, new beginnings, and the wind. All things which belong to the air—birds, clouds, stars, the planets—all belong in the domain of the east."

"I don't suppose it's coincidence that we're on the *Great Eastern* heading east," Corrine said.

Father Joe smiled. "Perhaps not." He indicated the hair charm around her throat. "Remove that for the moment. You must be free to see with your mind's eye."

Corrine pulled the fragile thing over her head and laid it on the bed.

"Now, close your eyes. As you breathe in, count to five. As you breathe out, count down from five."

Corrine closed her eyes and began counting.

"Feel the wind. Feel the breeze creeping in around the door, the joints at the ceiling, the edges of the porthole. Listen to the wind moving across the ocean outside, sliding past the ship's hull, catching her flags and guylines . . . Let that wind carry you . . ."

Corrine tried. She tried to feel the wind under her, carrying her as if she had wings, as if she could ride upon its back.

But she also kept thinking about Euan and the Unhallowed and the end of the mortal world. She felt herself plummeting toward the dark sea.

As if he'd anticipated this, Father Joe said, "If thoughts come to you, return to your breath. Keep counting up and down with each inhalation and exhalation. Keep riding the wind. Feel the moving stillness in your mind."

She counted. *One—two—three—four—five. Five—four* . . .

"Ride that wind. Feel your feathers steadying you on the air. Feel your wings reaching out toward the horizon. You notice that the stars are fading. The sun is rising. And just below the sun, you see dark towers rising. You want to go there. You must go there, for this is the home of the guardians of the east, the Lords of the Air . . ."

His voice trailed off, leaving Corrine gliding on a stream of air, far away from the maddening clinking noise. Her raven eyes focused only on the towers growing closer beneath the disc of the sun. She heard only the wind rushing under her feathers. Something was there. A hooded man. A veiled woman. She couldn't be sure until she was there. And then the face looked up at her, golden hair streaming into the sun, amber eyes burning with wicked delight.

Come, my little raven. Come, my pretty one.

Corrine's eyes flew open. Father Joe looked at her intently. The silver edge around his shadow glittered like glass on the wall behind him.

"The witch," Corrine said. "She wants me."

Father Joe's fingers shook and he clutched the edge of the bed to stop them.

"Leanan," he whispered.

SEVEN

January 9, 1866

THE NEXT DAY, DESPITE HER ACHING STOMACH, CORRINE went with Christina and Ilona to study in the salon. As she had before, she set up the writing case and unbundled the letters Miss Brown had placed in its inner pocket. She was ready to begin—her ink secure, her pen fixed with a fresh nib—but thoughts of what Father Joe had said about Hallowmere nagged at her. How would the human world end if the Unhallowed were able to retrieve all the rathstones? Why had the Unhallowed been unwilling to speak of Hallowmere to Angus? And why had the Prince been angry at the Captain for killing one of the Hallowed?

She slid the serpent-bound book from her pinafore pocket and opened it on her lap. Though Father Joe had given it to her to prove his trust in her, he was also uneasy about her possession of it. He didn't like her to read in it often, though he was pleased that she could read the Unhallowed language without much difficulty. Still, the book had a mind of its own, unwilling to reveal more than a little at a time to her. She sometimes felt that there was some key or spell she needed to unlock its deeper secrets, but she didn't know where such a thing might be found.

"Hallowmere," she whispered under her breath.
Letters swam and curled lazily to the page's surface.

Of Hallowmere

The first to establish domain over Hallowmere was
Mordroch, and as the true son of Mordroch, the Prince
declares his claim above all others. Mordroch it was who wrested
the Cauldron from the gods, and who used its power to elevate
their children to their rightful inheritance. Mordroch it was who
hid the Treas Ulaidh within the Cauldron, locking them away
from the gods and those who would use them to subjugate the
true Lords of the Earth. There the Ulaidh remain, locked
away from their rightful Lord. For the Great Deceiver,
in the guise of friendship, seized control of the gates through the
rathstones that opened them and sent his humans to scatter the
stones where the Lords could not find them. We have languished
long while these mortal locusts have eaten over the land, destroying
the sacred raths, polluting the lineage of the Blessed with
their paltry blood. But as the Great Deceiver is of
the Eldest race, the Prince is bound by the laws of his magic.
The stones may only be found by the Polluted Ones, those the
Great Deceiver calls the Half-Born.

Thus the Lords are watchful and wait for the signs of
their birth. They are most often female, for it is seldom that
a male mortal can tolerate the horrors of the power unleashed in

his wretched veins. These Half-Born are valuable only if they have achieved the higher magics through mastery of the upper elementals. If they have not, their path lies in madness and their blood is best drunk at the Prince's feasting table.

To each stone is tied a condition. And when the Half-Born has met it, only then will it be useful to her in opening the gate to Hallowmere.

The Great Deceiver says thus:

> One by thorn
> And one by stone
> One by blood
> And two by bone
> One by earth
> And one by sea
> By venom's sweet sting
> And the spider's dark art
> Between golden jaws
> Shall the mists depart
> And open the gates to treasures three
> So has it been
> So must it be

But to every destination there are many paths. And the Lords of the Earth have long known that the quickest means to immortality is by the blood of the Unblessed. Mordroch has

*said that the blood of sacrifice feeds the fires of the Cauldron.
If this be truth, then perhaps Hallowmere will open again
to its true rulers without need for the power of the polluted
Half-Born. And the Treas Ulaidh will be ours again,
at last.*

Corrine shut the book. She was surprised the book had
shown her anything, temperamental as it was. Half of what
she'd read she didn't understand. Who were the Half-Born?
When it spoke of mastery of magic, she could only think about
what Father Joe had said yesterday. And what he hadn't said.
Was she Half-Born? Was Mara? And what had it meant about
the path of madness best served at the Prince's feasting table?
The ever-present clinking receded beneath the spell that still
rang in her ears, as if someone had whispered it. "One by thorn
and one by stone . . ." Those two had already happened, she
realized. "One by blood . . ." She shuddered. So many questions.
And now, defenseless on this ship with the Unhallowed about
to strike at any moment, Corrine wondered how she would
ever know the truth.

The door to the salon slid open and Miss Brown and Father
Joe entered. They both came to sit with her at the table. Miss
Brown had dark circles under her eyes and Father Joe looked
as though he hadn't slept in days.

"Is something wrong?" Corrine asked.

Miss Brown sighed. "Siobhan seems very unsettled. Has she
said anything to you or the other girls about what's upsetting
her?" she asked Corrine.

"There has been a . . . sound," Corrine said. She was hesitant to try to explain; no one seemed to notice it except her
and Siobhan.

"A sound?" Father Joe asked.

"A clinking sound. I hear it all the time. The only time I don't is when I practice those breathing exercises you taught me, Father."

"A sound," Miss Brown murmured. "Is there something she's not telling us?"

"We could have Mara . . ." Father Joe began.

"No," Miss Brown said. "The iron is taking its toll on her." She glanced at Corrine. "I don't think asking her to do any other magical work would be good for her health."

Father Joe nodded, but his face was tight with frustration.

"I heard we've almost rounded the Irish north coast," Miss Brown said. "We'll be in Glasgow in two days perhaps."

"If the Unhallowed allow us to make it that far," Father Joe said.

"What?" Miss Brown smiled wanly. "A priest without faith?"

Father Joe's lips quirked, but then he glanced at Corrine and kept his expression neutral. Out of the corner of her eye, Corrine saw Ilona and Christina watching from their sofa, fretting because they couldn't hear what was being said.

"Merely being practical, my dear Thea."

It was the first time Corrine had ever heard the priest call someone "dear." She swallowed her snicker.

"Then we must hope your practicality is outweighed by my optimism," Miss Brown said.

Corrine thought of the mermaid and her toothy grin in the Grand Salon and couldn't agree more.

January 15, 1866

Sobbing woke Corrine, sobbing interwoven with the clinking noise that had become part of the fabric of Corrine's existence on board. Only the breathing exercises Father Joe had taught her to help her become more in tune with the east seemed to drive the sound from her mind. She tried the breathing now, sensing the faint breeze that blew into the cabin around the door and porthole seals, through the ventilation shafts. The ship rolled; she was edging along Scotland now, having crossed the deep and rounded the British coasts with only heavy winds to impede her. Most passengers now kept to their cabins; the grand promenade had lost its luster with the onset of the screaming northern winds.

Though the strange metallic rapping fell into the background as Corrine breathed, the sobbing continued unabated. Her throat itched where the hair charm scratched her skin, and she dug her fingers beneath it.

Come out.

The voice was right in her ear, the whisper of an old man. Corrine sat straight up and whacked her head hard against the top bunk. Terrified, she breathed shallowly while the pain bloomed in her skull. Neither Miss Brown nor Mara woke. Corrine hunkered back down again, pulling the wool blanket up to her chin and covering her ears with her hands.

Come out.

It reminded her far too much of those nights in her Falston attic room, when the wind rocked the great manor as though it were a ship and the moon ran guilty from pursuing clouds. The Prince would call her then, whispering for her to come to him. In her dreams she had often done so, and Falston had paid the price. Every fiber of her being, therefore, told her not to get out of her bunk and go to the door.

Yet, she found herself swinging her legs out from under the covers, carefully putting her feet on the cold floor, praying that she didn't somehow waken Mara or Miss Brown. Corrine felt her way to the door, listening to the latch groan open with gritted teeth.

She was a bit surprised when she found that the sobbing came from quite an ordinary source. Siobhan was hunched against the door of the cabin she shared with Christina and Ilona. She grasped the handle as though she was trying to get back in, but didn't have the strength.

"Siobhan?" Corrine knelt next to her.

Siobhan hid her face in the sleeve of her raised arm. "Don't let him get me," she sobbed.

"Him?" Corrine said. "Who?"

Me.

Corrine turned. The man she had seen in the mirror on that first evening stood in the corridor. He was pale as ice, with eyes black as the ocean's heart.

"Why are you bothering my friend?" Corrine said.

The man checked his pocket watch and smiled his shark's grin at her. *The time has come. Are you ready?*

The latches to all the doors of the hall sealed themselves from the outside, locking all their inhabitants inside. The clinking noise that had plagued Corrine for days banged at her skull. Corrine couldn't think. Siobhan moaned.

The ghost shifted into a cloud and flung himself at Corrine. Corrine felt a terrible tugging at her skin, as though something was trying to divide her spirit from her flesh. The necklace of interwoven hair burned white-hot against her throat. With a shivering wail, the ghost trickled down her arm and fell into Siobhan.

Siobhan stood and looked at her with the ghost's black and bottomless eyes. An unnatural, male grin tugged at her features.

"Siobhan!" Corrine grabbed the girl's elbows and shook her. Frost burned Corrine's hands as the cold spread across her body.

The girl who had been Siobhan pushed Corrine's hands off

with a smirk and moved on down the corridor, heedless of the dark or the ship's rolling.

"Siobhan!" Corrine called. She started after her, and then thought about Father Joe and Miss Brown's warnings.

She tried the latch of her room. Locked. Now from the inside. She beat at the door until her hands couldn't bear the pain. She ran to the men's quarters, finding Father Joe's door and banging on it weakly in the dark. Father Joe opened his door, peering at her in the darkness as he pulled a robe over his dressing gown and attempted to put on his spectacles. Euan rose from his cot, his scarred chest silver in the gaslights.

"Corrine, what . . .?" Father Joe said.

Corrine tried not to watch as Euan pulled a shirt over his old wounds. Was this the reason why he was often ill?

"Siobhan . . ." Corrine tried to clutch the door as the ship slid her toward the opposite wall.

"What about her? What are you doing in the corridor? It must be two o'clock in the morning!"

She didn't censor herself in front of Euan as she once might have. "The ghost, the man I saw in the mirror, he took Siobhan."

Father Joe crossed himself. "Heavenly Father protect us."

"I've tried to wake Miss Brown, but the door won't budge and no one answers."

Father Joe stood considering.

"Shouldn't we hurry?" Corrine said. "Siobhan . . ."

"Yes. Let me just get a few things, and then we'll go."

"I'll come with you," Euan said. "That girl's mad as a box of frogs. You may need help." Corrine was thankful that he didn't question her about the ghost, as another man might have. But why would he? He saw what she saw. How and why were still questions she couldn't answer.

Father Joe nodded and slid the door closed again.

Corrine looked down at her hands. The moon white frost was fading into black. The pain was so great she almost couldn't hear the hammering in her skull.

Father Joe and Euan emerged their cabin.

"Which way did she go?" Euan said.

Corrine pointed down the corridor. Euan started down and she followed with Father Joe, trying not to touch the wall. With the *Great Eastern*'s tremendous size, Corrine had no idea how they would ever find Siobhan if the ghost didn't want her to be found.

At one point, traversing the grand promenade above one of the great paddle wheels, they stopped to catch their breaths. Corrine worried that finding Siobhan was beyond hope.

"I want to warn you," Father Joe said, almost forced to shout above all the ship's noise, "this is probably a trap. But we will do what we can for Siobhan."

"Should I try to fetch the others?" Euan asked. "Perhaps the doors will open now."

Father Joe looked down the deck. "Yes," he shouted above the wind. "Tell Miss Brown to make ready to depart, in case the danger I spoke of is upon us. And bring Mara to us. She is the only other who can help us now."

Euan nodded. With a nod in Corrine's direction, he went back the way they'd come down the deck.

Father Joe led her along the galley. Then, finally, he stopped and looked at Corrine. "Can you still hear the noise you spoke of?" he asked.

She nodded.

"Is it getting louder?"

She listened, then shook her head.

"You lead, then," he said. "Follow it to the source. We may find her there."

Corrine turned her head this way and that, breathing the

cutting wind as deeply as she dared. Then she moved toward the first-class suite. They followed the sound until they came to a dead end. The metallic clanging was so loud now that Corrine could barely hear the ship or the wind that drove her. The only way around was to climb up to the broad deck and try to get their bearings from there.

They climbed up into the lashing wind and Corrine longed for her fur muff; her hands were numb as blocks of wood. And her feet, despite the woolen socks she wore, felt frozen to the salt-slick boards.

The deck rolled away into darkness, the gaslights pitching strange shadows. Corrine thought she saw something squiggle away as she walked with Father Joe, holding on to him for balance.

Corrine looked back. The mermaid's black-within-black eyes stared at her from around the corner of one of the deck-houses. Shreds of corpse white skin trailed from her shoulders onto the night-slick deck.

Corrine clutched at Father Joe. "Look!"

But before he could, the mermaid slithered out of view.

"What?"

"The mermaid," Corrine said. "She's here. You were right."

Father Joe nodded. "I assure you, I'm not pleased to be right in this matter. If for no other reason than the fact that I can't swim."

Corrine stared up at him, unsure whether to laugh or weep.

"We can do nothing against her until we find Siobhan," Father Joe said, and urged her forward to where they could climb down into the hull. The clanging was so loud that Corrine thought it might drive her eyes from her sockets. She clutched her head, then hissed and dropped her hands in pain.

"Are we nearly there?" Father Joe asked.

Before she could say yes, they heard footsteps on the ladder above them. Euan climbed down with Mara.

Mara eyed Corrine. "That hair charm work all right?" she said.

"It was the only thing that kept the ghost from getting me," Corrine said.

"Thought so." Mara's smile was small and eerie.

"But my hands," Corrine said, as Father Joe motioned them after him down the corridor. "They're frostbitten."

Mara nodded. "You tried to touch her, eh?"

"Yes."

"Don't want to be touching nobody that's ridden like that. 'Less you know how to handle them, that is." It sounded a little like a challenge.

Corrine had a strange notion of herself as a witch like Mara, with her frightening rituals and her clattering juju bags. Corrine gritted her teeth. She hoped it wouldn't happen that way. She continued down the ladder, Mara and Euan just behind her.

"Oh Lord," Mara said when they came to the landing.

Dim gaslight revealed Siobhan. She stood with her hand against the ship's iron hull, whispering. The metallic beating warped the air as though it were a sheet of tin. Even Father Joe and Mara could hear it now. Corrine guessed by the look on his face that Euan could too.

A shape drifted from the hull. The light glanced from slender bones before the skeleton leaped into Siobhan. The ghost-ridden girl cried out briefly in pain before the two spirits subsumed her. The clanging stopped.

As Siobhan noticed them, Mara opened her bag and fumbled through it. Corrine had never seen her nervous before, even when Falston was aflame and the ghostly Confederate cavalry rushed through the school's open gates.

"What's wrong?" Corrine said.

Siobhan swung her head between Father Joe and Mara like a bull deciding whom to charge.

"This won't work," Mara said. "Too many ghosts riding her."

"So, what will you do?"

Mara shook her head and pulled out her feathered chicken's foot. She dipped it into a bag of powder and began shaking it in Siobhan's direction. The girl's face rippled, flexing into a death's-head grin. She moved toward them. But then Euan stepped forward. Before Father Joe or Mara could do anything further, Siobhan shrieked—a long metallic wail that made the clanging seem melodious by comparison. She tore past them with a horrible strength that none of them dared to try to grasp.

Siobhan fled up the staircase. They raced after her—to the mid-level decks, along the paddle wheels, burrowing to the heart of the ship until they reached the boiler rooms. In the roaring light, the boiler-room men looked like nothing so much as devils shoveling damned souls into the fires of hell. Corrine could almost see horns flickering on their soot black brows, tails emerging from their worn clothes.

Euan hurled himself at Siobhan as she entered the boiler room. He shouted something that Corrine couldn't quite catch. Siobhan's head cracked against the iron floor and for a moment the maid's familiar panic-stricken gaze emerged.

"Here now!" the closest worker yelled. He reached for Euan's collar, but before he could close his grip, Siobhan threw the gamekeeper from her with terrifying strength.

Euan and the boiler man fell in a heap against some pipes. Father Joe rushed to aid them.

Mara swore. Corrine saw her reach into her bag again as the men tried to untangle themselves. Siobhan ran through the boiler room to a valve on the main boiler of one of the stacks. She turned the wheel with a wrench that nearly pulled it from its housing. Corrine watched open-mouthed. Men screamed, abandoning their pitchforks and running toward the girl.

In that moment, the ghost materialized before Corrine. He wore a top hat and broadly striped trousers. He checked his pocket watch. "You should seek cover," he said. "My ship is dying. The *Great Eastern* will soon be no more."

"Why?" Corrine shouted.

The whistling of steam pierced the gloom. The great engine pounded like an overworked heart.

"They would have torn her apart," the ghost said.

Corrine could see Mara edging closer to Siobhan through the rattling pipes. She held to a fitting, gasping against the stench of burning coal, the building pressure. Father Joe was pulling Euan across the trembling struts toward her.

"Who are you?" Corrine asked the ghost.

The ghost clucked. "I am Isambard Kingdom Brunel. And this is my ship, the *Leviathan*. My great babe."

Corrine shuddered. Father Joe had just told them on the docks how Brunel, who had poured his life into this ship, had collapsed shortly after his picture was taken on the grand promenade at the ship's completion. And now he was trapped here, unable to leave his beloved ship. She choked on the fumes and steam, hoping she could distract the ghost long enough to let Mara do her work. Father Joe pulled Euan into the cover of the stairs, while Mara snuck ever closer to Siobhan as she worked at the pressure valve of another boiler. Through the smoke, Corrine saw Mara dust Siobhan with the feathered claw.

"All of this matters little, I suppose. You are of the utmost importance. Be assured that you will be delivered. The witch has plans."

"The witch?" *Leanan.*

"In exchange for her queenship, the mermaid will deliver you to her."

"What?"

Taking a ship down is the only way a mermaid can become a queen. So Father Joe had said.

"You are the price. The witch swore to help the mermaid if she would deliver you to her."

His shark's grin spread from ear to ear. Then, he evaporated into the walls. Corrine ducked into the stairwell beside Euan and Father Joe and peered out between the iron-plated treads. Euan was muttering softly under his breath, clutching his chest and looking faintly ill.

Before Corrine could say anything, the boiler blew, the funnel rocketing from the first stack and tearing through the upper decks. The pressure shot all of them backward into a heap against some storage casks, but she felt an odd bubble closing around them, as though a shield had sprung up between them and the blasts of steam and hot iron. Mara pulled Siobhan toward them through the steam, a green light pulsing around them like a protective net. As Corrine untangled herself from Father Joe and Euan, she heard cries of agony, and then a man lurched down the walkway, his face almost unrecognizable from the scalding. Voices whispered from his charred throat—the crotchety protests of an old man arguing with a Cockney riveter. He stumbled past her, down the corridor toward the deck above the paddle wheels. She closed her eyes when she saw him jump, the ghosts still arguing.

Distant rain sang like the sound of many harps unstrung. Then Corrine realized it was falling glass. The *Great Eastern* shuddered, and Corrine clutched at the treads of the stairs. Steam and smoke streamed toward the graying sky through the new hole in the ship's deck. She put her hand against her pinafore pocket, seeking reassurance from the book that still rested there.

The ship listed badly. When would the witch come to claim her? Corrine almost slid down in a heap, but Euan was there, steadying her.

"Now is the time to trust me," he said. "Do you or don't you?"

His eyes were filled with a light that made them seem almost green in the fire glow. She tightened her grip on his hand and rose.

Father Joe helped an ailing boilerman up the stairs while Mara and Euan carried Siobhan between them. Corrine helped them as best she could.

The *Great Eastern* rolled in the slow dawn. The horizon was a red line drawn over the distant Scottish coast. The first stack lay on its side on the deck, entangled with the mast rigging. The dome of the Grand Salon was gone, its iron supports twisted into useless, arthritic fingers. People lay groaning on the deck in various states of pain, trying to staunch wounds or remove glass. Some were dead. A soft, sweet hum carried above the suffering, a sound Corrine couldn't quite place. Uninjured crew members moved through the crowd, offering assistance. Others scrambled to launch the relief boats and bring the passengers to them in an orderly fashion. Though there was a need to hurry, it wasn't the frenzy of people who knew a ship was sinking. They were stranded not far from the Scottish coast; it only remained to get the passengers into the boats and to land.

"Euan," Father Joe said. "Will you find a boat while I try to find Miss Brown and the girls?"

Euan nodded.

Corrine didn't know what compelled her to look up as she followed Father Joe's form down the deck. The six masts of the *Great Eastern* loomed strangely unharmed and silent above the felled stack. Corrine traced the rigging with her eyes, and then spotted a strange curving shape perched on one of the crossbeams.

Taking a ship down is the only way a mermaid can become queen. The words echoed again in Corrine's mind. The mermaid sat on the crossbeam, the wind tugging at the banners of her skin. She tasted the sea wind, the low, liquid humming cascading from her rubbery lips.

"Euan," Corrine said.

He turned and looked where she gestured. "We must hurry," he said.

Mara looked too, and shook her head, as she held Siobhan against her. "If only I had my mama's shotgun," she growled.

The mermaid's song grew louder. Corrine heard a strange churning, as if the paddle wheels had started again. *But that couldn't be* . . . She looked over the side of the ship and saw that the water was rising.

You were the price . . .

"Euan!"

He looked at the rising water and lifted Siobhan out of Mara's arms. He led them toward a relief boat that the crew had not yet untrammeled from its moorings. Corrine and Mara began working to unmoor the boat, while Euan laid Siobhan gently against the deck housing. They threw the oilcloth off as the mermaid's song swelled with the rising tide.

Euan lifted Siobhan into the boat. There were terrible steam burns on her arms and across her shoulders. After all Siobhan had suffered, Corrine worried her wounds might kill her.

Corrine, Mara, and Euan climbed into the boat. Mara looked out over the desolation of the *Great Eastern*, then cast a shrewd glance in Euan's direction.

"Someday you won't mind telling me just how you protected them from the blast," she said.

Euan half-smiled.

For a moment, Corrine thought she saw his profile shift in the dawn. She blinked, and whatever she'd seen fled. Mara's eyes narrowed a little.

"You aren't what you seem," Mara said.

Euan's smile grew larger. "Nor are you."

Mara conceded with a sharp nod. Corrine again felt that an entire conversation had passed without her hearing it. As the waves reached their gray fingers over the sides of the upper deck, Corrine couldn't suppress the nervous shuddering that overtook her. Where were Father Joe and everyone else? If they all died today, it would be her fault.

"Are you hurt, Corrine?" Euan asked.

"They want me," Corrine said.

"What?" Mara said, her gaze swinging away from Euan.

"I am the price for this, for the mermaid to become a queen. The Unhallowed helped her, if she would give me to them . . . after."

"How do you know that?" Mara said.

"The ghost told me," Corrine said.

"Which ghost?"

"The engineer who haunts this ship. The one who built her. Brunel."

Mara just shook her head.

"What if everyone dies today because of me?" she said.

Mara looked her squarely in the eyes. "You face it."

Euan leaned forward, pulling the oars from where they were stowed within the boat. "She will not take you."

His firm, quiet tone reassured Corrine in a way little had these past few months.

"We will get to shore," he said. "I will take you to Sir James's estate. That's what I came to do."

Corrine looked away from his penetrating gaze. She remembered his touch, how it crept through layers of cloth to her skin. Flushing, she concentrated on the surging water. If they didn't move soon, they'd be pulled down with the force of the ship's sinking.

"Where are they?" Corrine said. She bent and shook Siobhan, but the girl offered little response. Her skin was like ice. Corrine grabbed the oilcloth tarp and tucked it around her, making an awkward, bulky blanket.

When she looked up, a tall man was standing near the boat. He was dressed like an officer, but he had the hungry look of one who had gone mad. Euan's fingers shifted on the oar.

"Get out," he said. "Me and me mates are taking this boat."

Corrine froze. The mermaid's song was an eerie warble up in the rigging. The water was nearly to the deck.

"I beg to differ, lad," Euan said.

The man rushed them, and Corrine could see his mates slipping around the corners, sliding closer. She looked toward the stairs, hoping that she would see Father Joe.

Euan lifted the oar in an arc across the man's chest. He fell back, winded. Euan leaped over the side of the boat as the man got to his feet, snarling and slipping. He held the oar at the ready, as if it were a giant, flat sword.

Mara took up the other oar and stood defensively. "Get a weapon, dammit!" she hissed over her shoulder at Corrine.

Corrine realized that she had been sitting with her mouth open, feeling sure that nothing could be done. She bent and scrabbled for anything that she might possibly use.

She heard the *thwack* of wood on skin as the men came forward. Euan wielded the oar almost faster than she could see, slapping one man to his knees and catching another under the chin and sending him flying.

"Hurry!" Mara yelled.

Corrine peered down the deck and saw Father Joe, Miss Brown, Ilona, and Christina wading along the tilting deck.

They came as quickly as they could, burdened down with what belongings they had managed to carry. Corrine was relieved to see that Miss Brown had brought her writing case, and Father Joe carried, among other things, Euan's valise. The ladies climbed in, as the last of the sailors were backing away from Euan, unwilling to take more punishing blows from his oar. Father Joe and Euan then pushed the boat out as far as they could, before they climbed in, shivering and dripping. Miss Brown clucked over Siobhan, while Father Joe settled himself next to Corrine.

"William said you were a fine swordsman," Father Joe said. "If you can do that sort of thing with just an oar, I believe it!"

Euan nodded briskly and bent to the oars, pushing as hard as he could to get free of the ship's wake.

Corrine looked back. The ship was nearly gone, its deck completely underwater. Other rescue boats filled with survivors scurried away from the ship in all directions. Tall white flames hovered and danced above the shattered lattices of the Grand Salon's skylights. Ghosts, all tethered to the *Great Eastern*'s rusting hulk. They evaporated as the deck sank under the gray waves, but Corrine knew they would flit through the rotting velvet and corroding mirrors at the bottom of the sea for eternity. At last, the mermaid dove from the mast, a flick of foam the only sign to mark her passing. People struggled with the boats through the bits of flotsam, paddling as hard as they could to escape the ship's sinking wake. The red morning clouds stretched across the sea as it welcomed its new queen.

~ EIGHT ~

January 16, 1866

THEY DRIFTED FOR A DAY AND A NIGHT, WITH THE MEN and even Ilona and Miss Brown taking an occasional turn at the oars. They ate tinned food that they found stowed in a strong-box under one of the dinghy's benches. At night, as the stiff wind whipped the stars into the sky, the girls huddled together for warmth. Miss Brown held Siobhan to try to keep her warm. The maid groaned when Miss Brown accidentally touched her burns, but didn't wake. Corrine heard Miss Brown whispering prayers in the depths of the night. When Euan relinquished the oars to Father Joe, he took his flute from his case and played a soft, slow melody that soothed the girls into sleep.

By morning, the shore finally beckoned. The girls climbed from the boat onto the rocky beach, their boots splashing through the icy water. Father Joe and Euan made a fire from driftwood and Corrine warmed her hands before it. This wasn't how she'd imagined coming to Scotland, but then she hadn't imagined that a mermaid would try to kidnap her by sinking a ship either.

Euan volunteered to seek out the nearest village and bring back help for Siobhan. Corrine watched him go, pale and hunched against the cold. She still wasn't sure whether she could trust him. Rory had dealt her such a blow that she believed she'd never recover from it. She wanted to believe that Euan was genuine, that whatever he was, he truly was only trying to protect her. As he had pointed out, there had been many opportunities and he had taken none of them. In fact, he'd put himself in the gravest danger just to be sure she was safe.

While they waited for Euan to return, the girls and Miss Brown curled together under a wool blanket and the oilcloth tarp, trying to keep Siobhan warm. Corrine fell into a dream where skeletons danced in the drowned Salon.

She stood in the dead Unhallowed city again, watching the movement of the dancers as they twirled to the rhythm of the Prince's stone heart.

I see you escaped, *he said.*

She turned. Somehow she knew he smiled, though she couldn't see his face.

He took her arm and escorted her down a promenade on which the moon and sun shone with equal ferocity. Mermaids are the most unreliable of creatures.

She looked up, hoping the silver-gold light would reveal his face, but his features remained blurred.

The witch wants me, *she said.*

Everything shuddered, and she realized that what had seemed solid was merely an illusion he cast.

She shall not have you, *he said.*

But—*Corrine began.*

She shall not have you, *he said again.* You will come to me, Corrine. And you will stay.

He took her frostbitten hands in his. An unholy warmth coursed through them, a warmth that she fought even as she welcomed the release from the pain.

The sun was in her eyes as she woke, and she almost feared that she'd ended up in the clutches of the witch anyway. Then she realized where she was and she squinted against the light, the blown sand, the salty wind. She put her hand to her throat and felt around her tattered collar. The charm Mara had crafted was gone. *He can reach me again.* She sighed. Mara had said it would happen eventually; the charm couldn't hold out forever.

Her hands were as hot as if she'd put them into a fire. She had to get rid of the heat. She looked over at Siobhan, who still lay unconscious and pale, breathing shakily under the oilcloth. She put her hands on Siobhan's collarbones and *pushed*, trying to transfer the warmth she couldn't contain.

Color dawned on the girl's face. She breathed deeply and opened her eyes.

"Siobhan," Corrine said.

Traces of terror and pain crowded into Siobhan's eyes, but it was clear that she knew who she was. She also knew Corrine. She started back a little in fear. "You shouldn't use their magic," she said. "It's wrong."

Siobhan sat up. Red handprints darkened both sides of Siobhan's neck. Ilona had apparently already gotten up; there was only an impression left where she had slept on the sand.

"I'm sorry," Corrine said. "I wanted to help you."

Siobhan stared at her, but before either of them could speak again, Miss Brown knelt in front of them. She placed her hand on Siobhan's forehead before taking the maid's hands in hers.

"Siobhan! Are you feeling quite all right?"

Siobhan nodded slowly. Her face looked like it wanted to crumble into tears, but she managed to maintain her dignity and removed her hands from Miss Brown's grip.

"Only the burns, Miss Brown, they hurt something fierce."

"Can you stand? Once we find a village, we should be able to make our way to Sir James. Euan has gone for help. He should be back soon."

Siobhan tensed at the sound of Euan's name, but didn't say anything more. She managed to stand on her own without help. It was all Corrine could do to stand herself; every muscle in her body ached. The only parts of her that didn't ache, in fact, were her newly healed hands. Mara looked deeply tired, as well, as though she could use an extended holiday filled with warm springs and hot soup. Only Christina looked fresh and well rested, though Corrine knew her friend certainly wouldn't have wanted anyone fashionable to see her bedraggled curls or salt-stiffened dress.

Euan returned by midday with a fisherman who dragged a cart behind him through the sand. His brogue was so thick only Euan could understand him. When the fisherman saw that the girl he'd intended on carrying was well, he insisted on carting along their baggage instead.

They arrived in Oban perhaps two hours later, their boots full of sand and their hair stiff with salt. Everyone spoke with the same brogue, but they treated Euan with a deep deference, as though he were the son of a lord rather than a gamekeeper. Soon, one of the fishwives had settled the girls on a bench close to the fire and ladled out bowls of steaming fish stew to each of them. Despite Corrine's great distaste for fish, the salty stew was probably the best thing she'd ever eaten.

A couple of fishermen agreed to take them in their carts to Connel where they could find a stage to take them overland to Fearnan. The girls huddled miserably among the baskets of dried and fresh fish, trying not to let the smell overpower them, while the adults sat next to the cart drivers.

"Don't you dare faint," Ilona growled to Christina. "If I must bear this, so must you."

Christina stuck out the pink bud of her tongue in a most unladylike fashion. Corrine hid her grin in her salt-stiff sleeve.

In Connel, Euan hired two stages that would take them as far as Tyndrum, where they would change for Fearnan. Father Joe also hired a courier to ride ahead and let Sir James know they'd made landfall. People nodded to Euan, but whispered whenever they saw Father Joe with his cassock and rosary. Corrine couldn't be sure, because their accents were hard to decipher in their murmurs, but she thought she heard the word "papist." As they awaited the stage, Corrine wondered dully from which quarter the next attack would come. She hadn't thought of anything but keeping one step ahead of the Unhallowed for a long time. Would that feeling ever end?

Euan brought her a warm meat pie from a vendor he'd found outside. Corrine cradled its warmth in her palms. He unwrapped a scarf from around his neck and tucked it around her unguarded throat. "You look cold," he said. "Keep this. My mother knitted it, long ago."

"Thank you," Corrine said. She bit into the steaming pastry, but not before she saw Christina and Ilona elbow each other. Ilona winked. Corrine rolled her eyes and chewed the tough meat, glad of its warmth.

The stage ride passed in a blur of cold and melancholy. The countryside with its snow-crested hills and deep, gray rivers was beautiful, but she couldn't find much joy in it. Christina and Ilona murmured to each other. Siobhan stared out of the window, her fingers twisting nervously in her lap. Mara's customary silence seemed tinged by what Corrine could only guess was homesickness. She looked lost in the sea of white faces, the brooding landscapes. Corrine imagined her belonging somewhere hot, like a deep swamp, not here in the cold, fretful moors of Scotland. A familiar vision opened: a tall tree wading through black water, trailing lianas and Spanish moss in its gnarled branches. Corrine wondered what it meant. She remembered someone saying once that Father Joe had rescued

Mara from New Orleans. Had she grown up in a bayou? And why did Corrine always see a walking tree whenever she focused on Mara?

Deep in the night, with the horses near exhaustion, the coaches finally turned onto the long drive of the Campbell estate at Fearnan. Corrine roused enough to be embarrassed by her stiff dress, the stench of sweat, soot, and ocean that clung to her. There had been no time to change and certainly none to bathe in for several days. She hoped Sir James would forgive them all their improprieties.

The carriage halted before the doors of the manor, where a butler named Mr. Turnbull waited to receive them. Mr. Turnbull greet Euan heartily, and then Euan opened the carriage door to help everyone out.

"I'll take my leave of you now," Euan said to Father Joe.

Father Joe nodded. "We'll talk in the morning. We have much to discuss."

Euan nodded and hefted his valise. "A good night to you all," he said.

Corrine was disappointed that he avoided her attempts to make eye contact.

"Follow me, please," the butler said.

He led them up the stairs and through the grand foyer to a staircase of dark, polished wood that curved away into the gloom. A matronly woman bearing a lantern came from upstairs.

"I'm Mrs. Guthrie, Sir James's head housekeeper," she said. "If your servants will follow Mr. Turnbull to their quarters, I'll show you to your rooms upstairs. Tea's on and hot baths will be brought to your rooms soon."

Mara and Siobhan disappeared into the gloom down the hallway, following Mr. Turnbull. Corrine felt guilty that they would certainly not enjoy the niceties she would. She hoped someone would take care of Siobhan, who seemed barely capable of walking with Mara's support.

She followed Mrs. Guthrie with the others up the stairs, overcome by yawning. She had seldom seen anything much more welcome than the fire that blazed on her room's hearth or the white down coverlet that waited for her nearby. Everything still shifted and tilted, like a rocking carriage or a listing ship. She sat in a chair by the fire and before she could lean forward to pour tea into her cup, she was asleep.

January 17, 1866

In the morning, bathed, dressed in fresh clothes, and refreshed from sleep in a luxurious and unmoving, if creaky, bed, Corrine wandered downstairs. Mr. Turnbull directed her to the dining room, where mounted heads of every sort of animal Corrine could imagine stared down at the long, dark table.

Father Joe entered just after her, his dark hair still wet from washing.

A portly man rose from the head of the table to greet them. White muttonchop sideburns framed a reddish face above a maroon silk dressing gown.

"Sir James," Father Joe said, relief evident in his voice.

"Father," Sir James said, coming around the table and clapping him on the back. "I never would have thought to see you again in these parts."

Father Joe nodded. "Times change, I'm afraid."

Sir James turned to Corrine. "And you must be William's niece?" He took her hand between his meaty palms. The gesture was endearing, but Corrine was taken aback by the cold, dark feeling that washed through her. She looked at him and thought she saw a faint shadow, like the shadow she'd seen around Father Joe. And yet unlike it too.

"Glad to meet you," he said, his dark eyes holding hers. His accent sounded more English than Euan's Scottish lilt; she was reminded forcibly of her uncle. He squeezed her hand almost until it hurt, but released it quickly as Miss Brown entered the room with Ilona and Christina.

"Miss Brown," he said, making a courtly bow in her direction, "how delightful to meet you at last."

"My pleasure," she said. "These are our students." She introduced them in turn. Christina, of course, gave a graceful curtsey, while Ilona bobbed her head.

"A pleasure. Please come and sit. Breakfast will arrive soon."

Corrine observed Sir James, trying to make out the shadow she'd thought she'd seen. She felt terribly unsafe, but there wasn't anything she could pinpoint. The weak morning sun streamed in through the windows. Mrs. Guthrie carried in the breakfast things covered with white napkins on a silver tray. The staring heads of elk and red stags were eerie, but not threatening.

Sir James seemed to catch her thought, for as he returned to his seat, he looked at her and said, "Don't worry, young lady; you'll be safe here. The Council laid strong wards all about these grounds centuries ago. Nothing gets in or out of here without my knowing about it." Corrine thought of the daoi she'd seen at Uncle William's and shuddered.

"Thank you."

"I know your uncle," he said. "If you're anything like him, you worry far too much."

Corrine nodded. Was it worry that drove her uncle to be so brusque and distant? She couldn't imagine.

Dish after dish was placed on the table, so that Corrine wondered if she'd ever need to eat again. There were scones with real butter and preserves, steaming fried eggs, great bowls of porridge, and blood pudding. After the thin gruel on the ship, Corrine wanted at least one of everything.

Sir James signaled and Mr. Turnbull came around to fill their cups with tea or coffee as they desired. "I've been thinking of a suitable way to welcome you and help you meet everyone here," he said. "And I've thought that perhaps I shall have a ceilidh so that you can all get acquainted. What do you think?"

"Well, after the accident, we're hardly equipped for a dance—" Miss Brown began.

"Pish. There's a perfectly good tailor in Kenmore; I'll have him call round this week." Sir James seemed so pleased with himself over the notion that there were no more refusals. "I'll have Mrs. Guthrie spread the word that we'll hold it on the first of February. A good, solid day for a ceilidh, with music and dancing and haggis. Mustn't forget the haggis!" Sir James beamed.

Miss Brown nodded, smiling.

Christina clapped her hands. "A dance! How perfect! And we can celebrate Corrine's birthday at the same time."

Corrine blushed. She'd almost forgotten that her sixteenth birthday was two weeks away. With all that had changed, birthdays didn't seem to matter that much. She was surprised that Christina had remembered.

"Your birthday, is it?" Sir James said. "Even greater cause for celebration. We shall have to send to Clan McPhee for a proper tartan sash for you."

"Thank you," Corrine said. She'd never thought much of her heritage on her mother's side and her uncle, of course, was not forthcoming about his knowledge of it.

Ilona pushed her spoon around her porridge bowl, hiding behind her hair. Corrine guessed she was less enthused about the prospect of dancing, as she had hated dancing class at

Falston. Mrs. Alexander, the dance mistress, had mortified her far too often.

After breakfast, Miss Brown asked Mrs. Guthrie to lead them to the room on the ground floor that had been set aside for the girls to study. Its great windows looked out on a labyrinth of hedges dusted with snow. Miss Brown distributed primers she had conjured from her rescued carpetbag, and Corrine tried not to groan. Of all the things to be rescued from the ship, why had these survived?

"Though Falston is gone, nothing has changed," Miss Brown said. "You all still have need of a good education."

Thus began the familiar French declensions, the algebra problems, the painful recitation of botanical names. Corrine's gaze wandered often to the winter garden. A gazebo rose at the center of the labyrinth, its edges softened by snow. Three black ravens sat at the apex of its roof.

She was walking again along the fog-ridden lake. A loon's cry echoed in the stillness. In the distance, something moved and Corrine stepped off the path. The three ladies veiled in black walked along the road. One of them carried a shield. Another carried a spear. The last carried a mask that trailed ribbons like living snakes into the mud—

". . . Corrine, what do you say?"

Corrine shook her head and saw Miss Brown watching her with a slight frown.

"I asked if you'd like to walk about a bit," Miss Brown said.

Corrine nodded. Maybe the cold air would clear her head.

"You must use what Father Joe is teaching you."

"I'm trying, Miss Brown; I just . . ."

"No need to explain. Come out with us. The fresh air will do us good, I imagine."

Miss Brown gathered her shawl about her and crossed the room to open the French doors. The air rushed in with a damp chill that made the lanterns flicker. Corrine took a throw that Ilona offered and wrapped it around her shoulders. The air breathed through the room like a living thing; Corrine envisioned an enormous daoi stretching a web of cold through the room and shivered.

The stone steps were swept clean of snow, but frost still crackled under the girls' boot heels. The ravens took flight, gliding toward the twisted, leafless depths of the forest along the river. As she walked along the border of the labyrinth, Corrine watched the forest following her. She felt sure she had seen this forest before. The day she had first seen her father walking away from her uncle's house . . . she had dreamed not long afterward that the trees had trapped her deep in their roots. It was then that the Prince had come to her and bid her drink.

Strange metallic sounds rang through the cold. Corrine wondered for a moment if somehow the *Great Eastern's* skeletal riveter had followed her here. As they rounded a low wall, though, she realized that what she'd heard was more of a singing hiss than the clang of a wrench against pipes. She first saw a young boy, perhaps thirteen or fourteen, lifting a thin foil that seemed almost as long as he was tall with a guard that completely swallowed his wrist. Ilona nearly dragged her the rest of the way. Euan blocked the boy with an odd, copper-colored foil.

"Euan!" Ilona said.

The boy's foil tangled with Euan's. Euan shook him off.

The boy looked up as the girls stopped. His face was already red with cold, but the blush deepened when he realized he'd had an audience. Ilona stood next to Corrine, her body tilted forward and quivering like a dog's. There was a beauty in her attention, her dark, sparkling eyes, that Corrine realized most people would probably never see. Fascinated, it was all Corrine could do to tear her gaze from her friend to Euan. He saluted all of them with his foil, his other hand hovering over his chest. He coughed aside lightly as the boy stepped back and lifted his foil in the guard position.

Corrine tried to guess Euan's age, as she had tried through-out the sea voyage, but failed utterly. The ease of his pose, his mussed hair, the way he wore his thick gauntlets—all seemed to belie his youth. But there was something about his sharp face and hazel eyes that made her wonder again if he was older than he seemed. For just a moment, shadows gathered around him, warping the day into a cloak of night. She rubbed a hand across her eyes to try to clear them.

"Good morning, ladies," Euan said, bowing in their direc-tion. The boy followed suit. Euan's eyes didn't rest on anyone in particular.

"I see you're well rested, Mr. MacDougal," Miss Brown called, half-laughing.

The wind kicked up and tugged at Miss Brown's bonnet, forcing her to put a hand to her head to keep the bonnet from blowing backward. Snow skirled against Corrine's lips, tasting of metal and worn stone.

"I'm giving my assistant Kenneth here a little lesson in fight-ing in the weather," Euan said. "Only trouble is that the weather seems to be besting both of us." He coughed again. "Kenneth will need a new partner at this rate."

"Is there anything we can do to help?" Miss Brown said.

"Tell him there's no need to practice in the snow?" Ken-neth asked, ducking away when Euan shook his foil at him good-naturedly.

Miss Brown smiled. "Perhaps you should consider taking a breather, Mr. MacDougal. Surely your health was taxed by our recent misadventure."

"I could fight him," Ilona muttered under her breath.

Euan considered Ilona with a gaze that made Christina blush

and duck her head. But Ilona remained steady.

"Could you, now?" he said.

There was a challenge in his voice, but also an invitation. Ilona rose to it. "I could."

Corrine looked at Miss Brown, wondering what she thought, and was surprised to see a grin hiding in the depths of her bonnet. Perhaps she, like Corrine, was thinking of how Ilona had come to be at Falston in the first place—fighting with a girl at her former school in Norfolk.

"Well, then," Euan said, "perhaps Miss Brown and I shall speak about this further. I have no objection. Women can be natural fencers. Would spare me to work Kenneth all the harder in the forest."

Kenneth made a face, but did not seem truly averse to the idea. "I look forward to the chance, Miss . . . ?"

"Takar," Miss Brown volunteered.

"Takar," Kenneth said, saluting her.

Ilona nodded gruffly, trying to hide behind her usual rough demeanor. Corrine imagined Ilona with a foil in her hand and didn't know whether to smile or shudder. She remembered a bit of an old vision wherein Ilona stood like Joan of Arc, shining in silver armor against a great darkness, defending a cowering girl with her sword and shield. She had seemed so young and strong all at once.

"We'll think on it," Miss Brown said. "But we should leave you to your practice now."

Euan smiled and nodded. His smile was not as captivating as Rory's had been, nor were his eyes as enticing. But there was something about the way he lifted his foil, the way the wind touched his rough huntsman's coat that made him seem more genuine than Rory had ever been. She was surprised to realize that she trusted him. Surprised and just a little angry. She didn't want to be vulnerable like that ever again.

Kenneth sighed and saluted Euan, ready to begin their match anew.

Miss Brown ushered the girls along the path. The damp cold seemed intent on inserting itself into Corrine's bones.

Christina pouted. Corrine guessed that she was a bit put out by the fact that Euan had never fawned or doted on her. Christina liked the effect she had on people, though her joy was quite subtle in comparison to Melanie's, who had always flaunted her curls and curves whenever she'd had the opportunity. The thought of Melanie made her mouth sour. Corrine didn't want to think about Melanie, even though she was quite certain she'd not seen the last of her.

Something brushed Corrine's peripheral vision; a strong, powdery wind touched her cheeks. Wings snapped around her temples. She felt rather than saw the claws flexing toward her eye. Someone shouted. One of the ravens that had been roosting earlier on the gazebo roof lifted off into the growing fog, its claws curled.

"Corrine!" Christina said.

As she fell, Corrine wondered when Christina would faint.

Miss Brown caught her before the day went dark.

NINE

January 20, 1866

H E SAT ON HIS THRONE AGAIN, BUT HE NO LONGER WEPT. *Instead, she was trying to weep. But all Corrine felt in her right eye was a dry itching. Her eye socket was a puckered crater beneath her hand.*

Why?

This was not my work, *he said.*

Then who?

I think you know. *He rose. She tried in vain to see his face.*

The witch. But what have I done to her? Why can you not stop her?

He crossed the echoing chamber and she felt the sadness in his touch, though she couldn't see it on his face. I can only protect you if you come to me. There is no other way.

Anger beat blindly through her skull. I gave you your heart! *she shouted.* Surely that's worth a little of your regard! *The throne room warped, as though she looked at it through ancient glass.*

But you haven't given me yours, *he said.* I require more than stone, little one.

No, I won't give you that. I will never give that to anyone again.

He laughed. His fingers cupped the dry, burning socket. With his other hand, he brushed her hair away from her throat.

Never? Never is a painful word.

She tried to use Father Joe's breathing exercises, but the teeth of never slid into her throat, choking her breath, darkening her heart.

A thread of light bled into Corrine's slumber. Someone waved a candle flame in front of her eye, tracking her vision. She shrank, as though the fire might leap in and steal her last bit of sight.

A man spoke in such a thick brogue that all she could make out was the gist. Her eye wasn't permanently damaged. It would heal. She felt again the dry crater of her dream, the Prince's hand over its burning cavity.

She couldn't follow any more of what the doctor said and eased back against the pillow, longing for him to just put the bandage over her eye again and be done.

Miss Brown appeared; twigs of pain clawed the surface of her eye as Corrine tried to focus.

"Corrine, don't try so hard; I'm sure it's painful." The edge of Miss Brown's hand curved briefly over her temple.

The skin felt tight under her eye. She put her hand to it and felt more bandages.

"The raven clawed your cheek; we're hoping it won't scar too badly."

"Too badly?" Corrine repeated.

The tears came then, and with them, the pain.

Miss Brown sat with her. "The doctor says it's good if you cry now and then. The tears clean out the wound."

Such matter-of-factness made Corrine long for her mother. She reached to pull the sheet over her head, to shut out the world and be alone with her pain. But the doctor was there, turning her, tilting her head, forcing the tears to pool in her eye before he allowed them to run down her cheek. Then, he bandaged her and left without saying good-bye.

Miss Brown was still looking down at her. "You'll have to wear the bandage for several weeks until the eye heals fully."

"Weeks?" Corrine said. Her mouth felt stuffed with cotton.

She remembered the impending ceilidh. This time, she pulled the covers all the way over her head and refused to speak further. The door groaned as Miss Brown left the room.

January 21, 1866

In a day's time, Corrine felt like a caged bird. Miss Brown wanted her to wait one more day to adjust before she resumed normal activity. Corrine remembered all too well her long recovery from the swamp fever and didn't want to ever spend that much time in bed ever again. But she acquiesced grudgingly and was glad when Ilona and Christina sneaked in for a visit.

"Miss Brown didn't want us to bother you," Christina said. "But we thought you might want the company."

Corrine tried to nod, but the pain stopped her. "Yes," she said.

"Are you well?" Ilona said. "I could not believe it when . . ." Corrine held up her hand, and Ilona went silent. Corrine didn't want details.

"I'll be well; the doctor said the eye would heal. It's just scratched." She put her hand carefully over the bandage. "I suppose I won't be attending the ceilidh, though." She clasped her hands in the hollow of the blankets over her lap. With her good eye, she watched her fingers form a claw, like the raven's.

Christina took her hands. "Ah, but of course you will, my friend!"

Corrine looked at the faint roses in her cheeks, the alluring dark eyes, and sighed. "But this patch—" She began.

"Perhaps we'll dress you like a pirate," Ilona said.

Corrine gave her what she hoped was a patently unimpressed stare, but she doubted she could achieve much beyond comical with the white bandage.

Christina looked at Ilona with admiration. "Ilona, what an idea!"

"What?" Ilona said dubiously.

"We could ask Sir James to make it a costume ball! That way Corrine won't feel out of place. She could be a pirate or . . ."—Cristina caught Corrine's glance—"or . . . wear a mask."

"This is silly," Corrine said. "Sir James shouldn't change the ceilidh just because of me. I'll just stay here. You can tell me all about it afterward."

The thought made her unhappy for some reason, which also confused her. Why did she care about a silly dance? What difference did it make? Euan's face came to mind, but she quickly pushed it away. Why should I care if he's there?

"No, that just won't do at all," Christina said. "It's your birthday. You're going. We'll find a way."

Corrine opened her mouth to speak, but closed it as Ilona said, "If I have to go, you're going. That's it."

The door opened and Ilona and Christina froze. Father Joe entered, followed by Siobhan. Corrine hadn't seen the maid since their arrival at Fearnan. Siobhan still looked paler than usual, her eyes too sunken, her wrists a little too bony. Corrine couldn't imagine what the multiple possessions aboard the steamship had done to the already fragile girl. She mused that the scratch on her eye was small in comparison to Siobhan's hurts.

"What's 'it'?" Father Joe asked. A rare smile hovered about his lips.

Christina had recovered herself and was turning on the charm.

"We wanted to make sure that Corrine wasn't trying to get out of going to the dance, Father," Christina said, smiling and bowing her head.

"Was she trying to?"

"Yes, but Ilona found a marvelous solution."

"Oh?" Father Joe removed his glasses. Corrine half-smiled. Talk of such feminine things seemed to make him nervous. She wondered how he had managed working so long at a girls' school if he was still this unaccustomed to female interests.

"Yes," Christina continued. "We shall ask Sir James to make it a masquerade. Corrine can go as a pirate."

At the word *masquerade*, Corrine another Christina float into her vision in front of the real one.

A much older version of Christina, wearing a wine red gown that drank in the light of a thousand candles, held a gold-ribboned mask by her side. She pushed through a crowd of masked dancers, frantically searching for someone in the sparkling reflections of gems pasted to hanging silks. A man in a midnight velvet coat and doublet stepped forward. Ah, my queen. At last I find you . . .

Corrine clutched the blankets, willing herself back into the present moment. The dry pain in her head made it easier to accomplish. Siobhan hovered like a ghost by the door.

Father Joe was smiling at something Christina had said, but Corrine saw uncertainty in his eyes. She could almost hear his thoughts. *Then anyone might sneak in . . .* Shadows of suspicion played around him, but he said, "I suppose it wouldn't hurt to ask about the masquerade. Perhaps at dinner?"

Christina made a small curtsey of appreciation.

"And now, shouldn't the two of you be studying?" he asked.

Christina and Ilona looked at each other. Ilona pressed her shoulder, and then the two girls departed, looking appropriately contrite. Ilona gave Corrine a wicked grin before she shut the door.

Father Joe pulled up a chair at the left side of the bed. Siobhan came forward to change Corrine's bandages. Corrine shut her eyes, trying to avoid the light seeping into her wound. She resisted the urge to put a hand to her cheek. She was afraid of feeling the puckering scab there.

"Let Siobhan wash your wounds," Father Joe said. "The doctor said the herbs would help them heal faster."

Corrine leaned her head back in Siobhan's hands. Siobhan shakily dripped the cold tincture into her wounds, soaking up the excess with a cloth she held at Corrine's temple. There was too much in the girl's eyes. Corrine saw that Siobhan was on the verge of vision, and she reached to grip her hands to stop them from shaking.

"Don't let it take you," she said.

"I'm sorry, miss," Siobhan said.

"It gives them too much power," Corrine said, realizing it for the first time as she said the words. She thought of how her wish to stop seeing had come so oddly and painfully true. She was beginning to think that she should stop wishing entirely. A wish had begun all of this. And yet, with the perversity of the Fey, she could imagine what would happen if she wished for nothing.

"I know," Siobhan whispered. "I just don't know how to stop them."

"I can help you, Siobhan," Father Joe said. "If you'll let me."

Corrine released Siobhan's hands, and the girl began replacing the bandages on Corrine's cheek and eye.

Siobhan half-shook her head. "No magic, Father. It's the work of the devil Unhallowed. I'll not stoop to it."

Father Joe sighed heavily. "Surely you can guess what will

become of you if you don't learn to control this gift?"

Siobhan nodded. Her lips were tight; she looked like she might cry.

"Then, I strongly encourage you to consider my offer."

"I will, sir." But Corrine could see that she wouldn't.

Siobhan placed all the bandages in her basket and set the tincture on Corrine's nightstand. "May I be dismissed, Father?"

"Yes, of course," Father Joe said.

She left without looking at either of them.

"Is there anything that can be done to help her?" Corrine asked after the door had closed.

"Not without her consent," Father Joe said. "One of the banes of magic is that good must be participatory. Siobhan must participate in her own change."

"And, yet with a curse . . ." Corrine began. She was thinking of Rory, of how they had cursed him in Virginia and how he had fled to Scotland. As far as she knew, he still hadn't been found despite the searches the Council had been conducting of the surrounding area.

"With a curse, no participation is required. It is easy to do evil at a distance. Not so with good."

"Then, what do we do?"

"To help Siobhan? Nothing unless she wills it. We must keep her safe, of course, but we cannot aid her if she doesn't wish to be aided. But for ourselves—for you and the other members of the Council—there's still much we can do to hold back the dark."

"What can we do?" Corrine asked.

"Learn the magic. Be wary of those who would charm you to their purposes. Most important, retrieve the stones and find a way to keep the Unhallowed from Hallowmere forever."

Corrine clutched again at the bedclothes. With so much

against her, she didn't see how she could possibly win. "I still don't see how," she said.

But Father Joe cut in before she could finish. "Much is still unclear, even to us. Have you had more dreams? Does the Prince still speak to you?"

She heard the Prince again. *"Never" is a painful word.*

"Yes."

"What does he want?" Father Joe said.

Corrine felt suddenly embarrassed, remembering how the Prince had drawn her hair away from her throat in her dream, how she had given in to his goading. How did he always manage to unsettle her? She shook her head.

"Has he led you to any of the rathstones or tried to make you take the wards from Fearnan?"

"Not yet," Corrine said. Then she found a little of her courage. "He still tells me to come to him."

"Does he say why?" Father Joe leaned forward intently, a predatory gleam sharpening the angles of his face.

"He says it's to protect me," she said. "From her. From the witch." Every time she spoke of the Prince, she worried she'd be forced to admit that she had given him such tremendous power by giving him the stone. Even before Rory had taken the stone from her at Falston, she had placed it in the cavity of the Prince's chest in her dreams. Thus had begun the music that rebirthed his empire. What more did he need of her now?

Something in Father Joe's face shifted. It was almost imperceptible, and she had the odd feeling that she would have seen it for certain had she been able to look upon him with what her mother had called her "fairy eye." The eye the raven had tried to take. The eye that wept quietly into its bandage now.

"Who am I?" she asked.

He startled, as though she'd caught him reading a forbidden text. Snippets of conversation chased back through her mind.

Just after the destruction of Falston, when the bloodmark had been discovered in her strange eye, Father Joe had said, *I have been given reason to believe* . . . And he had kept Miss Brown from speaking on the subject further. The argument heard from outside Uncle William's study door about her power. The need for magical training. The reference in the serpent-bound book to those the Unhallowed called the Half-Born. *The stones may only be found by the Polluted Ones, those the Great Deceiver calls the Half-Born.*

"What do you mean?" Father Joe asked.

"I mean, who am I, what am I, that the Unhallowed won't let me be?" She thought again of the witch Leanan. *Come to me, my little raven.*

"Corrine, if I——" She had never seen Father Joe quite so flummoxed.

She imagined her voice going shrill before she even spoke, but a swift knock came and the door opened.

Euan took off his gamekeeper's cap and made a small, careful bow. He came forward and hesitantly laid a sprig of something green at the foot of Corrine's bed. His dark hair was mussed, his cheeks red with cold or exertion.

"Euan," Father Joe said, relieved.

"Father," Euan said. "Corrine. Forgive me for interrupting. I wanted to be assured Corrine was well after the accident."

Corrine sat as straight as she could. "Yes, quite," she said. She had seen Christina act haughty once; she hoped she could do the same passably. She didn't know why she felt the need to, except that her dream had given her even more determination. She trusted Euan, but trust and love were two very different things. She would not fall prey to love so easily again.

"I brought you a sprig o' juniper," he said. "Something the old folks around here use for protection against beasties like the one that attacked you."

Corrine nodded.

"They say you should pin it in a fold of your shawl and no harm will come to you." Though he stood quite still, he was tense as a caged cat. He looked as though he very much wanted to say more, but wouldn't say it in Father Joe's presence.

"Thank you," Corrine said. She let the sprig with its shriveled blue berries rest on the counterpane.

Euan waited as though he thought she'd speak more. She offered nothing but silence.

"Well then," Euan said. "I'd best be getting back to my work."

Father Joe nodded.

After the door closed behind Euan, the silence was too thick to be broken.

Father Joe said at last, "I wish I could tell you what you want to know. But I cannot. I have only suspicions—it would not be fair."

Corrine turned her head so sharply that the pain bloomed anew in her head.

"We must find Rory. He can explain what we don't yet understand. If he can be compelled to do so."

Corrine's teeth gritted at the thought of seeing Rory again.

Father Joe stood. "I'll leave you now. Mara or Siobhan will bring your dinner soon. Until then, practice the concentration exercises I taught you. We'll resume your studies tomorrow."

As he left the room, Corrine's gaze fell on the juniper sprig. She picked it up and slid out of bed. She trod the cold stones to the hearth and tossed the sprig on the fire. She might trust him, but she was tired of hiding behind someone else's protection. The flames sizzled and popped as they consumed it, and the sharp scent of juniper made Corrine's unbandaged eye water. The fire sighed as she turned back to her bed.

January 22, 1866

Corrine waited for Father Joe in the small turret room on the upper floor of the manse. There were ancient books aplenty here; the smell of them was comforting. She strained to see their titles in the gray afternoon light. She didn't anticipate enjoying this training session much. Meeting Leanan in her vision on the ship had not been pleasant. She stood and went to one of the high windows.

Other than her ill-fated walk along the edge of the labyrinth, it was the first time she'd seen the estate grounds. The labyrinth twisted in knots below her, the gazebo rising like a stone heart at its center. Alongside it, a narrow path cut through the hedges and over a dark stream. The path continued through the leafless forest. Smoke curled up from the trees—the cottage of some servant or other groundskeeper, she imagined. The brown line of the Scottish Highlands rolled off in the distance.

She expected a cloaked figure to raise his bloody hand to her, but the landscape offered up nothing threatening. She put her hand thoughtfully against the serpent-bound book in her pocket. Since the mermaid had failed to deliver her to Leanan, she wondered about the next move of the Unhallowed. From what corner would they strike next? And how could she be ready?

Father Joe entered then, and she turned from the window as he offered her a chair at the table. "You've continued your practice with the wind, yes?" he said.

Corrine nodded. She had, though possibly not as frequently as he had meant her to. The great towers at the edge of the world still frightened her. She feared what awaited.

"Good. Keep up the practice. Breath is the fuel for all other acts of magic," he said. "Today, we want to move into the next domain, the domain of fire." He held a piece of paper in front of her. "Set this on fire."

She gaped at him. "How?"

"Use your breath. Use your mind."

Corrine closed her eyes and began the breath-count. She felt herself taking flight, gliding toward the castle in the dawn.

"Now, go beyond the castle. Go into the sun," Father Joe said.

She lifted high above the turrets, steadfastly refusing to look down in case something unpleasant waited there. Instead, she flew on toward the burning eye of the sun. But the light blinded her. The heat melted the feathers and flesh from her bones. Her breath quickened with the pain.

She opened her eyes.

"You must fly through it. Embrace the light and heat," he said. "Try again."

She shut her eyes and counted down. She skimmed over the limitless ocean toward the castle.

"Are you near to the sun?" he asked.

She nodded.

"You are clutching something in your talons," he said.

And she was. It was heavy and sticky, like a ball of tar. It had been weighing her down without her knowledge.

"This is your resistance," Father Joe said. "Let it go."

She struggled. The tar-thing didn't want to leave her grasp. Like a rathstone, it knew her touch.

"Let it go, Corrine. You will not pass the test of the sun if you don't."

The sun swallowed the horizon. Its rays reached out for her with blazing tentacles.

"Release it!" Father Joe said.

As the light seared through her skull, she willed her claws to open. The thing caught fire and fell like a black comet into the well of the sun.

There was a moment of pain and a heat even greater than

the explosion of the *Great Eastern*. She gasped and nearly lost her concentration, but managed to sail through.

"Where are you?" Father Joe said.

When she answered, her voice didn't sound like her own. "In a garden. It's . . . There are roses." She crouched in a blossom-shrouded bower. It was noon and the welcome summer heat made sweat stand out on her skin, even in the shade. Bumblebees floated out beyond the curtain of roses and June bugs skimmed the green grass between the flower stems. A hummingbird darted in through the curtain to look at her, then zipped away again. As she watched, everything fizzed with a slow, green energy. It moved up the thorny stem of a rose near her into the bee that dug for its nectar. The bee floated away with green sparks dancing between its wings.

"You're seeing the fire of life," Father Joe said. "It moves through everything and joins all things in its web. Look out of the bower. What do you see?"

"Yes!" she said. "I see a green net. It moves through everything . . . Wait."

"What's happening?"

"Something . . . Someone is coming. The edge of the garden is curling up, like burning paper. It's dark and gray."

"Can you make out who?"

"No, I can't see. The roses . . . They're full of blood!"

"Come back," Father Joe said urgently. He gripped her arm. She inhaled deeply and opened her eye. Her bandaged eye stung unmercifully.

"What happened? Have I done something wrong again?" she asked.

Father Joe shook his head. "The natural order of things is upset. We shall have to work on protection charms. The taint of the Unhallowed reaches everywhere."

Corrine thought of the juniper sprig she had burned. Euan

had said it was for protection, but she'd resisted the deeper intimations of what he'd offered. She wished now that she'd kept it.

"What?" Father Joe said.

Blushing, she told him about burning the sprig.

"That's unfortunate," Father Joe said, opening one of the books. "But I'm certain we'll find a charm in here. It will be good practice for you." He splayed his fingers across one illuminated page. "You could do worse than to trust him, you know," he said, carefully avoiding her gaze.

Her blush deepened. *But that trust could not become more.*

"He was at your side first after the attack. He carried you to your room, and gave the doctor the herbs he needed for the tincture."

"He did?" No one had spoken of it before.

"Not to mention all that he did for you on the ship. Though I'm still puzzled as to the origins of his magic."

Corrine gaped at him. "You know about the magic?"

Father Joe looked up from his book with a snort of exasperation. "Of course I do! We should have boiled alive when that stack blew. Mara was barely able to protect Siobhan and herself from the blast. There's no chance she could have protected us too. My powers are bound and you are still far too unskilled. That leaves only him."

"Your powers are bound?" Corrine thought of the silver outline she'd seen surrounding his shadow on board the *Great Eastern*.

"Yes." Father Joe removed his spectacles and rubbed at his temples. "But it matters little now." He sighed and looked up at her. "I suppose Euan asked for your silence?"

Corrine didn't say anything.

"Well. I won't force you to break your word. But this may become important to the Council. Yet I have only ever known one man besides myself with such power, and he died long ago."

Angus, Corrine thought.

"I don't know if Sir James is aware of this, though I can't imagine that he isn't. There may come a time when you will need to seek information for us."

"You want me to spy for you?" Corrine asked, incredulous.

"For the Council," he corrected. "Not at the moment, but the time may come. If what you saw in the domain of fire is true, then the situation is growing ever more desperate. We must find Rory and retrieve those rathstones."

Corrine remembered how he had forbid her to eavesdrop, how he had told her that such dishonesty never helped a person to prosper. And now he might ask her to spy on someone she was growing to trust, even if she refused to love him. A creeping sensation skittered over her skin as though a daoi watched her again. The thought that she might become a spy like one of them was even more unsettling.

"Corrine, I know this is difficult. We're unprepared for what is coming and we have little time left. Please trust me and the Council on this. Do as we ask. More lives than you know depend on it."

Corrine nodded. She wasn't sure she was convinced, but she knew the consequences of misplaced trust from her time at Falston. Father Joe was right about the dangers.

"I'm going to call a Council meeting tonight to discuss what you saw today. Then, perhaps I can also retrieve the key to the Council chamber from Sir James and seek more information about protection charms."

"The Council chamber?" Corrine asked.

"When they built this estate, Sir James's forefathers built a secret octagonal chamber at its heart, a repository for all the Council's knowledge. For a long time, the letters of Angus and

Brighde were stored there, and it was under great duress that Sir James agreed to your uncle's proposition to take Angus's letters to America for further study. I should like to return them as soon as you're finished copying them. And to browse the chamber for spells or charms that might aid you. There may be something we're missing here."

Corrine's fingertips zinged as though she had touched the serpent-bound book. A secret chamber full of forbidden knowledge. She couldn't think of any greater temptation.

"May I see it?" she asked.

"If Sir James allows it," Father Joe said.

Already, Corrine envisioned sneaking off with Ilona and Christina to find the chamber in the middle of the night. What murky dungeons would they have to pass through? What buried halls filled with chests of treasure? The trip to Scotland had certainly never endowed her with such anticipation. She tried to keep her expression neutral.

"However," Father Joe said, "we shall start with this stack of books. Look for lesser level protection spells. They'll most likely be herbal charms. Mark them out for Miss Brown. She is collecting charms to make a special grimoire. And copy those letters! We need them back in the archives as soon as possible."

"Yes, Father."

He sighed then and rose. "You'll be fine on your own?"

"Yes, Father." She looked down at the books he pushed toward her. Her sight swam with pain, but no vision came.

"I shall go then and be sure everyone else is willing to meet tonight."

She nodded.

He was almost to the door before he stopped and said, "You would not be the first to do something unscrupulous in the service of higher principles, Corrine. I once stole the book you carry in your pocket—you do carry it still, don't you?—because I believed it should be out in the world. Neither the Council nor the Unhallowed knows where it is. Both would desperately like to have it." He smiled conspiratorially. "I should think being a spy is a tad better than a thief."

And then he was gone, leaving Corrine to sift through the charms without the faintest clue of what she was looking for. The piece of paper Father Joe had asked her to set on fire mocked her from the table. She turned to another letter for escape.

[Trans. note: End missing]

September 1357

To Sister Brighde, Isle of the Female Saints, from Brother Angus, Kirk of St. Fillan, greetings.

My beloved —

How cheered I am to at last read your words again! Please do not fear me—never would I do or say anything in word or deed to hurt you. I so long for you to trust the Fey as I do, to see how kind and good they have been to me now that I have left the monastery entirely. Each day, I receive their goodness like manna from Heaven. I am even as Thomas the Rhymer, who of old was beloved to the Elf Queen and received her gifts for being her faithful servant. It saddens me that you do not know these gifts yourself already. You hold such power. The Fey recognize it and call it good. Why should you think otherwise?

I am perplexed, though, that you say you have seen me more than once since Midsummer, and so there seemed no need to write. I am bound here until the doors of this world—or rath, as they call their homes—open. I could not have come to you at the time you mentioned. Perhaps it is just that we dream of each other, and the power of our longing is somehow made greater by its depth. Neither of us can deny what is in us. And since you will not have it that we leave together to find a new life elsewhere, there is but one choice—to enter into the kingdoms where we can walk together unseen . . .

January 22, 1866

That evening was the first time that Corrine rejoined everyone for dinner. Sir James greeted her heartily, apologizing for her injury and saying that he'd sent Euan to shoot every raven he could find. Corrine winced at the thought. She doubted any ordinary raven had done this. Every raven at the estate shouldn't die for Unhallowed trickery.

The glassy eyes of the mounts watched her as she spooned the thick soup into her mouth. There was an abundance of mashed things, among them turnips and potatoes, or "neep" and "tatties," as Sir James called them. There was roast venison. "Shot by Euan this morning," Sir James said.

Corrine kept her gaze on her soup bowl, but saw Euan's face in her mind's eye instead. She wished that he ate with them, though she strangely couldn't recall having eaten with him on the ship but once or twice. He had always been too ill. She dismissed her wish as foolishness and reached for more bread. How could he possibly find her interesting? Rory had only pretended to be interested for the sake of what he could get from her. And Euan seemed to know far more about her than even she did. What might he possibly want? She couldn't even begin to guess. She tore the piece of bread into small, frustrated bits.

"Sir James," Christina said.

All eyes turned to the ambassador's daughter, whose glossy curls shone in the lamplight.

"We wondered if we could ask a special favor on Corrine's behalf. She's too shy to ask it herself, so I hope you won't find it improper if I do."

Sir James chewed and swallowed. "Ask away, my dear." Corrine peered at him, trying to see the shadow she had seen on the first day she'd met him. There was nothing. Her wounded eye throbbed and itched.

"Well,"—Christina glanced down the table at Corrine— "we wondered if you would consider making the ceilidh you proposed a masquerade, as a birthday favor to Corrine."

"A masquerade?"

"Christina," Father Joe said, "considering the danger, I don't think a masquerade is a very good idea. Anyone could walk into this hall. A ceilidh is risky enough."

Sir James waved Father Joe into silence with his napkin. "A masquerade, eh?" He took a swig of wine from his glass. "I think that's a fine idea. I shall have Mrs. Guthrie send word. What occasioned it, if I may ask?"

Christina looked at him with her most charming smile.

"Corrine felt she shouldn't appear at the ceilidh in her condition. And I . . . we . . . thought it would be sad if she were to miss the night of her coming out into society and her birthday celebration because of an unfortunate mishap."

Sir James smiled. "Yes, ever has happiness been sacrificed before the altar of vanity." He laughed, pleased at his own pithiness. Corrine was a little incensed at the insinuation that she was vain, but the pleased look on Christina's face outweighed her objections. Her friend had won. And now, whether she liked it or not, she would be forced to attend the ball.

"A masquerade ball," Sir James said. "I must have Mr. Turnbull find a suitable costume. Perhaps something from a fairy tale?"

And then he expounded for several long minutes on what character he might choose and why, with Christina nodding vigorously while Ilona slashed at her venison as if it were an enemy she would very much like to dissect.

After dinner, Christina and Ilona were sent to a parlor to play baccarat until Mrs. Guthrie escorted them to bed. Miss Brown, Father Joe, and Corrine followed Sir James to his study, and Mara joined them after a few moments. Corrine's gladness in seeing her conflicted with her guilt at Mara's stiffly starched uniform. She wished there were some way for Mara to be free of her employment, but Corrine couldn't imagine how. Although she was free from slavery, she was still a slave to the necessity of fending for herself.

They seated themselves at a round, teak-inlaid table. Heavy, burgundy curtains were drawn over the windows. A few lamps shone here and there, but the greatest source of light was the fire that snapped on the hearth. A portrait of a Scottish lord and his hunting dogs—some ancestor of Sir James—hung above the marble mantel.

"I call this meeting open," Father Joe said. "As we've no

way to summon the spirit of Elaphe any longer"—he avoided looking at Corrine—"shall we discuss concerns?"

Everyone nodded.

"Mara?" Miss Brown said. "Would you speak first?"

Mara shifted in her seat, her maid's cap incongruous with the dark gleam of magic in her eyes. "I've sought Mr. Rory high and low, scried, asked some of the servants, laid a root even. Nothing."

Sir James coughed. Corrine would have thought he had giggled if she hadn't seen him cover his mouth with his handkerchief. He cleared his throat and said, "The MacLeods are well-known in these parts. If he was at MacLeod Castle, I'm sure I would've heard by now."

"Then where is he?" Father Joe said.

"I know he's here, Father," Mara said. Her fist clenched on the table. "I just don't know where."

"Can you lay another root tonight? The moon is full; it should aid your power," Miss Brown said.

"I can try," Mara said.

"Good," Father Joe said. "We need him here. We need to know how we can retrieve those rathstones from the Prince. We need to know the Prince's plans." He stopped and took off his spectacles. "This is not news, I'm afraid."

No one said anything.

"Madame DuBois sends word that all is progressing well in London," Miss Brown said.

"Have you received word from William?" Father Joe asked.

"I've not heard from him since we left," Miss Brown said. She looked down at the table.

"Unfortunately," Father Joe said, "I think there is movement in the astral domains. Corrine, tell them what you saw today during our training exercise."

Corrine related how she had seen the edges of the green

garden curling and burning, and someone walking toward her in a dark, buzzing cloud. She was fairly certain she knew who it was; if the Captain couldn't stalk her in the physical world, she knew he would come to her in her mind. In her first encounter with the Unhallowed, the hawthorn people had told her that the Captain served the witch. She wondered now if the witch Leanan had been after her all along.

"I believe this means that the Unhallowed are gaining even more power," Father Joe said. "They have made their presence known at both tests of the elements. I fear to see how they will manifest themselves for the last three. This is why I'm concerned about this masquerade. Elaphe only knows what the Unhallowed might do once they get word of this. I've been trying to find protection charms but none seem quite to suit. Sir James, would it be possible for us to browse in the Council chamber?"

Sir James sighed and folded his hands on the table. "Yes," he said." It would be possible. If . . ."

"If?" Father Joe prompted.

"If I still had the key."

There were several heartbeats of silence in which Corrine felt the bound power building in Father Joe like a thunderstorm. Her spine ached with it, until at last he drew a breath and pushed back from the table. His spectacles skittered across the table like a frightened animal. He went to the fireplace and leaned on the mantel.

"Joseph," Miss Brown said.

"What happened to the key, Sir James?" Father Joe said, staring at the portrait above him.

"It's gone," Sir James said. "Believe me, I've searched hither and yon for it and there's not a trace of it. It's not in any of the old hiding places."

"Without the key, we cannot even find the chamber," Father Joe said.

"I know," Sir James said in a small voice.

"Then, I suppose," he said, turning to Mara, "you must also lay a root to find the key as well as Rory."

"Yessir," Mara said.

"Corrine and Thea, if you will keep searching for the protection charm we need, I will see if there is any news of Rory to be had. Unless he is hidden deep within the Prince's rath, there must be some way of locating him."

"You'll find him somehow, Joseph," Miss Brown said. "All hope can't yet be lost."

"No," Father Joe said, his eyes locking with Corrine's. "Not yet."

~ TEN ~

January 28, 1866

THE CONTINUED COLD KEPT THE GIRLS INDOORS. THE
Council also forbade Corrine to go outside until her eye healed
or at least until they could be assured that Mara could put a
root of protection on Corrine. Sir James was still chagrined
about Corrine's injury. "Wards are set," he said almost daily
at breakfast when he looked at Corrine. "The Unhallowed
couldn't have done it. It must have just been a mad raven."

The kind of raven that just attacks people with strange eyes, Corrine
thought.

Corrine spent the morning poring over charms in the turret
room, until her head ached. She turned back to the translations,
sifting through to Angus's next letter.

[October 1559]

My beloved —

*I am deeply disheartened to hear that you are ill these many
days, and that the weather has turned as dark and dreary as the*

133

heart of winter. I wish you would see the Fey physic; he is a good doctor and his cures may do you good. It is difficult for him to travel between the rath and mortal worlds, however, so I fear you may have lost any chance of seeing him for quite a while.

It seems that it is left to me to provide comfort, cold though it may be when we are so removed from one another. If you would but remove the barrier in your heart, how close we could be again! It is summer here and if you would consent to come, you could feel the sun's warmth eternally on your face and hear the birds chattering in the shining trees. You could dance with the nixes on the heath at night, while stars weave themselves in your hair. I have told you of the wondrous foods here, the daily feasts, but there the Fey have given me something even more exquisite of late, a food they call chocolat. It is rich and dark, and the taste! Sweeter and more mellow than the finest honey-cake. It comes from another world their brethren have discovered, another land they say that is rich in gold and curious animals and all sorts of wonderful new foods. They promise more soon to come, and say that if I remain in the Prince's favor, I may attend a Hunt in this new world someday.

There is no end to the happiness here. Every day is filled with new wonders. Paradise opens before me. I do not know how I bore the days in our world before I met these good folk. I do not know why our people tried so hard to destroy them long

134

ago. Nor can I understand your resistance to the happiness you might have if only you would allow yourself. All would welcome you here with open arms. Have you never thought perhaps this is the Lord's way of giving you bliss on earth? I will not deny this gift. I beg you to open your heart and come to me.

Yours in Hope,
Angus

Corrine grimaced. Angus was worse than Rory with all his charming phrases and promises of magic. He'd even tried to lure the poor nun with chocolate! Still, she wondered how Brighde had managed to resist him, cloistered alone on her dreary isle. Corrine wasn't sure that she could have.

In the afternoon, when she couldn't bear to look at the written word any longer, Miss Brown came and told her it was time for a recess. The headmistress escorted

Corrine and Christina to the gallery to watch Ilona and Kenneth fence, and then left them muttering something about Council business. Miss Brown had reluctantly agreed to Ilona's training, as long as it wasn't bandied about the estate everywhere that one of the young ladies was being trained to fence with the men. Corrine had never seen Ilona more profusely grateful in her life than when Miss Brown had given her permission. The girl had practically gone to the ground and kissed Miss Brown's walking shoes, her face flushed with excitement.

Euan put Ilona and Kenneth through their paces up and down the long, low hall. The dusty suits of armor rang faintly with the clash of Ilona's and Kenneth's foils. Corrine realized now that the odd foil she'd noticed on the day of the attack was some form of reinforced copper, and Euan used it quite liberally to thrash his students when they made mistakes.

Ilona's height gave her an advantage over Kenneth, but she often wasted it, wielding her foil like a woodsman's ax. Finally, Euan whipped her on the arm with the foil and cried out in exasperation, "Do you not know how to dance? Dance with that foil; don't chop wood with it!"

Christina gasped, covering her mouth with her hands and looking over at Corrine. Ilona's face went red then; Corrine wondered if the girl would retort with just how much she hated dancing. But she said nothing and pressed harder, trying to hold the foil lightly. Not long afterward, Euan broke off their match, and set them to doing drills again. He showed Ilona how to better hold the foil so that it seemed an extension of her arm rather than a block of wood. "The movements must come from deeper than your wrist," he said.

Kenneth moved back and forth across the floor, obviously trying for the crablike precision of more skilled fencers. Euan watched him for a moment before coming to where Corrine and Christina sat near the fire.

"Of all of us in this match, you two certainly have the greatest advantage," he said, holding his hands out to the flames. He turned to watch his students. His angular profile caught the flames.

"How so?" Corrine said, hoping her voice sounded disinterested.

"You have the fire," Euan said. "We're about to chatter our teeth out down there."

"And you have both eyes," she said.

"Some things are taken only for a little while, Corrine," he said. His hazel eyes searched her face. He put his hand out as if he would touch the bandage and try to soothe the hurt, but his fingers fell back against his side.

"And some are taken forever," she said, fixing him with her one good eye in what she hoped was a baleful glare.

"Some. It is true," he said. His gaze fell on Christina, who remained silent. Jealousy scratched at her chest. "But others return to you, almost mysteriously, often unlooked for. Have faith in that mystery."

Corrine wanted to retort further, but she looked down at her hands instead, which were clasped in her lap. Her ankle burned fiercely for some reason, as it hadn't in a long while. She interlaced her fingers to keep from reaching down to her boot to scratch it.

"I should return to my pupils," Euan said.

Corrine looked up at his rapier-thin smile and nodded.

He gave Christina a short bow before striding back across the hall to his charges.

She followed her father along the edge of a loch. He walked far ahead of her, and no matter how fast she tried to run, she couldn't catch up to him. Fog rolled in off the loch and swallowed him. She was alone. She hugged herself against the damp cold. Freezing mud oozed between her toes. She looked down and saw that roses bloomed again around her ankle.

Something was coming behind her. She climbed up into the brush on the hillside to hide. She walked through spruce boughs that soaked her shoulders. A mound loomed through the trees, guarded on either side by pylons of crumbling stone. Its entrance led deep into the earth. She had a strange terror of being swallowed by it. The more she looked upon it, in fact, the more it seemed like a mouth, the pylons like fangs in the upper jaw.

It drew her to it. She crept closer, but as she came between the pillars, a sharp pain in her ankle nearly sent her sprawling. She tried to move forward, but it was as though a wall of glass rose between her and the dark portal. Something glimmered, as of a reflection from a mirror in the mound's depths.

There was a roaring in her ears. Her stomach dropped as though she plummeted down a well. She saw a tiny church rising on a hill . . .

Someone applauded her. She pushed out of her dream to find Christina bending over her, clapping her hands in her face, her arms draped with swathes of fabric. Ilona stood beside her, clasping a pile of musty old dresses that rose almost to her chin.

"This is no time for napping! We must start on your costume before supper," Christina said. She draped the things in her arms over the end of the bed, while Ilona piled hers over a chair.

Corrine slid the serpent-bound book where it rested next to her deeper under the covers. She had been trying to glean more information from it, but as it had done every time lately, it had given her nothing but garbled words and nonsense. She looked at the piles of fabric dubiously.

"Where did you get all of this?"

Christina smiled. "There are trunks all over this manor."

"And she went through almost all of them," Ilona said. She cursed in Hungarian and sneezed.

"Do we need that much?" Corrine asked. The thought of being swathed in so many layers, colors, and patterns made her wince.

"Silly girl, no," Christina said. "But we will need to test various designs, of course, to see which most suits a pirate queen."

"But I'm not—" But it was best to go along with Christina in her present mood. It had been a while since she had seen her friend this happy. Who was she to squelch Christina's enthusiasm, even if she didn't quite share it?

Corrine let Christina fuss over her as though she were a living doll. Ilona swooped in to pin things here and there when decisions were made.

Christina led Corrine to a tarnished standing mirror near a squat, ancient wardrobe. Lions were carved above the wardrobe's doors and thistles blossomed into door handles. Corrine found the wardrobe far more interesting than her own reflection, but Christina turned her head and forced her to look.

They had found an old black silk bodice, which they laced up over a white shirt with ruffled cuffs and puffed sleeves. The skirt was old green velvet with a few moth holes near the waist and down the back, which Christina hoped to conceal by an elaborate drapery of a musty fox stole.

"Do you really think pirate queens wore fur?" Corrine asked.

Christina gave her a disapproving look and pulled the old black ribbon from Corrine's hair. She ran her fingers through the heavy, brownish locks until Corrine's hair floated softly around her face. Corrine looked down at the green velvet hem in the mirror. She felt ridiculous, even more so when she looked at Christina's rapt beauty over her shoulder in the mirror.

"We shall put ringlets in, of course," Christina said. "Perhaps draw it back, like so . . ." She gathered a few strands of hair, tried to arrange a few others as though they curled. "Does your hair hold curl well?"

"I don't know," Corrine said. She had never had occasion to have it curled.

"Of course, you must carry a sword and wear an eye patch. Or do you prefer a mask?"

"I don't know," Corrine said again. She sighed.

"Come, come," Christina said. "We are making a good costume for you. Are you not happy with our work?"

Corrine couldn't bear for Christina to think her work was unappreciated.

"No, it's not that . . . it's just . . . Am I really the sort for a pirate queen? Shouldn't I be . . . a shepherdess or something?"

"A one-eyed shepherdess?" Christina's lips flattened. "What, was she blinded by her crook?"

Corrine couldn't answer. Ilona grinned behind her hair.

"No. You are a pirate queen," Christina said. "And every man at the masquerade will want to dance with you; your card will be full in no time!"

The thought brought on a new restlessness. How was she to dance without tripping over herself or someone else? Dancing was hard enough when her vision was intact, much less with just one eye. But Christina wouldn't hear further protests.

"And what will you two be?" Corrine asked.

"A Cossack," Ilona said, bowing.

"A shepherdess," Christina said. She grinned and then giggled, and Corrine laughed in spite of herself.

Christina's eyes narrowed and she gave Corrine a measuring look.

"Something is missing," Christina said. "Turn round."

Corrine twirled, nearly tripping over the long, heavy hem.

"Don't you think something is missing?" Christina asked Ilona.

Ilona grinned. "Yes, I think so."

"Every pirate queen needs a crown," Christina said.

It was deep in the night. Ilona and Christina ghosted down the stairs in front of her in their white nightgowns.

"Are you sure this is a good idea?" Corrine whispered at them.

"Shhh," they said almost simultaneously.

"This is an old castle," Christina said. "There must be treasure of the sort we need in it somewhere."

"But won't Sir James be angry?" Corrine asked.

Christina waved the thought away and gestured for her to follow.

They were going down the back stairs at the end of the hall. Ilona went first with the shuttered lantern. The stairway deposited them into what Corrine guessed was the back hall leading to the kitchens.

"Do you know where you're going?" Corrine asked.

Ilona glared at her.

They peered up and down the hallway. There was another door not far down on the left. Ilona gestured that they stay put and went to test it. Corrine saw her shine the lantern down in it.

"Are you sure an attic wouldn't be better?" she whispered to Christina.

Christina looked at her. "Silly girl, they never keep things like that in an attic! Now, shush!"

Ilona waved for them to come and the two of them skittered across the marble. Ilona shut the door behind them.

They spiraled down into the darkness and silence. Several landings branched off into low tunnels, but Christina insisted they go all the way down. They passed the entrance to a place that looked as though it housed an old dungeon. Cold energy stirred there, much like that surrounding the ghosts of John Pelham or Isambard Brunel. Corrine shivered.

"Keep going," she whispered. "There are bad things in there."

At last they came to the bottom of the stairs. It was impossible to see much beyond the circle of the lantern's light, but Corrine could see the glimmer of unhewn stone, almost as though they'd entered some sort of cavern. The floor was uneven and damp beneath her feet. They walked out into the echoing darkness. Christina tripped, and when Ilona shone the light in her direction, they saw the humped shadows of discarded furniture, old wine casks, rusting iron chains.

Corrine heard a long, low moaning from the other end of the hall. She clenched Ilona's arm. "Do you hear that?" she whispered.

"Hear what?"

"Shutter the lantern!" Corrine hissed. She suddenly longed for Mara.

Ilona shuttered the lantern completely, pitching them into abyssal night.

Corrine peered toward the other end of the cavern. Weak light beckoned.

"Wait here," Corrine said.

"Corrine!" Ilona said.

"Don't you think—" Christina started.

"If there's something bad down here," Corrine said, "much as I don't want to, only I can see it. Don't put yourselves in danger. Wait here for me. Unshutter the lantern just a little, so I can find my way back."

"This is foolish," Ilona said.

"Yes," Corrine said. "But I have to do it."

She turned toward the other end of the cave and peeled the bandage from her wounded eye. A halo of reddish energy pulsed, almost bright enough for her to see by. She saw that the chamber narrowed eventually, spilling out into what looked like a vast hall. She clambered as best she could across the wasteland of broken things, her heart thrashing against her ribs.

The low moaning resolved itself into an eerie, singsong sobbing. Corrine came at last to the wall and hugged it, skirting a pile of rotting wooden spindles. At first, she couldn't make sense of what she saw—a balloon of deeper darkness throbbed above the well of red light. Light shone also from brackets in the walls, a cold, magical light that stung her damaged eye.

There was a scrabbling sound, like claws digging into rock. She looked up. A giant scorpion-like thing hung from the ceiling, its pincers scraping uselessly against the stone. It had many little heads all along its back and their mouths were sighing, "Where-o-where-o-where-o-where," like little moaning birds over and over.

Corrine held to the wall as tightly as possible to keep from falling. The thing's whiptail hung down from the ceiling, glistening with hundreds of barbs that seemed longer than she was tall.

"Where-o-where-o-where-o-where . . ."

Corrine gulped. *Move, feet,* she thought. But they didn't move.

She shut her eyes. Fear-sweat dripped down her arm despite the chill.

Move.

Slowly, her feet obliged.

She started back across the chamber, holding to the faint star of Ilona's lantern with all the hope she had left. She was halfway across when she heard the moaning song change. "The key! The key? The KEY!" the little heads cried.

Corrine ran. She exchanged stealth for speed, picking up her nightgown and running as fast as she could, heedless of the things she kicked or broke in her passage.

"Run!" she said when she got near Ilona's lantern.

Neither of them questioned her.

They ran all the way up the stairs, feet slapping in the emptiness. They slammed the door in the hall, not caring if anyone heard, and raced back up to their rooms. Corrine sensed that the thing would not follow them up into the house, that the wards prevented it from doing so. Even so, she asked the girls to stay in her room with her and bolted the door and made sure the shutters were closed over the windows.

As she crawled under the covers, Christina said breathlessly, "I think a pirate queen can do without a crown after all."

Corrine couldn't help but agree.

Eleven

January 29, 1866

"CORRINE! WHAT IS GOING ON HERE?" MISS BROWN demanded.

Corrine rubbed her eyes and winced at the pain; she'd forgotten about tearing the bandage from her eye last night. She squinted at Miss Brown, immaculately dressed in a brown velvet jacket and matching skirt, leaning over her bed.

"A while ago, your door was locked, and just this moment, I found Ilona and Christina sneaking out of your room!"

Corrine dragged at the bedcovers, and then sat up.

"And where has your bandage gone?"

"I can explain, Miss Brown. But first, you have to know—there's an Unhallowed creature hiding in the dungeon."

"Are you sure?" she said.

Corrine started to nod, but pain shot through her head. "Yes," she said. She put her hands to her temples.

"I'll tell Father Joe," Miss Brown said. "What did it want? Did it see you or hurt you?"

Corrine was grateful Miss Brown didn't ask her to describe it. The thought of the many-headed scorpion made her nerves fire with terror. She released her temples and smoothed her hands over the white coverlet.

"I think it might have been looking for the chamber," she said. "It kept moaning about a key. It didn't hurt us, but it knew I was there." She heard its chirping screams again. *The key! The key? The KEY!*

She met Miss Brown's worried gaze. "We were so scared we slept in here last night and locked the door in case it came after us. I promise, Miss Brown, I will never ever go exploring like that again."

Miss Brown smiled briefly. "Well, I'm not sure I welcome all you endured to come to that conclusion, but I'll take you at your word." She squeezed Corrine's shoulder.

She looked at Corrine's eye, reaching for her chin and tilting it so she could examine the wound. "I'll send someone up to replace the bandage. It looks as though it'll all be healed soon. I think your cheek may not scar after all."

Miss Brown ran through a hall of mirrors. A white wave crashed down after her.

Corrine blinked. She reached for Miss Brown's hand and clasped it tightly. *It's not my fault,* she wanted to say, even though she'd no idea what she'd be apologizing for.

"What, Corrine?" Miss Brown said.

Corrine released her hand. "Nothing," she said, scrabbling her hands uselessly over the coverlet.

"Well, then. I'll alert Father Joe. I suspect he'll want to work with you in the training room this afternoon," Miss Brown said. "Only two days until the masquerade. And your birthday. Try not to worry so!" And she smiled before she left.

Corrine waited to dress until after Mara had come to her to medicate and re-bandage her eye. The tincture cooled the gritty itch that had begun when she'd rubbed it. Corrine told her about the thing lurking in the cavern below the dungeons.

"You're just damn lucky it didn't catch you," Mara said.

"I know."

"Teach you to mind, though." Mara gathered up the extra strips of linen and replaced them in her basket.

"Did you find Rory?" Corrine asked, trying to change the subject.

"I laid down a root," Mara said. "Should work." She smiled. Corrine shivered a little to remember what the last was supposed to have done. Rory should have felt as though his bones had melted to jelly. He should have crawled up the steps of the Fearnan manor begging to be released from it. But he hadn't.

"Soon," Mara said. And then she too was gone.

After breakfast, instead of copying the letters quietly in her room, Corrine idled around the ballroom, wanting to be close to normal human activity. The Fearnan servants were decorating the ballroom for the masquerade with colorful drapes and rosettes of tissue paper; the room looked almost like the domain of fire in full bloom. Corrine chose a corner chair out of the way from which to enjoy the hubbub. No one, of course, asked for her help; her injury still precluded her of being much use.

She slid the serpent-bound book out of her pocket, curious as to what the book might show her today. It refused again to show her any more than garble. She couldn't make out the wavering lines of script no matter how much she stared or turned the page this way and that. She finally shut the book in exasperation.

Kenneth and Sir James hailed her then and paused in their pacing of the ballroom floor to speak to her. Kenneth had been drafted into helping with the decorations.

"I'm here in a purely managerial role, of course," Sir James said, beaming. His gaze fell on the book on her lap. His eyes narrowed. She covered the serpents as best she could with her hands, though they squirmed beneath her fingers.

"What's that you've got there?" Sir James asked.

"Oh," she said. "Just some studying. Something Father Joe wants me to read." She cursed herself internally. *Wretched fool.*

Sir James seemed to take the hint, however. Just then, something clattered to the floor at the far end of the hall and Sir James hustled across the parquet floor, shouting in dismay.

Kenneth grinned at her. "All the same, these lairds."

Corrine swallowed and nodded.

"Well, then. I'd best get along and help," the boy said. "Enjoy your reading, Miss Corrine."

"Thank you, Kenneth," she said. He sauntered over to a group of women who were struggling with a banner. If she'd had a little brother, Corrine would have wanted him to be just like Kenneth. He had been nothing but helpful and kind—and just a little mischievous—since she'd arrived.

She hid the book back in her pocket as inconspicuously as she could. Maybe she'd been lucky. Maybe Sir James hadn't really seen it. Then she saw Sir James assessing her from across the hall. The damage was already done.

After studying algebra and literature with Ilona and Christina in the early afternoon, Corrine awaited Father Joe in the turret room. The drizzly day didn't beckon her to the windows, so she turned the pages of the charm books idly, wondering if the servants ever read them, if there were rumors circulating throughout this estate the way the rumors had moved through Falston. *They must think us all odd indeed. Me with this eye, Sir James with his secrets, Father Joe . . .*

The priest entered the room, burdened again with books. "I'm beginning to think it would be easier to meet in Sir James's study instead," he said, as he dumped them onto the scarred table in a puff of dust.

"Miss Brown tells me you saw something below the dungeons," Father Joe said.

"Yes, Father." Corrine told him about the scorpion-thing, its many wizened, chirping heads.

Father Joe looked over her head toward the window, as though he could see the Unhallowed nightmare crawling up through the gloomy day. "You're certain that's what you saw."

"As certain as I am of the daoi I saw at Uncle William's." Corrine tried to shut the twittering screams from her mind.

Father Joe pulled out a chair and sat down woodenly. She thought for a moment that he might put his head in his hands, but he just continued to stare toward the windows.

"Father Joe?"

"If you saw what I think you did, the safety of this house has been compromised and we are all in great danger."

"What did I see?" Corrine asked.

Father Joe's fingers stumbled over the edges of one of the dusty grimoires. "It's called a cuideag. They are Unhallowed shape-shifters. Once they taste the blood of their victims, they can assume that person's shape, mannerisms, speech—everything. Leanan created them to infiltrate the courts of the Hallowed and bring them under her sway. The Prince has sometimes used them to shift the balance of mortal events in his favor, but only when he was at his most powerful. The dark magic required for their shape-shifting takes much energy to sustain. What you saw was the cuideag's true form, to which it must revert every full moon. How it got here in the house, I don't know. But someone is not who he or she claims."

"How do we find out who it is?" Corrine said. "And how do we destroy it?"

"Mara could cast a root," Father Joe said. "But it would be difficult and dangerous. The cuideag would know that we were trying to flush it out. There may be other lesser magics to at least tell if a person is false or not who he or she seems. We shall have to seek a charm for that as well as for your magical protection." He opened one of the books roughly, its spine cracking in protest. "We may need one for physical protection, as well," he muttered.

Corrine nodded.

Father Joe sighed, struggling visibly to collect himself after such bad news.

"Speaking of charms," he said, "have you made any progress with the protection charm?"

Corrine shook her head. "I don't know what I'm looking for," she admitted.

"Something that will protect you when you move between the elemental domains. There is too much Unhallowed incursion, either in the domains or in your mind. We need to block them from entering where you're attempting to train."

Corrine looked at the page where charms for seeing fairies listed various herbs to be used at different times of the year. Seeing more of the Fey was the last thing she wanted to do. She closed the book.

"Without such a charm, I'm reluctant to send you into further domains. Have you been practicing your breathing exercises? Have you worked more in the domain of fire?"

Corrine nodded, even though she really hadn't. "A little."

"But not much, eh? Thinking a little too much about the ball?"

Corrine blushed.

"Well, then," he said, "I think you should spend the rest of the afternoon seeking a few charms that we can work with, and then working in the domain of fire once that charm is found."

He rose from his chair, gripping the back of it too tightly.

"I will consult with Mara about the cuideag. In the meantime, *do not* go exploring either by yourself or with the other girls. And do not trust anyone."

"Even you, Father?"

Her spine pulsed at his glance. "Even me."

February 1, 1866: Candlemas

Corrine's birthday dawned clear and cold. She woke with echoes of the Prince's voice. *Tonight*, he whispered. *Tonight.* Despite that, she had to admit she'd slept better for the first night since discovering the cuideag. Sir James, when they'd told him of it in a Council meeting, had merely reemphasized the fact that he had set powerful wards before they arrived. If nothing else, the rathstone hidden deep in the Council's chamber would protect them.

Ah. That's why he doesn't want anyone near it. And why the Unhallowed want into the chamber so badly.

He'd looked hard at Corrine. "Mind that you don't sneak about anymore, young lady." He'd said nothing about the serpent-bound book.

Throughout the day, Corrine tried to focus on her breath and find her way into the garden beyond the sun. She tried to dip her fingers into the green fire of life, letting it rest in her palms. Sometimes she heard the fire, sometimes she felt it dance between her fingers. Other times, as now, she felt nothing at all, just a disturbing emptiness, as though she'd tried for hours to light the spark in herself and there was no ember with which to light it.

She opened her uninjured eye and looked around at the study. Sir James disturbed her, but everyone else on the Council trusted him, claimed he was a known quantity. She considered the others in the house. Of them all, she was certain of one thing. Euan was not what he seemed. And though she had grown to trust him, she needed to know who or what he was.

She flipped through the charm grimoire, then picked up *The Secret History of Magical Herbs and Their Uses*. She scanned the pages until she came to an entry that read:

To test if a person be false or not what he seems
On a piece of pure lamb skin, write the name of the person.
Light a beeswax candle. Burn the lamb skin carefully, catching
all of the ashes. Place the ashes along with a goose feather in an
oaken box.
Whisper this charm:

Flame and ash, thistle and seed,
By heart of oak and feather bright
Reveal the truth by the moon's full light.

Set the ashes and the feather along with a bit of thistle in
the oaken box and leave the box in the windowsill where the moon
can gaze upon it. By the turning of the next full moon, if the
feather is black, you will know the person is false to you.

Just a few months ago, Corrine would not have believed that any such nonsense would work. But now, she was beginning to believe Father Joe's admonition that magic was her only possible refuge against the Unhallowed, and perhaps her only weapon too. And perhaps it was also the one thing that could tell whether she could truly trust Euan.

She copied out the spell on a piece of scratch paper and took it to her room. She hoped, despite how Siobhan felt about magic, that she'd consent to fetch the items discreetly. She went to her room to stow the spell in her desk, then walked to the window to gaze at the shivering twilit landscape, the fog creeping up from the black stream. Corrine thought she saw movement there, something scavenging through the mist, something lean and predatory seizing another form, but there was nothing. She hadn't seen or felt the Captain in quite a while.

She guessed Sir James must have been telling the truth. The wards were working. The shadow she saw resolved itself into Euan, the feathered bodies of several pheasants slung over his shoulder. She watched how he walked, no artifice or swagger in his gait, just simple purpose and a gliding ease that again made her feel he was much older than he appeared. She thought again about what he had said on the ship, that she had no notion of what she truly was. Father Joe had avoided the question and Mara, she knew, would probably never answer her. She turned the strange phrase from the serpent-bound book over in her mind. *Half-Born.*

Just then, Christina came knocking. Ilona trailed behind her, already dressed in her Cossack's flowing coat and high fur hat. She stroked a false black beard that flowed over her chin and nearly to her chest. Corrine hid her smile behind her hand. Christina had donned her shepherdess costume, with its tiered, belling skirts that stopped just short of her calves and gave a beguiling glimpse of her pantaloons. On anyone else, Corrine thought, it would have seemed improper, but somehow on Christina the costume was charming.

Christina carried a curling iron to the fire, the end of which she carefully set into the rim of the flame to heat.

"And now, oh pirate queen," Christina said, "your subjects await you in the hall!"

Corrine tried not to protest as the girls helped her into the bodice and skirt, as they draped the folds of musty fox fur over her. They removed her bandage, replacing it with a black eye patch. Christina fastened the ends securely under her hair.

Next came the curling iron. Ilona led her to a seat, and Corrine sat dubiously as Christina rolled and set the curls herself. The smell of singed hair hung around Corrine's head to the point where she worried that Christina had burned off the ends. She watched in awe when Christina went to the mirror and curled ringlets into her own hair, better than the most competent maid. Corrine couldn't imagine having such skill in her own toilette.

The last touch was a buccaneer hat that Ilona pulled from under her Cossack's coat. "Better than the finest crown," she said, as she set it on Corrine's head.

"Better than trying to find the finest crown," she said, shuddering at the memory of the horrible creature pulsing on the stone ceiling above her.

"Now, come," Christina said, leading her to the mirror.

Corrine stared at herself for several moments, a hand going to her mouth.

"I can't possibly . . ." she said.

"What?" Christina said. She was already near the door, gathering up her crook, her layered skirts crackling like crushed snow.

"I can't go," Corrine said, clutching at her throat. The fox stole mostly covered the plunging neckline, but she could still see the outline of her breasts above the black bodice, the slender arrow of her waistline before the skirts trailed behind her in waves of green.

"Why ever not?" Christina said.

"Miss Brown . . . Father Joe . . . what will they say?" *What would my mother say? My father?*

Ilona smiled. "Heh. I am wearing trousers and a beard, my friend. And carrying a toy gun! That is far more scandalous."

"But," Corrine said, gesturing at the neckline of her dress, the incriminating bustle.

153

"And my ankles are showing!" Christina said. "What a troop of harlots we are! Now, come, or we'll miss the ball entirely!" As if on cue, Ilona took one of Corrine's arms while Christina took the other. The two ushered her out, her protests falling on deaf ears.

Even down the hall, they could hear the sounds of guests being welcomed into the grand foyer below. Christina rushed them down, even as Miss Brown came up the stairs to meet them. She wore what looked like an older blue gown that had been overlaid with a net of glittering gauze. She carried a mask shaped like a crescent moon from which silver and midnight blue ribbons dangled.

"The night sky," Corrine said.

"Happy birthday," Miss Brown said, as she made a short bow. In her half-smile, Corrine glimpsed a repressed happiness. She thought of the picture that had once rested on her uncle's desk. How long had it been since Miss Brown had dressed in fancy clothes or danced at a ball? How long since she had been truly happy? Corrine couldn't imagine.

"Thank you," Corrine said.

"Where is Father Joe?" Christina asked.

Miss Brown looked at Christina's exposed ankles and raised a brow, but said only, "This isn't really the type of function for a priest, I don't think."

"But . . ." Corrine felt a little unprotected knowing that Father Joe wouldn't be there.

"Come now," Miss Brown said, "let's pick up our dance cards and make our way to the ballroom."

The girls followed Miss Brown down the broad, spiraling steps. Corrine gulped when she saw all the people hurrying in from the damp chill of the February evening, laughing, and crowding the hall. The array of costumes was complex—from simple peasant to Turkish sultan. All the costumes were improvised, like hers, of course; the country folk Sir James had invited probably had little means to outfit themselves in spectacular garb. Many of the men wore Italian dominoes, full cloaks that extended from the crown of the head to the ankles, revealing only a carefully chosen mask. There were blustery faces of the West Wind, faces cold and remote as Miss Brown's moon mask; one man even wore the burnished mask of Apollo. But she could see that the women often wore remade gowns like hers or Miss Brown's—stains or moth holes covered with rosettes or bows or ribbons, whatever remnants they had to hand.

Even Mara and Siobhan greeted the guests in costume, wearing the stiff, high collars and voluminous gowns of the Elizabethan court. Corrine wondered if they also had been digging through Sir James's trunks. She smiled at them and Siobhan looked at her nervously; she still looked pale and unwell. Mara answered her smile with her dangerous grin.

Corrine felt ridiculous as she picked up her dance card and swiveled to find a young man eagerly trampling her hem, asking to sign. It took her a moment to realize that the young man was Kenneth. He was well disguised as a Viking; the braided beard, however false, significantly altered the shape of his face.

Corrine let him sign, trying to smile and finding it still a little awkward. If Christina had worn this costume, she would be playing the part—talking boisterously, charming everyone with a flash of her dark eye, a bounce of her curls. But Corrine found herself shrinking, drowning in velvet and fur.

"Oh, and I've a birthday present for you," Kenneth said. He pulled something out of his Viking vest. "Well, at least . . . it's actually really yours, but you mightn't have realized you lost it."

He put the serpent-bound book in her palms.

"I found it in Sir James's study when I went to get something for him a while ago. I thought maybe you'd want it back, since you haven't had a chance to write in it yet."

So he *had* noticed.

Corrine managed a smile and slipped the book into a fold of her stole, hoping it would stay. "Thank you, Kenneth. Yes, I have many things to write in it now, not the least of which is your kindness in returning it to me."

He blushed.

Something shivered across her shoulders and she looked around with her good eye. Nothing was there, but she would have sworn for a moment that she'd had the feeling she sometimes got around Mara or Father Joe or Euan. Siobhan caught her eye. The maid's hand was over her mouth. Then, she picked up her skirts and fled from the room. Several people turned to watch her go. Mara frowned and stood a little straighter, as if to pronounce that she wouldn't leave her post.

"Siobhan," Corrine called out.

She was about to go after her when Sir James appeared at her side, dressed rather oddly as a fairy-tale frog prince. Two large papier-mâché eyes stared down from his forehead where he had pushed his mask back. A gold foil crown hung down his back from a string. He steered her away from Kenneth. "Come, my girl," he said, taking her elbow.

She planted her feet, and he loosened his grip. The bright green velvet strained across his chest. "Come with me," he said. "We must announce the reason for this celebration, after all."

He didn't touch her again and she followed him uncertainly through to where people milled about the ballroom, waiting for the first waltz. The musicians were tuning their instruments on the stage at the far end of the room, and it was to this that Sir James led her. He climbed up and offered her his hand, but she refused it.

"An announcement!" Sir James shouted. "I've an announcement to make."

Conversation ceased and everyone turned. There seemed to be a thousand masked people staring at her, though Corrine knew logically that the number was far less. Dreams of the Prince's dancers, their owl eyes and horned masks, haunted her. She focused on Kenneth, who grinned close to the stage. Otherwise, she feared the crowd would make her ill.

"Tonight is a special night," Sir James said, the frog eyes bobbing maniacally on his head. "Not only do we welcome our newest guests, as well as all of you"—he gestured at the crowd—"to Fearnan but it is the birthday of Miss Corrine Jameson, the orphaned niece of a very dear friend."

Corrine gritted her teeth at the word "orphaned." She hated that word, even as she realized that she was beginning to believe it was true.

Mr. Turnbull came alongside the stage with a length of blue-gray plaid in his hands.

"In addition, it is also the occasion of her sixteenth birthday, her debut into society." There were scattered claps of approval. Corrine blushed and wished she could sink through the floor, until she remembered what lurked below the dungeons.

"Thus,"—Sir James waved Mr. Turnbull forward—"we have sent to her mother's clan, Clan McPhee, for this tartan to commemorate this very special day."

The entire hall erupted in applause, with a few scattered catcalls. Sir James took the tartan sash and draped it from her shoulder to her waist over the fox stole. He patted her waist heavily as he arranged it. He was searching for the book. She looked into his eyes and felt that blackness again. He only smiled at her and turned back to the crowd.

"Let the dancing begin!"

Everyone turned away, resuming private conversations. The

musicians finished their last bit of tuning as Mr. Turnbull helped Sir James and Corrine off the stage. Corrine glimpsed Euan entering the hall, dressed as a young shepherd, complete even with a snow white lamb he'd led in from the pasture. A young woman was on his arm. Christina. They laughed together, obviously pleased at their shared taste in costumes. Corrine felt ridiculous for hoping that Euan might have sought her out first.

"Corrine?" Kenneth said next to her, as the strains to the waltz began, "May I have this dance?"

For answer, she took his arm and let him lead, trying to pretend that she wasn't taller than him, that he wasn't treading on her gown, that his beard wasn't slipping dangerously off the left side of his face. He had returned the book to her when she hadn't even realized it was gone. And he had anchored her during what felt like the greatest humiliation of her life. For that, she owed him every dance on her card if he asked for them.

Kenneth took her through the first waltz, and she couldn't help but laugh at what a pair the two of them made between his stumbling and her blindness. She had to turn very carefully or else miss her mark, and yet if she didn't turn fast enough, she would throw off the entire rhythm of the dance. They didn't speak much, but Corrine was busy trying not to tumble to the floor in gales of laughter. She'd almost forgotten Euan and Christina entirely. When the dance was over, Kenneth took her to where Miss Brown and Ilona sat watching the spectacle.

"You're next," he said grinning at Ilona. "But before that, Miss Corrine, would you like some punch?"

Corrine nodded, attempting to catch her breath. "Thank you," she gasped. She hadn't felt so winded since she'd fallen ill with the swamp fever. She longed to take the buccaneer hat off and fan herself with it, but smoothed her skirts and sat next to Miss Brown instead. A tall, gangly man came to ask Miss Brown to join him. Kenneth was back with a crystal cup of punch, which he nearly spilled into Corrine's hands before he turned to Ilona and pulled her out onto the dance floor. The tall Cossack and Viking bowed to each other, their beards getting tangled in the process. Corrine smiled as they tried to untangle themselves and avoid being trampled by the other couples at the same time.

She saw a flash of white pantaloons and realized she hadn't seen Christina and Euan since they had entered the ballroom together. She thought of the juniper sprig Euan had given her and how she had watched it burn. Her happiness melted as quickly as the ice in her punch. She considered returning to her room, but reminded herself that she was not interested in Euan or any other man. She turned to look at the hangings of the ballroom, half-listening to the fact that one waltz was ending and the dancers were straying to new partners, the buffet table, or outside for a bit of fresh air. The chandeliers were pulled down and every other candle snuffed out; romantic shadows danced down the walls and across the ancient portraits of the hall.

Corrine noted the portrait of one lady with a particular smile, a lady who wore white, and whose frame was graced with an embroidered scarf. She set her cup down on a nearby chair, wanting to go nearer the portrait and study it further. The musicians tuned their instruments again; the violins were strident as cats until they found their pitch and sang. A voice came from just beyond her shoulder, a voice that made her skin resonate like the strings as the bows flew across them.

"Corrine."

For a moment, she thought she'd imagined it. So many times had this voice called to her in her dreams.

The Fey Prince said her name again. She whipped around.

159

He was tall, as she'd guessed, but not so tall as he'd seemed in her dreams. He was swathed in a black domino cloak that revealed only the barest outlines of his shape, muscled shoulders, corded arms . . . She searched his face, but his mask, fashioned into the image of a black fox, obscured all his features. All save the eyes. She had never seen such eyes in her life. The pupils rippled and wavered; she couldn't have said if they were more like a cat's or a goat's. His irises were similarly quixotic—one moment they seemed green, another hazel, another gold. All the colors of a summer forest and yet none.

"How . . ." was all she could manage.

"You have made me stronger than ever before," he said. "And it is the night of Imbolc, the night of the old gods, when the dark son is born to the goddess."

Corrine shook her head. She had no idea what he meant. Hearing his voice was strange enough without trying to parse out his meaning. His very presence paralyzed her.

"The doors to some raths are open," he said.

She looked up quickly, understanding this time. If he had the power to walk free this night, then perhaps that explained how the Unhallowed had crept below the manor. Unless it had been trapped there long ago. But if that beast and the Prince could get into the manor, the witch could too. She stepped back.

But he anticipated her thought and reached for her arm. "The witch cannot harm you while I am here. I come this night in peace. I wish only to dance with you. No more. Will you not indulge me in that one small request?"

"I . . ." Though there was velvet and leather between his skin and hers, she could still feel the sweet sting of his touch.

"Do you have any idea what I could do if I wished, little pirate queen?" The air shifted and resolved itself into a wind that threatened the candlelight. In that moment, the walls trembled as though they were water.

She was tempted to snap at him, to rip her arm from his grasp and simply walk away, not caring whether he brought the entire manor down around their ears. But it was the sadness in his eyes that held her, a sadness as immortal as the world itself.

The eddies of wind stilled; the candle flames leaped with renewed vigor. "And yet, I will not." He was about to release her, but she let her hand slide down to rest in his.

He led her onto the floor, and it seemed as though the music was for them, the other dancers but pale shadows who waltzed around their living flame. No one had ever been so close to her; she felt the precision of his muscles leading her through the figures, guiding her beyond the blind spot of her injured eye.

"Why did you come?" she asked as she turned in his arms.

"You have forced me to it," he said.

"I have?"

"You have shut yourself off from me. Your dreams are dark to me."

"Why does it matter?" she squeaked. Normal speech escaped her.

"Because dreams are doors to the soul." She felt his attention shift; he was looking above her head as she turned yet again, as though the walls were transparent.

In her turning, she saw Father Joe standing in the doorway. She felt the Prince's body tighten; he hissed under his mask.

"I must go," he said. "Follow my lead toward the banquet table. I will leave you there."

"But . . ."

"I cannot stay any longer. But know that I came to you." She turned with him through the waltz to the edge of the floor, feeling the shadows gather. There was an exit onto the veranda not far from where servants waited with punch and sponge cake.

"Next time," he said, "you will come to me." She thought she heard a smile in his voice, but when she looked into his eyes, their grief stole her breath.

"Farewell, little pirate queen."

Before she could answer, he had melted out through the door and she was left at the edge of the dance floor, clutching emptiness between her palms.

"Corrine?"

She heard Father Joe, but didn't turn.

He came up beside her. She was still looking at her palms, feeling the strange heat still cupped in creases of her gloves. He hadn't touched her skin, and yet it still felt as though his touch was more real than anything or anyone that had ever touched her in her life. She thought of Rory's rough kiss long ago at Falston. How untrue that had been.

"Corrine? Who were you dancing with just now?" Father Joe asked.

She would have liked to lie, but she lacked the artifice. "The Prince," she said.

She watched Father Joe's face grow still and hard. Then, he took her hand and dragged her toward the door onto the patio. "How did he leave? This way?"

"Yes—no—Father, stop!" She tried to plant her feet and pull her hand out of his.

"Show me where he went," he said. His grip was relentless; he dragged her out into the night.

Fog curled up from the trees, through the labyrinth, curling its fingers through the marble porch railings. Corrine looked to one side and saw Ilona, Euan, and Kenneth chatting. Euan stepped aside a little when he saw Father Joe. Christina was nowhere to be seen.

The priest turned this way and that, as though scenting his prey. Stars glittered briefly before the fog closed over them.

"Did you see anyone?" he asked. "Did anyone leave through this door?"

"No, Father," Kenneth said.

Ilona shook her head, her beard wilting against her chest.

"No, sir," Euan said. "We only just came out ourselves."

"You are certain?"

"Corrine, was someone troubling you?" Euan asked. He had sworn to protect her on the *Great Eastern*. But she wondered if he could protect her from herself.

"No," she said. "There was no bother." She still felt the Prince's hand upon her waist, the command of his voice. *You will come to me . . .*

She was glad no one could see her face in the dark.

"Sit," Father Joe said, indicating one of Sir James's leather chairs near the study fireplace. He set a glass down rather hard on the sideboard and sloshed brandy into it from a nearby decanter.

When he returned, he took a sip and sat before her on the edge of his seat.

"Now," he said, "tell me what happened."

She told him about the Fey Prince, feeling again how she had whirled effortlessly in his arms, the low resonance of his voice, his strange, mesmerizing eyes. She couldn't tell him why she hadn't run away, though. She didn't know herself.

"Do you know what he wants with you?" Father Joe asked.

"Me," Corrine said, her voice straining. She found it difficult to repeat what he had said—it seemed too personal, too deeply intimate, and far too frightening. *He wants me.* She twisted her hands in the folds of the fox fur, reaching for the reassurance of the book that hugged her ribs. "I think he still wants me to come to him, but I don't know why."

Father Joe was growing angry. She could tell by the way he finished his brandy quickly and turned the glass in his hands, bands of light coruscating across his fingers.

"So, what now?" she asked. "What do I do?"

"That he came to you through the wards when I and other Council members were near, in the flesh." He stopped turning the glass, stood, and went over to the mantel, as he had when Sir James had confessed he'd lost the key to the Council chamber. He stared again at the portrait of the Scottish lord and his dogs. "It bodes very ill, Corrine. Perhaps your Uncle William was right."

She was desperate to get the subject off the Prince's attraction to her. "But can't we use this to our advantage?" she asked. She didn't want to have to say any more about him, about how she still felt his hands burning at her waist and palm, about how light she had felt . . .

Father Joe looked at her with a measuring stare and she worked hard not to flinch.

"It's possible. We could use you as bait, to lure him out again. But your uncle would not like it at all. And frankly, I don't either. That has been tried, and we failed miserably."

Corrine realized he was speaking of Melanie. Corrine almost didn't blame her for hating the Council so much. They had used her but given her nothing. And she had promised to repay Corrine for it. She shook her head. The feather plume on her hat tickled her nose. She pulled it off and set it beside her on the chair arm.

"That won't work. He said he came because I would not, and that the next time, I would come to him."

Father Joe mused. She waited for him to remove his spectacles and polish them on his cassock, but he didn't. "Is there something you propose?"

"I could go to him. I could try to find the stones and take

them back from him——" *I could cut out his heart . . .* The thought made her queasy.

"You could," Father Joe said. "You could indeed. But how would you resist him? He has all the powers and charms of millennia. You haven't completed training in the lesser magics."

Corrine was silent. Tonight, she knew, it would have been so easy. If Father Joe had not entered, if they had been left to the dance, she wondered if he would have taken her back into the rath with him. She was quite certain she would have gone. Even now, she felt the heat of his hands tugging at her, whispering to her to come out into the fog, come out under the cold moon.

"There must be some sort of charm," Corrine began.

"Not nearly enough to combat as powerful a creature as the Unhallowed Prince! If you thought the cuideag was terrifying, you should think again. Its power is nothing compared to his. How do you think you'd keep him from taking your mind and making you his slave? Believe me, Corrine, he will do it if he can." Anguish flitted across his face, and she saw Leanan, weaving flowers into his hair.

"Why me? Why do I matter?" Anger stronger than brandy coursed through Corrine.

Father Joe looked as though he wanted to say something, but his eyes slid away from hers. "I don't know," he said.

"Yes, you do! You've known since Falston!" she said. "Why won't you tell me the truth?" Her voice cracked on the last word, and his face grew stern.

"I suspect, Corrine. And I will taint neither you nor the Council with little more than vague imaginings until I have proof."

"How long must I wait for you to tell me?" she demanded.

"I had hoped to find what I needed in the Council chamber. But since the key has been lost, I am unsure now what I should do. There are tests." He looked as though he wanted to say more, but instead he ran a hand through his dark hair.

She thought of all the times things had happened before that she hadn't had the knowledge to understand and didn't have the power to prevent. How her father's absence had translated itself somehow into his death; how her mother had died without saying good-bye. How she'd been sent to Falston and all that had happened there. "Test or no test, I want to know now! Why does the Prince keep haunting me? What does he want? Who does he think I am? Why won't anyone tell me?" Tears streamed; her eye itched and burned. She choked at the pain.

"Corrine . . ." Father Joe began.

The door opened and Miss Brown came in, the netting of her skirt sparkling in the low light. She looked a little surprised to see Corrine, but when she saw her tears, she came to her side.

"Why are you crying, Corrine?" She touched Corrine's singed curls briefly, hesitantly.

"He won't tell—I want to know—" Corrine sobbed and tried to catch her breath.

Miss Brown reached into a pocket of her bodice and handed Corrine a handkerchief.

"What have you said to her, Joseph?" There was a flat anger in the headmistress's voice that brought Corrine up short. Corrine had never heard her use his name in that fashion.

"It appears that what I've not said is at issue," he said. Corrine sensed something more in his words than just a reference to his evasiveness with her. Weariness lined his face, and Corrine wondered again at his true age as she wiped at her eyes with the handkerchief.

Miss Brown glanced at Father Joe, and Corrine saw that nameless, maddening thing move between them. *Lover's quarrel?*

"The Prince came," Father Joe said before Corrine could say anything.

Miss Brown's face became hard and delicate as porcelain. "What happened?" she asked Corrine.

"We danced," Corrine said, hiccupping slightly. She held the handkerchief over her mouth to keep from saying more. *We danced and he spoke my name and wants me to come to him and I really want to even though I don't know why . . .*

"You're fortunate you escaped him," Miss Brown said with a trace of admiration.

"I'm quite sure she wouldn't have if I hadn't come when I did," Father Joe said.

"He said he came in peace," Corrine said.

"And you believed him?" Father Joe asked.

"At least he tells me the truth!"

The words echoed. The Scottish lord above the mantel sneered.

Father Joe bristled, but all he said was, "Good night then," and started toward the door.

"Wait," Miss Brown said. "I must tell you what—whom—I saw."

Father Joe stopped and turned.

"I'm sorry, Corrine, to interrupt your conversation, but you must both know—Rory was here tonight."

Corrine's heart throbbed in her mouth.

"Are you certain?" Father Joe said.

Miss Brown nodded.

"When?"

"Just now," she said. "I tried to follow him, but he saw me and slipped away. Whether he's returned in a different costume, I don't know."

"I should try to find him. He will not evade my questions this time."

Not as you've evaded mine, Corrine thought. Anger beat at her, like a bird trapped in her chest.

Father Joe left, not bothering to glance at either of them before he was out of the door.

"You should go to bed now," Miss Brown said. "We'll sort all this out at the next Council meeting." She pulled her sparkling shawl more tightly about her. Her mask hung forlornly at her side.

Corrine nodded and stood. As she turned to leave, she felt Miss Brown's hand on her arm.

"You should forgive Father Joe for his . . . control of certain subjects. It could be dangerous to you to let even a rumor of these notions into the open. We're thinking of your safety."

Corrine thought about Falston—all the lies, all the hiding of information and the disastrous results. "Hiding things was the way you lost Falston," she said. And she gathered her skirts and departed before Miss Brown could reply.

The heat in her face gathered under her eye patch. She tore off the patch as she went toward the stairs, heedless of who might be watching. The revelers were departing the ball in pairs and small groups.

"Corrine," a male voice said. She swung around, covering her injured eye quickly with her hand, praying that it wasn't Rory. Kenneth approached, and she sighed in relief.

"I just wanted to wish you good night," he said. "I hope you had a happy birthday celebration." His earnest face, his uncertain tone, seemed comical behind the beard.

"Thank you," Corrine said. Her pent-up anger loosened into tears she didn't want him to see. "Good night," she said and hurried up the stairs.

"Good night," he called after her.

Tears blurred her sight. When she cleared the landing, she thought she saw three black shapes down the corridor. Corrine blinked and saw only shadows from the gas lanterns. She rushed into her room and shut the door as loudly as she dared.

She drew the serpent-bound book from her stole, longing to feel its terrifying cover, to see if she could read anything new—perhaps a spell that would reveal the cuideag or force everyone around her to tell the truth. Perhaps she could finally discover if she was someone other than the plain, orphaned farm girl. Half-Born. Or something even better.

But the book revealed nothing, even when she whispered to it. Its letters remained stoically indecipherable. Frustrated, she threw it across the room into a dark corner.

"Some birthday," she said.

All night long, the serpents slithered helplessly around and around the cover.

TWELVE

February 2, 1866

CORRINE'S STOMACH CHURNED AT BREAKFAST, AND SHE couldn't tell if this was from her growing distaste for salty porridge or the brittle tension around the table. No one spoke, not even Sir James. Corrine guessed Father Joe had told him of the two unwanted guests—not to mention the horrible thing Corrine had seen beneath the manor—who had shown up despite his wards. She was sure Sir James was angry with himself and wondered if he realized how Father Joe's trust in him was faltering. How could he not see it?

Her eye itched where she had clumsily replaced her bandage before coming down to breakfast. She longed to rub at it, but clenched her spoon more tightly and dug through her porridge.

There were voices at the door, and Corrine looked up to see Euan entering the dining room, his hat in his hands. His face was flushed, his eyes terribly bright. She remembered how he had spurned her last night at the dance and scowled.

"Sir James, Father, ladies," he said, looking around. His gaze lit briefly on Christina, but she didn't meet his gaze for more than a moment. Corrine couldn't reconcile last night's laughing shepherd with this morning's nervous gamekeeper. Nor could she see the steady fencing master who ran his charges through their drills almost mercilessly.

"Euan!" Sir James said. "Do sit. Have you eaten, lad?"

Euan shook his head. "I'm sorry I can't join you. I came, rather, to ask you to release some men to me. Kenneth's missing."

"What?" Sir James set down the jam spoon carefully.

"Kenneth . . . he didn't meet me this morning where we agreed to. I went to his room. The door was open, the room empty." He glanced around the table. "I also found a deer that looked like it had been slaughtered by wild dogs. I'm just worried for Kenneth's safety, sir. Strange things were afoot last night."

Looking at Corrine, Father Joe said, "Indeed."

"Corrine," Euan said, "do you know where Kenneth might be? The last time I saw him, he was with you."

Corrine shrank into her chair. Euan seemed to be judging her, sizing up her deficiencies and finding her wanting. If she had felt ridiculous as a pirate queen, she felt even more so now.

"No," she said in a small voice, "I don't know. I only said good night briefly before I went to my room."

Euan nodded. "May I commandeer some men then, sir? I don't think he would have just run off. That's not like him."

"Certainly," Sir James said.

"And I'll help," Father Joe said.

"So will I," Ilona said.

Miss Brown seemed about to protest, but Christina chimed in, "And me."

"And me," Corrine said.

"I'm not sure this is the proper sort of thing for young ladies," Sir James said.

"Quite honestly, sir, the more people we have, the sooner we find him," Euan said.

"Or discover where he went," Father Joe said.

Sir James nodded. "Well then . . ." He stood, pulling the napkin from under his collar and in the seat of his chair. "Let's meet in the downstairs drawing room in a half hour's time. Euan, you'll have a map with you, eh?"

"Yes, sir," Euan said. Corrine thought again how strange it was that he looked so well when the news he gave was so terrible. *Another disappearance.* Thoughts of Jeanette and Penelope and all those who had gone before flooded Corrine's mind, girls she'd tried to forget for so long. And now Kenneth too. She remembered his face behind the false beard as he'd returned the book to her, his uncertain voice as he'd said good night. She wondered if the book could help her find him. If only it would allow her to read it as it had before.

As they filed out of the room, Miss Brown said, "Corrine, are you certain? With your eye . . ."

Corrine stood a little straighter. "I was the last person to see him. He deserves my help, I think."

Miss Brown nodded. "Very well. Go get your things."

Corrine went to her room. She caught Siobhan coming down the stairs with an armload of laundry and stopped her. The maid looked like she wanted to run away, so Corrine held her by the elbow.

"Siobhan," she said, "can you find these things for me?"

She slipped the list of spell items in Siobhan's apron pocket. "I'll make sure you get extra pay for your troubles." She wasn't sure how, but she promised herself firmly that she would.

"What is it?" Siobhan eyed her.

"Just some things I need for . . . an art project."

"When they send me to market next, miss, I'll search them out."

"Thank you." Corrine released her and watched her go carefully down the stairs, her head almost entirely hidden behind the pile of laundry she carried.

When she got to her room, she looked first in the desk drawer, and then remembered that she'd thrown the book into a corner in her exasperation last night. She went to where she thought she'd thrown it. But there was nothing there. She searched the room carefully, but the serpent-bound book was gone.

Christina and Ilona came knocking, bundled in scarves and mittens. Corrine picked up the scarf Euan had given her after the wreck of the *Great Eastern* and wrapped it around her throat. She'd have to search for the book again later.

Corrine and the other girls hurried down the stairs to the drawing room. They stood behind the men, listening as Euan directed them about which paths to take.

"Some will do a perimeter sweep," he said. "I'll take the dogs through the center. Ladies"—he turned to Corrine, Christina, Ilona, and Miss Brown—"if you would kindly take this path here, that would help immensely."

"Isn't it possible that he just ran off?" Father Joe asked.

Euan shook his head. He looked feral, his eyes almost green under his fur cap. "He was apprenticed to me so that he could return to the estate where his old father works as a carter. He was trying to learn fencing to earn more money in matches to send back to the old man. I doubt he'd abandon him."

"Yes, then," Sir James said, "off with all of you. I shall have Mrs. Guthrie order a great supper for you. Hopefully this mess will be resolved by then." He was not going along. She noticed he also didn't say anything about how perfectly safe his estate was. Maybe by now he'd figured out that it wasn't as safe as he claimed. She couldn't help wondering if he now had the book locked somewhere she'd never find it. And because it had been stolen from the chamber in the first place, she knew she couldn't ask.

They marched out into the cold February damp. She heard the Prince's voice in her ear. *This is the time when the goddess gives birth to her dark son.* Whatever had he meant by that?

Euan led them to where a handler waited with the dogs. The group walked along the bridle path to the stream, the dogs sniffing and crossing over the ground in front of them. Corrine walked very carefully with Ilona at her side to keep her from tripping. The group straggled in a line along the path until they came to a small bridge. The trees loomed, twisted and ancient, before them. A shape flickered farther along the path. A man, walking away from them . . .

She caught hold of Ilona's arm, remembering the old dream of being in the forest, suffocated in the earth's great coils while her father screamed in a distant grove.

"What is it?" Ilona asked.

"I just . . . I tripped," Corrine said. She released Ilona and hugged herself against the cold.

Ilona's face was grim with memories of the times she'd searched for her disappeared friends at Falston.

Corrine wondered if they would find another white tree, another buzzing horde of angry Unhallowed as they had in the school's last days. She prayed not. And yet, if that would make it possible that Kenneth was alive somewhere, she would bear it.

Before the bridge, Euan stopped. "Ladies," he said, pitching his voice so Miss Brown and the girls could hear, "the path is across the bridge and to the left—see the opening in the trees?"

They all nodded or said yes.

"Everyone knows where to go, then?" he asked.

As everyone confirmed, he knelt and showed the lead dog a shirt of Kenneth's. The handler released the dogs with a command, and they dashed off over the bridge.

"You will be well?" Father Joe said to Miss Brown before he went with the other men.

She nodded.

"Here," Father Joe said. He reached for Miss Brown's hand and placed something in her palm; Corrine saw a round flash, like a marble made of mirrors, before Miss Brown's fingers closed over it.

"Mara made this," he said. "Say the word I taught you, if you are in need."

"But I'm not—"

"Even if you are not . . ." He glanced around at the girls. "Even if . . . It will work for you."

"I see," she said. She didn't look directly at him. The stream spoke of dark things at the forest's heart.

"Right then," he said. He went to the other men who had spread out on either side of the stream.

"Come, girls," Miss Brown said. She led them across the bridge. Corrine flinched when she saw three ravens lift off from one of the nearest trees and disappear across the canopy into the fog.

The distant shouts of searchers, the occasional baying of the hounds fell away along the path until there was almost absolute silence. Very occasionally, the sound of rain dripping from limbs to stone or the wet crunch of a twig cracking underfoot relieved the monotony of silence.

"We shouldn't be here," Corrine said, more to herself than anyone else. Her teeth buzzed with cold.

But Miss Brown heard her. "We have no other choice," the headmistress said. "Kenneth must be found."

"If he can be found," Ilona said under her breath.

Miss Brown glanced at her. "Let us hope it hasn't come to that."

No one said anything else after that; Christina looked especially pale at the thought. Remarkably, she hadn't fainted since leaving Falston, though Corrine guessed that was mostly attributable to being freed from doing things she didn't want to do. *Dear Lord*, Corrine thought, *not now. Don't faint now.*

Something—a shadow?—sped away on Corrine's left, running low through the trees.

"Ilona," she said.

Ilona nodded. "Should have brought my foil," she said. She tried to smile, but the two of them felt the same. This was obviously a trap. But who had set it? Rory? The Prince? The witch?

Whispers gibbered through the forest. Miss Brown and Christina walked ahead of Ilona and Corrine, their skirts dragging across the leaves. They rounded a bend in the path that led into a little dell lined with birch trees.

Feeling as though she needed all her sight, Corrine ripped the bandage from her eye. At first, the gray light made her wince. She still could not focus; it felt as though sand were lodged in her pupil.

Then she looked overhead. A horde of black shapes wreathed and circled through the trees. She was about to shout, when she heard a scream.

Ilona grabbed her arm and dragged her forward as they ran.

When they entered the dell, Christina had already fainted. Miss Brown was bending over her, but movement at the far end of the dell caught Corrine's attention.

A great black shape knelt over something white and red. White was scattered around the dell, little mounds white as snow. Corrine saw white fingers curling up from the leaf litter—all that was left of Kenneth's hand. Her breakfast rumbled up her throat and she retched, her vision going black for a moment. But she refused to faint.

Kenneth's body was scattered all throughout the dell. The Captain had been kneeling over the mangled torso, but now he rose and came toward them.

He croaked something, an odd word that sounded almost like "possum."

"Corrine!" Miss Brown said.

The Captain grunted again, as if he couldn't properly make use of his tongue. Kenneth's dead eyes looked at her from the bracken.

The green fire of life crept through the trees and the leaf litter, avoiding the places where Kenneth's body lay. Corrine thought of pulling the net of fire to her then, of building it into a hot, healthy blaze that would consume this place, hallowing this desecrated ground. It wreathed through her mind and out through her fingers. A line of green flame raced toward the Captain.

He stumbled backward like a dancing bear. As the flame struck the edge of his cape, he condensed into a winged shadow. He flew above her head, and as he passed, she heard a plaintive croak. "Possum!"

"Corrine!" Miss Brown said.

Corrine turned, her mind still in flames.

"Come here," Miss Brown said more gently. Corrine went. She knelt in the wet leaves beside Miss Brown and Christina, whose eyelids were fluttering rapidly.

Ilona stood frozen at the lip of the dell.

"Ilona," Miss Brown called.

But at the same moment, Euan called Ilona's name. He entered the clearing from the west, surrounded by dogs.

"I heard screaming," he said. Then he stopped and stared.

177

The dogs were milling and sniffing, and then one set up a bay that echoed like a funeral dirge through the naked trees.

"Great Mother," Euan said.

Ilona didn't move.

Euan went to her. Corrine watched him reach for Ilona's arm. "Come away, lass," he said. "There's naught we can do for him."

Ilona allowed herself to be turned. They came toward Corrine, but she couldn't meet the grief in Ilona's eyes.

She thought of dancing with Kenneth, how he had tripped on her hem and nearly spilled punch on her. She remembered his laughter and the way he'd so innocently returned the Unhallowed book. And Corrine also remembered Falston, watching the pine tree collapse on Dolores and the helpless inevitability of her death. The line of green fire moved again across the ground of her mind.

"We heard the scream and smelled the smoke as we got closer," Euan said.

Miss Brown helped Christina to sit and dusted damp leaves from the back of her coat.

"Miss Brown," Christina said. There were tears in her eyes.

"Kenneth—" Corrine choked.

"Did you see anything, Corrine?" Euan said. "It doesn't look . . . immediate. Perhaps last night—"

Perhaps just after we said good night.

Out of the corner of her eye, Corrine saw Miss Brown shake her head slightly. She wasn't to tell anyone about the Captain.

The only other person who might have seen him was Ilona, but Corrine doubted it, since it seemed few people could actually see the Unhallowed. Ilona was still silent, unable to acknowledge anything, even the fact that she had apparently lost a mitten and stood with one hand turning red from the cold.

"No," Corrine said. "We just saw what you saw."

"I'm sorry you had to see that," Euan said. "I never thought . . . I saw that deer this morning, and I worried that there might be wild dogs about, but I never really dreamed something so horrible could have happened."

"What do you think did this?" Miss Brown asked.

A strange look passed through Euan's eyes. He shook his head. "We shall have to investigate further. In the meantime," he said, his eyes going to each of the girls in turn, "you ladies should all stay inside the manor to make sure you're safe." He drew a horn from the hunting satchel at his side. "I'll call the others."

Miss Brown nodded.

He lifted the horn to his lips and blew a short, harsh blast that rolled through the naked trees.

Father Joe and the others who had agreed to patrol the perimeter arrived not long after, their voices rising in horror when they saw the devastation of the clearing. Corrine stayed with Miss Brown and the others below the lip of the dell. She squinted up through the trees. The black shapes were gone.

She heard Father Joe saying prayers over what remained of Kenneth; someone was sent to fetch sheets to cover whatever Corrine's fire hadn't burned. Euan strode around the perimeter of the clearing, restless as one of the hunting dogs.

Father Joe approached the girls. "Come, I'll take you back to the manor."

Christina sobbed softly into Miss Brown's shoulder, but allowed herself to be led away.

Ilona stood like a statue. Corrine reached out to her, but the tall girl didn't move when she touched her.

"Ilona," she said.

"They slaughtered him," Ilona said. There was so much rage in her voice that Corrine withdrew her fingers, as though she might be burned. The fire rose in her mind again.

They followed Father Joe, Miss Brown, and Christina back down the path.

"Like cattle, like a piece of meat . . ." Ilona said.

"He was, to them." Corrine shuddered. She recalled how the serpent-bound book had called humans "mortal locusts." The book that was gone now. The book that, Corrine was certain, Kenneth had died for, though she couldn't say how or why.

"Corrine," Ilona grasped her hand. "I want to help you. I want to stop them. Just tell me how."

Corrine squeezed Ilona's cold hand in her own. "Become a great swordswoman. So that when we can't use magic, you can at least defend us."

"So will I do. I swear by Mary the Virgin herself."

Corrine nodded then, and they walked hand in hand silently back to the manor.

It was only when she was in her room alone again, after she had searched for the book in vain, after she had cried for poor, honest Kenneth so horribly murdered, that she remembered the Captain's plaintive cry. She went to her window and looked down on the forest, where a team of inspectors was now tromping along the bridge toward the murder site.

Possum, he had called her. Only her father had ever called her that. A painful thought caused her eyes to sting with tears again. Had the Captain murdered her father too? Had he spoken of his Possum with his last breath? Perhaps she was truly an orphan now, as Sir James had made known to all of Fearnan.

A Council meeting was called after midnight. Mara woke Corrine from a restless sleep, helped her dress, and led her to Sir James's study. Father Joe, Miss Brown, and Sir James had just settled themselves around a table near the fire when the girls arrived. They looked as though they'd been arguing; Sir James refused to look at Father Joe.

Corrine and Mara seated themselves. Corrine rubbed gently at her eye; she hadn't replaced the bandage since this morning's horrible discovery.

"Well, let's get right down to it, shall we?" Sir James said.

He leaned across the table and thrust a photograph at Corrine. A young woman looked out at her, her casque-style bonnet perched low on her forehead to show off her intricately coiled chignon. Corrine was sure the chignon must have been a hairpiece; no one could possibly have that much hair! The lady wore a smart walking suit and her hands were clasped over an umbrella handle inlaid with mother-of-pearl, as though she were just about to step out for a turn around the grounds. An odd ring of silver knots and sapphires shone on one of her hands.

"This is Cecily Dalrymple, the barrister's daughter in Killin. She disappeared yesterday."

Corrine tried to block the sight of Kenneth's body from her mind and failed.

"Was she—was she at the ball?" Corrine asked.

"Yes," Sir James said. "You might have seen her; she was dressed as a Turkish sultan."

Corrine shook her head. If she had seen this girl, she would have remembered.

"Margaret Sullivan—the miller's daughter in Killin—has also disappeared," Sir James said. He put his head in his hands. His voice was muffled when he spoke. "I set wards. They should have worked. The rathstone in the chamber should be enough, even without them."

"Apparently, none of those things are enough," Father Joe said. "And I warned you not to be foolish by thinking you would keep the Unhallowed from entering here if they wished.

The ball was a mistake, especially with a cuideag about, and I told you that from the first."

Sir James glared at Father Joe so venomously that Corrine shrank against her chair. A black well engulfed her eyesight. But then it was gone, and Corrine wondered if it was a trick of the firelight or her harrowed imagination. She took five deep breaths. Sir James was a Council member. Would he possibly betray them? She thought of Miss de Mornay, her old teacher at Falston, opening the gates for the Unhallowed and the ghostly Confederate cavalry. Had Sir James also fallen under the spell of the Unhallowed? Surely not. And yet, somehow the book had been in his study when Kenneth found it and decided to return it to her. And now Kenneth was dead. To what purpose?

Corrine shook her head. Miss Brown was saying something about how the ball had been well-intentioned. "We all enjoyed it; I just think we once again underestimated our ability to withstand the Unhallowed."

"The point is," Sir James said, "what do we do now? Kenneth is dead. Two more girls are missing. And there are rumors of another that have not yet been confirmed."

"And Rory and the Prince were here, as well as a cuideag we have yet to find." Father Joe sighed. "Your root worked," he said, turning to Mara. "Though perhaps not in the way we'd hoped."

Mara frowned, but said nothing.

"We must focus our efforts on retrieving that chamber key and the rathstones. We must find a way to get information from Rory. The presence of the cuideag means that we are in a race against time," Father Joe said.

"But we can't simply leave these girls to their fates," Miss Brown said. "We've sacrificed them too often for the greater goal. Is there a way for us to find them?"

"I could scry . . ." Mara said.

"Finding the girls will not aid the larger problem!" Father Joe said, his voice rising. Corrine could hear the echoes of bound power in it. She wondered how powerful he would be if he ever regained the full use of his magic. She wasn't sure she wanted to know.

"Perhaps, perhaps not," Miss Brown said.

"We are responsible," Sir James said, adjusting his waistcoat. "If we won't help them, who will?"

Father Joe bristled. He looked like he wanted to throw or hit something; Corrine wasn't sure which.

"Surely a little scrying can't hurt, Joseph," Miss Brown said. "Then we can discuss the 'larger problem,' as you call it." She lifted her hand as though to touch his arm, but the look he gave her forbade it.

Father Joe sighed. "I suppose it won't take long. And perhaps it would be a good lesson for Corrine. But we really must find the key, the stones, Rory—" He put his head in his hands.

"Soon," Miss Brown said. And this time she rested her hand lightly on his forearm.

Everyone looked at Mara then.

"I'll need a mirror, fresh water, salt . . ." she said, rising from the table. She went to stand near the fire. "We'll do it here on the hearth."

Miss Brown departed to fetch the supplies Mara named.

Sir James went to the sideboard for whiskey. Father Joe shook his head when he offered, though he looked as though he very much wanted some.

Corrine's eye stung and she touched it again carefully. She still could only see blurry reflections with it. She began to fear that perhaps it wouldn't heal as the doctor had promised. No one spoke. The fire was the only thing that moved in the room.

When Miss Brown returned, Mara took the mirror and laid it on the hearthstone. She gestured to Corrine. "Come over here if you want to learn."

Corrine moved to stand beside her, mesmerized by the reflected flames. Mara sprinkled salt around the two of them in a little circle. She let three drops of water fall on the mirror, tilting it so the water ran through shadow and light, then whispered words Corrine couldn't quite catch.

Mara stared at the mirror for a long time. Corrine looked down, assuming she should stay in the circle but unsure whether Mara would draw on her for power or simply ignore her. Corrine also wasn't sure she would see anything in the mirror's waterlogged flames. She squinted and tried to look out of her injured eye. The fire lost its shape in the mirror; it became the fog-shrouded lake.

She walked again toward the mound, and she saw the dancing glimmer deep within it. And the guardian came again, a fanged, eyeless thing that nevertheless knew her every movement. He was waiting for something. A sign from her, perhaps, or some word. But she didn't know it.

Suddenly, she was falling, helplessly tumbling into a void that rushed to swallow her. The fall stopped when three veiled women caught her. With her limbs hanging loose and unhinged, they carried her to a mossy altar, cracked and crawling with long-legged things that scattered as they placed her on it. Then the shadows took shape. The masked coterie of the Prince's court marched around her, their skirts and capes dragging the forest floor.

Then, he came. And for a moment, she almost saw his face, almost saw . . . the erratic pupils, the thin curve of a smile. And beneath that—vines, an oaken skeleton, a weeping heart of stone.

He held his hand over her eyes. Stop. You must not see . . .

She stepped back. The mirror flashed as though struck by lightning, and then went black. It shattered on the hearth into thousands of singing shards.

"Corrine?" Father Joe said. He held her up. She couldn't speak. Father Joe helped her to a chair.

"Mara, did you see anything?" Miss Brown asked, while Corrine caught her breath.

The maid shook her head. "My mojo ain't been right since the steamship. I can't see anything here. But she did."

Corrine felt Mara's frustration as a physical sensation, a throbbing in her knees.

"Did you find Cecily, Corrine?" Sir James asked.

Why did he care so much about this girl? "I don't know," she said. "But I know what's happening."

The words from the serpent-bound book flashed behind her eyes. "The blood of sacrifice feeds the fires of the Cauldron. If this is truth, then perhaps Hallowmere will open again to its true rulers . . ." She looked up at Father Joe, and then at the rest of the room. "They're sacrificing these girls to try to open Hallowmere."

Thirteen

February 3, 1866

Horrified silence pervaded the room. Then everyone began speaking at once. "What do you mean?" "How do you know?" "Why?" When they slowed, Corrine was at last able to tell them what she'd seen—the mound, the mossy glade, and its sacrificial altar. She could barely speak of the Prince. She had been told what he was capable of—how often had she heard it?—but she still had trouble believing it.

It is not meant for you. She thought she heard him sigh across the distances of her mind.

"Sacrificing girls? Is that what happened to Jeanette? And Penelope? And those before them?" Miss Brown said in half-shadow near the fire.

Is that what will happen to me? Corrine thought.

Miss Brown came forward, her face anguished. "Why would they do that? How would their blood open Hallowmere?"

"It seemed like a test," Corrine said. "And when she failed . . ." She couldn't finish. And she knew she couldn't tell what she'd read in the serpent-bound book with Sir James standing there.

"But what kind of test?" Miss Brown said. "What could they

be testing for? They must have the stones to open Hallowmere; they know that!"

Father Joe bowed his head. "We have never known why they took those girls. If only Melanie had been able to discover the reason! It may be that they need someone to . . ."—he looked at Corrine with dawning comprehension—"to open the way to Hallowmere. Someone . . ."

"What?" Corrine said.

Mara looked at them like she knew all too well what he was talking about.

"Corrine, do you have the book I gave you at Falston?"

Corrine clutched at the arms of her chair. "No."

"Are you well enough to fetch it?"

Corrine swallowed. A wild hope that whoever had taken it would have put it back by now beat in her chest.

"I can try," she said. She avoided looking at Sir James.

"Do you need help?" Miss Brown asked Corrine.

He must have it. "No, ma'am," she said. *But why?*

Miss Brown returned to the chair in which she had been seated at the table. "Hurry back then," Miss Brown said. "Mara, would you mind bringing us some tea?"

Corrine left the room and walked down the corridor toward the steps as slowly as she could. She knew she wouldn't find the book, but she was glad to be out of that room for a while. She was surprised to find Christina ascending the stairs. When her friend saw her, she turned her face away. Her lips were swollen and red as rubies; her cheeks flushed with cold . . . or heat. Christina slowed reluctantly to let Corrine catch up.

"Corrine," she said.

"Where were you?" Corrine said.

"Ah, I was . . . ah . . ."

"Were you listening to us?" Corrine asked.

Christina's eyes shifted away from her, then back. "Yes," she admitted. Her smile was tempered by embarrassment.

Corrine was puzzled. "Well, you know of course I'll tell you everything I can. There's no need for eavesdropping."

"Oh . . . ah . . . well . . . we like to know what's going on for ourselves, Ilona and I," Christina said. She linked arms with Corrine as they continued up the stairs. "Now I shall know whether or not you tell the truth," she said, winking.

Corrine smiled, but couldn't help feeling as though Christina was lying.

When Corrine got back to her room, she looked in all the places she had looked when she had first discovered the book was missing—in the corner, in the drawer, in the wardrobe, under the bed. She paced back and forth, stalling, trying to think up a reasonable story. All she could think of, though, was to pretend that she'd only just discovered its absence, that she hadn't been as vigilant as she should have. Everything she thought of, though, seemed incriminating in one way or another. Did Sir James have the book? What would he want with it? And had Kenneth truly died for it?

Finally, with much difficulty, she forced herself back out of the door, down the stairs, and into the study. It felt like her first day at Falston with all those pairs of eyes watching her as she stepped into the laboratory.

She shut the study door and stood with her back against it. She almost wanted to put her hand on the latch in case she had to run. She didn't know why she was so afraid.

"Corrine? Did you find it?" Father Joe said. She could tell that he was in a difficult position.

She looked down at the place where the worn rug met the stone floor.

"No," she said. "It's not anywhere in my room."

"Wait," Sir James said. "What are you two talking about?"

She glanced up and blinked against the blackness.

"Do you know what happened to it?" Father Joe said, ignoring Sir James with an exaggerated calmness.

"No. I've looked everywhere."

"What the devil are you both on about?" Sir James said, louder this time.

Miss Brown looked at her hands. Father Joe sighed. "I stole the Unhallowed book long ago from the Council chamber because I believed it best for us to know our enemy. But, with my powers bound, I could make no sense of the Unhallowed language. I gave it to Corrine at Falston as a test, to see if she was capable of reading it. She has carried it ever since."

Sir James's face grew so red Corrine thought he might explode like the boiler of the *Great Eastern*.

"First the rathstones and now this!" Sir James shouted. "Oh, aye," he said when Father Joe attempted to interrupt, "William admitted whose fault the loss of the stones was in a letter last year. What a fine mess you've gotten us into, Miss Jameson!"

Corrine looked at him in shock.

"Sir James!" Miss Brown said.

"You've all been dancing about the subject, but I think it must be said. This girl is the reason for all our problems. She is directly responsible for the loss of not one, but two—two!—rathstones, and now she has lost the book, the book which by all rights would have been safe if it were still in the chamber where it belongs!"

"Sir James," Father Joe said.

But Sir James overrode him, rising from his chair and pointing a stubby finger at Corrine. "It's because of you that all this has happened—that Kenneth was ripped to pieces and Cecily and Margaret are gone! And now the book is missing! You are responsible!"

Corrine shrank against the door, confused. His anger seemed genuine. Did he or did he not have the book? How could she accuse him of Kenneth's death if he didn't have the book? And if he didn't, who did?

"That's quite enough!" Father Joe shouted.

"I won't stand for this!" Sir James marched over to Corrine, his great belly shaking beneath his smoking jacket. "I have done a great deal for you, even held that ridiculous masquerade—I dressed as a frog, for heaven's sake—because of my fondness for your uncle. But this goes beyond the pale! While you are a guest in my house, you will not attend Council meetings. You and Mara will work to find Cecily and Margaret and you will do so immediately! And you," he whirled to Father Joe, "you will find that book you stole. Or I will eject all of you from this house!"

All Corrine saw through her tears was darkness. No one bothered to remind Sir James that he had lost the key to the room that would have given them all the knowledge they needed. Her left eye burned.

She turned and threw open the door.

"Corrine!" Miss Brown called her name, but it was too late. Corrine flew out of the study, down the corridor to the main entrance. She picked up her scarf where she had left it on the foyer bench after returning from searching for Kenneth. She threw the latch and was outside before anyone could stop her.

Tears obscured her vision. Corrine slowed to a walk. The cold gripped her in its iron corset, thinning out her sobs. She inhaled snowflakes, felt them melting on her hot cheeks. She wiped at her eyes and wound the scarf around her throat. She didn't know where she was going. Sir James's words beat at her like fists. *It's because of you that all this happened. You are responsible!*

Maybe I should just go to the Prince and get it over with, she thought. *What reason do I have to stay?* Maybe she was fighting the inevitable.

A soft mewling cry startled her. She stopped. She realized that she'd walked along the bridle path and was now at the bridge. Beyond the dark stream, the forest held its breath in the flurrying snow.

The cry came again from just within the trees.

Trap? Corrine set her teeth and stepped on the bridge. If it was a trap, she would walk into it gladly. By the Council's lights, did they not view her as a traitor anyway?

The sound of her boots on the bridge seemed like a death knell. Soon, the Captain would come. Soon, perhaps, she would know what his garbled croaks meant, why he called her Possum. Soon the triumphant Prince would come, perhaps to sacrifice her, just as he had done with all those other girls.

The silence held as she entered the tree line. She heard the cry, fainter this time and off to her left. She followed it, chagrined by the crackling of leaves and twigs under her boots. A dim light led her, like a trace of starlight hanging just above the ground. Or a diamond sparkle, or the glassy light of falling water.

As she came closer, Corrine could make out a tiny figure, the angles of arms and legs, the glimmer of drooping wings. She wanted to laugh at her first thought. *A fairy.* She had stopped believing in fairy tales the day she'd discovered they were real, the day the Unhallowed had first spoken to her from under the hawthorn bush. Yet here one was. And she was in trouble.

The pixie was bound with wire to an iron stake driven deep in the dirt. Her hair hung around her bowed head like dead vines in the drifting snow. The source of the light was the strange, shimmering blood that flowed rainbow-slick from her hands and feet.

Corrine didn't know what to say. She knelt and reached out to the creature, her sorrows subsumed in the desire to help. When Corrine touched her, the fairy screamed—a high, silver peal. Like a bell in snow. Or nails on ice. Corrine fell back in the frozen leaves.

"Do not," the pixie said, and her voice froze in Corrine's ears.

"But I want to help you," Corrine whispered.

"You cannot," the pixie said. "I am dying. Soon, I will be gone forevermore."

"Surely if I free you—"

The pixie shook her head, but Corrine was already at the wires. They were twisted tight around the pixie's shoulders and legs, and they were sharp. Corrine's numb hands split; her own chilled blood flowed out of the cuts.

Once she worked off the second wire, she cupped her palm and the pixie crumpled onto it like a wet leaf.

"Why did they do this to you?" Corrine asked.

The pixie considered her a moment, then winced in pain. "Your mortal blood is painful to me, but the fact that you see me, that you hear—" She struggled to catch her breath and Corrine tried to hold as still as she could.

"They caught me on one of their Hunts," the pixie said. "They did this because I would not tell them where the key is hidden."

The key? Corrine frowned. She heard the cuideag again, its many heads screaming, *The key! The key? The KEY!*

"The key to the Council chamber?"

"Clever child," the pixie said. She shifted restlessly on Corrine's palm.

"And will you tell me?" Corrine asked.

"By the Law, what one Friend of Elaphe asks is freely given by another," the pixie said. Corrine noticed that her tiny fingers and toes were turning white, as though she were frostbitten or burning to ash in a hot fire.

"The fools locked the key with my cousin in an iron box on the Isle of Female Saints. If he still lives, he may be persuaded to give you the key when he is released." She struggled against the pain in her wings and extremities. "You must help us, help the Hallowed kin that remain, find Hallowmere before they do. There is evil in that house; it seeks you. You must be strong . . ." But the withering took her before she could finish speaking.

The pixie shriveled into a puddle of shining blood in her hands. Corrine's fingers warmed briefly; the cuts healed even as her tears started afresh. She remembered the shining blood of the two-headed serpent that she knew had tried to save her from the ghost of John Pelham at Kelly's Ford. It had died, presumably killed by Rory when she'd fainted. And here was another Hallowed being who had died in her hands.

A snap made her turn. A lantern swung along the path, and she was surprised when the light revealed Euan, peering at her out of the dark.

"Corrine? Bloody hell! What are you doing here?" He came toward her, reaching for her bare hands. "I thought you had better sense than to come here!" he said, as he wrapped her hands in his own.

"I was just . . . I . . ." Her teeth were chattering too much to speak.

He seemed angry, but she felt his fingers trembling over her own, as though he wrestled with something. He glanced at the iron stake. "What's this?" he asked.

She wanted to trust him. She remembered how Rory had found her wandering in the dark and closed her eyes.

"There was a pixie," she said slowly. "Someone had hurt her. She died in my hands."

She opened her eyes. His squeezed her hands. "The Elder Ones are constantly being hunted down. I'm sorry you witnessed that," he said. *This is not meant for you,* she heard the Prince say.

"Something has gone really wrong in the house, Euan. First Kenneth, and now Sir James—" she began.

His expression was grim. "I know. I promise you I'm doing what I can."

"Doing what you can? What can you possibly do?" she asked.

"Remember how I asked you to trust me on the ship, Corrine? Remember how I protected you?"

His hand sent tingles rippling through her arms and shoulders. She nodded.

"I need you to trust me now more than ever. If I am to help you, you must leave me to my methods. And you must stop putting yourself in harm's way like this."

"Who are you?" she said. It was all she could think to ask. He looked in her eyes and she shivered as she had when she'd danced with the Prince.

He bowed his head. "I am your friend," he said. His thumb traced spirals over her bare hand before he dropped it. "Now, let's get you back inside."

He lifted the lantern and led her out of the woods and across the bridge. Along the bridle path, another light swung toward them, showing the shadows of Father Joe's face in sharp relief.

"Corrine!" He came forward, reaching as though he wanted to embrace her or take her hands. "I thought you'd gone to . . . We were all so worried!"

"Even Sir James?" Corrine asked, her lips stiff with cold.

"Corrine, I think—ah," Father Joe looked over at Euan, who stood watching them as the wind ruffled his collar and the snow sparkled in his hazel eyes.

"Let's go inside to talk, shall we?" Father Joe said. "Thank you, Euan. It was fortunate that you were about at this time of night."

"Yes, well, ever since Kenneth—" He cleared his throat. "I keep hoping that perhaps I'll chance on the creature that killed him, Father."

"I can imagine," Father Joe said.

"Well, then," Euan said, looking at Corrine.

Corrine put her hands into the scarf at her throat.

"Good night." He nodded to both of them, and turned to go back to the bridge. The wind followed him, ruffling his hair while snow danced around him.

"Come," Father Joe said, taking her arm. "We must get you warm."

Father Joe took her straight up to her room. Miss Brown was already there, laying out her nightgown and robe on the edge of the bed. The warming pan stood ready by the fire.

"Corrine," Miss Brown rushed to her and enfolded her in a rustle of taffeta and wool.

Surprised, Corrine returned the embrace tentatively, thinking of her mother. But Miss Brown smelled of dusty things, a hint of lavender, not the exotic, sweet smell her mother had carried on her like a perfume.

"We thought you'd given up and finally gone to him," Miss Brown murmured.

Corrine withdrew from the embrace as soon as she could; the longing for her mother overwhelmed her.

"No," she said.

"Here," Miss Brown said, leading her to a chair by the fire. "Come, sit."

Corrine settled herself in the chair, holding out her boots toward the fire. She looked down at the scarf, still tangled around one hand.

Father Joe said, "I am sorry for Sir James's behavior. He was unkind."

Is Sir James sorry? Corrine wondered. But she didn't ask, just nodded.

It seemed that Father Joe might berate her, but he sighed and just shook his head.

"I'm sorry about the book," she said in a small voice.

"Was that the first time you'd noticed it missing?" Miss Brown asked.

Mara came in with a tea tray.

"Yes," Corrine said.

Father Joe bowed his head. "The stones, the key, the book. So many deaths," he whispered. He shook his head and looked up at Corrine.

"The book is most likely lost to us. We must retrieve those rathstones. And find the key, if we can." He removed his spectacles. "But first, unfortunately, I think we must appease Sir James somewhat. You and Mara shall go into Killin and try to find those girls. I'm afraid Sir James won't feel much like cooperating with the rest of the Council until we at least try."

"Father Joe," she said. She was afraid to mention anything about Sir James, but she felt she had to. She had withheld her thoughts so many times before because no one would listen to them. She hoped now that perhaps they would. "About Sir James—"

"Yes?"

"I think he may have taken the book," Corrine said. She explained how Sir James had seen her with the book before the ball, how Kenneth had returned it to her when she hadn't even realized it was missing. "And then he died. And after that, the book was gone again."

Father Joe removed his spectacles and bowed his head.

He sighed. "Are you saying you think that Sir James had Kenneth killed?"

Corrine bit her lip and nodded.

"But William's known him since he was a young man. His family has kept the Council chamber for generations," Miss Brown said.

"Yes," Father Joe said. "I just don't see how, why—"

Mara brought her tea and their eyes locked. The maid shook her head slightly and Corrine wondered if perhaps she should have maintained her silence about Sir James.

"There are many possible explanations," Father Joe said finally. "The Unhallowed could be trying to divert our attention onto Sir James and make him look like the culprit. Did you actually see Sir James with the book?"

"No," Corrine admitted. "But Kenneth found it in his study and brought it to me because he thought I'd forgotten it. He was just trying to be kind, and—"

"We know, Corrine," Miss Brown said. "This is how the Unhallowed operate."

"Indeed," Father Joe said. "They repay kindness with malice, trust with treachery. That is why it's difficult to believe Sir James would suddenly alter his alliance. He's always been faithful to us. He put himself in danger for your uncle and the Council many times. The behavior you describe just isn't like him. I can't imagine he'd be so angry about the book that he'd have someone killed over it! No," he said. "This has the stench of the Unhallowed about it."

Corrine nodded. She appreciated that Father Joe had considered what she said but was disappointed by his conclusion. Yet, what he said was true. She had no real proof. Only these strange feelings and hints of shadows.

"Thank goodness Euan found you when he did," Miss Brown said.

"Yes," Father Joe said. "Why did you go into the forest? You know how dangerous it is!"

Corrine thought of the pixie and her hands started shaking so much that she had to put her teacup beside her. She threaded the scarf around her palms. "I saw a pixie," she said. "One of the Hallowed. They had left her on an iron stake to die."

Father Joe clutched at the chair behind which he stood. "They have been known to do such things. As I said, they delight in cruelty to those who have rejected them."

"She said they tortured her because she knew where the key was."

There was a moment of silence. "And did she tell you?" Father Joe asked.

"Yes," Corrine said.

Father Joe glanced at the door, the walls, as though they were listening. "Not here," he said. "Not now."

"They want me to help them," Corrine said. "But how can I? Unless I can get the rathstones back."

"It may be that you will be needed for that task," Father Joe said. He paused, choosing his words carefully. "For now, though, let us focus on finding these girls, if we can. We need Sir James on our side in this."

Corrine nodded. But she was more determined than ever to find the rathstones and take them back from the Unhallowed.

FOURTEEN

February 4, 1866

CORRINE IMAGINED THAT THE TRIP INTO KILLIN WOULD
have been quite pleasant in another season. She was sure the
hills and trees, the thatched cottages and gray river would all
have benefited from summer sunshine. As it was, she sank
down as deeply into the carriage seat as she could with the rug
over her knees, listening to Christina and Ilona chat about the
dismal weather. Christina's voice was unusually high-pitched
and bright, as though she was speaking quickly to distract
them from something else. Mara remained silent beside Miss
Brown. She drew the dowsing rods they would try to use to
find Cecily from her bag and examined them in the dim light.
She'd whittled them from rowan. Normally, dowsing rods were
used to find water, but Mara had said she hoped this might
work where scrying had not.

The carriage halted before a tailor's shop, ostensibly the
reason for their visit. Now that Corrine had reached her sixteenth birthday, she would no longer wear the pinafore of a little
girl. They were shopping for fabric to make new dresses for her,
dresses that would reach the floor, like the mourning dress she
had worn so briefly before returning to the pinafore at Falston.
She supposed this also meant she would finally succumb to

wearing a corset, which was truly a dismal thought. The girls piled out of the carriage and Miss Brown spoke to the driver about where and when to meet them for the return trip. Then the carriage was off; the driver undoubtedly bound for some tavern to have a few pints while he waited.

The gray day streamed into the tailor's shop through dusty windows. There were a few gleams of silk and organza, but the fabrics were generally sensible—wools, calicos, muslin. The tailor popped out from the back of the shop as the door opened. He was a little man with mouse-bright eyes who pulled bolts of fabric down at Christina's insistence. While he was busy with Christina, Corrine got as close to Miss Brown as she could and rose on her tiptoes to whisper in her ear.

"The key is on the Isle of Female Saints," she said. Father Joe had told Corrine to tell Miss Brown at some point while they were away from the house.

Miss Brown nodded and whispered back, "Off you go."

Slowly, Mara and Corrine edged backward. Mara whispered, "hush," and as she opened the door, the bells shivered but remained silent.

Then they were alone out in the drizzle. Mara pulled Corrine away from the shop windows, toward a little alley. She passed Corrine a dowsing rod.

"Hold it under your coat," she said, "and just do what I told you."

Corrine held the rod under her coat, wondering if it looked like a revolver pointing through the wool. She was still unsure why the Council thought this would be safe, leaving the two of them to go alone through the village seeking the whereabouts of some girls who she was sure must be long dead.

"All right then," Mara said. "I'll look for the other girl. You look for that Cecily one."

Corrine nodded. She held the image of Cecily in her mind.

"Find," she whispered. The dowsing rod pulled her out of the alley, straining like a blind dog on the scent. It veered to the right, resisting her when she tried to go left. Mara's pulled her straight across the street. They looked at each other one last time before they lost each other in the row houses and spitting rain.

Father Joe had said that the dowsing rods would probably only lead them to a location. "You are not to go inside, nor to try saving these girls yourselves. Just tell us where the rod takes you. We'll do the rest."

"But how will I even know where I am?" Corrine wondered aloud.

The rod pulled her down the street, through coal-smudged row houses and shops with windows thick with dirt. She could feel the River Tay nearby, and how the rod seemed to want to go to it, as though finding water was much more natural to it than finding a person.

The few people who had ventured out in the weather stared at her as she passed, her steps forced unnaturally by the rod's strength. The tension in her wrist made her want to let go, but Mara had said it would be very difficult to get the rod moving again if she released it or lost concentration.

"Cecily," she whispered to herself, trying not to feel the cold stares, the unfamiliar buildings squatting over her in the rain.

At the top of a small rise in the street, the rod pulled her hard to the left, forcing her to cross the road, barely allowing her to pause before a carriage hurtled up over the hill. Muddy water drenched Corrine, seeping through her stockings and running down her legs into her boots. But the rod dragged her on, into a long, winding alley filled with debris and stinking of human waste. Growing more worried by the second, she followed the alley to its crooked end between two buildings. There was a little door built into the crumbling brick. The sky spat rain between the buildings—the water puddling in a pile of sodden blankets near the door. There was a heavy, rotten smell in the air. The dowsing rod vibrated as if it would burst.

Corrine jumped when the door opened and a little girl stumbled outside. She smiled vapidly, her eyes unfocused. She had little blonde curls that reminded Corrine of Penelope, who had disappeared at Falston around Thanksgiving. But this girl was younger, her face thinner. Corrine at first thought she wore a red collar or scarf before she realized that the girl's neck was scarlet with blood.

"Dear Lord!" She rushed forward, taking the little girl in her arms.

And then Corrine saw the blackened hand protruding from the pile of blankets. On it, a ring of silver knots laced with sapphires shone dimly in the rain. *Cecily.*

She remembered another hand, rising from the leaves of the forest floor, Kenneth's severed hand so obscenely devoid of life. Ilona, she knew, would have gone over, probably removed the blankets to be absolutely certain of the corpse's identity, but Corrine stood frozen. Who else would have worn a ring like that? She crouched against the wall, holding the little girl who hummed softly in the growing twilight. She couldn't look away from the winking ring or the blankets that hid the rest of Cecily's body. For a moment, she thought that she was like Christina after all, too weak to control the urge to faint.

Someone stepped out of the dark doorway. There was only one place to hide, and Corrine refused it. She stood against the wall, holding the child instead. *Let it come, whatever it is.*

She knew the black cloak, the hooded figure, the outstretched red hand almost before she saw it. She felt the deep trembling in her knees and leaned as hard as she could against the wall, sucking in the damp, cold air. The Captain had cornered her at last. It was over.

She felt his power looping out in great coils around him. He threw back his hood. The Captain's black tongue lolled from his mouth, and charred, patchy hair erupted from his pale skull. His flesh was wriggled and contorted as though it had tried to leave his bones. She thought she glimpsed something . . . or someone . . . beneath it. She shuddered and looked away.

She knew it was time for him to take her, but she wanted to save the little girl if she could. She shook her where she drowsed in her arms. "Run," Corrine said. "Run. If you run, he'll let you go."

The little girl didn't respond. Her blonde curls were matted with red. Corrine shook her again as the Captain advanced. Corrine choked. The little girl was dead.

"Possum."

She glanced at him, at his warped, burned face. His jaw was twisted, his black tongue incapable of forming the words he so desperately wanted to speak. She had never seen his eyes before. They looked unnervingly human, sad and mild as a dog's.

He lifted his hand, wet with fresh blood—the blood of the little girl who stiffened now in Corrine's arms.

She screamed and thrust the little girl's body at him. The green fire built in her mind. It raced through the air, dowsing him in emerald flame as he caught the girl awkwardly.

A sharp word crackled across the damp air.

The Captain moaned. He flinched as though he had been lashed with a whip.

"Corrine?" At first the voice sounded oddly filtered, not like any voice she knew at all.

Then she saw him standing slightly behind and to the right of the Captain.

"Euan?"

The Captain froze, his tongue working, his red hand out-stretched, the other clasping the little girl.

Go.

The Captain turned and ran out of the alley, clutching the little girl like a dead doll.

Corrine stared at Euan.

"How is it that I always find you where I'm least expecting you?" he asked.

I might ask the same of you, she thought. But she just shook her head.

"Why are you here?" He came a little closer. She saw the high flush on his cheeks again, that abnormally well look she had seen once or twice before.

"I . . . got lost," she said.

"Corrine . . ."

Moisture from the bricks seeped through her coat and into her dress. And before she knew it she was struggling to breathe, sobbing, feeling the little girl in her arms again before she realized she was dead.

"Corrine, Corrine." Murmuring her name like a lullaby, he drew her into his arms. She wished she didn't feel the comfort of it, wished his arms didn't seem so warm and protective, that his heartbeat wasn't like a soothing song.

"That little girl," she sobbed. "He took her! He killed her!"

He shushed her. He nestled his hand against the back of her neck. Somehow, just his touch felt even more intimate than the kiss she had shared with Rory that cold night at Falston.

She slid out of his embrace, embarrassed.

"Now, tell me," he said, as she wiped at her eyes, "what were you about here? Why did I find you cornered by the Captain?"

She gaped. "You know the Captain?"

"But of course," he said. He handed her a handkerchief from the pouch slung across his shoulders.

"How?" she said. "And how did you know how to call him off?"

"I know what all of those like us know." He looked at her sidelong.

"Like us? What are you saying?" She dabbed at her face, but the drizzling rain didn't allow her to stay dry for very long.

"You knew something was different about me from the first, didn't you?" Euan asked. He drew her to a stoop around the corner, so that the pile of blankets, the charred fingertips, were out of sight.

Corrine looked down at her sleeve and saw a red line of blood. She swallowed hard. There was nothing she could do. Wherever he had gone, the Captain had taken the little girl with him.

"Didn't you?" Euan prodded.

She nodded slightly.

"And you've always known something was different about the priest, haven't you?"

"Yes," she said.

"And you've felt there's something different about you, something no one will explain to you, something that makes them all look at you with pity and fear, yes?"

She looked at him. "Me? What do you mean?" She thought of the entry in the serpent-bound book. *Half-Born?*

"I mean . . . that like Father Joe and Mara, you are half-Fey."

Images and bits of conversation poured through Corrine's head . . . the ghost of John Pelham calling her *fairy girl* at Kelly's Ford, Mara and Father Joe exchanging glances . . . the fact that only she, Father Joe, and Mara could do magic . . . her "fairy eye" . . . all the silencing looks and half-finished sentences . . .

"Half-Fey? You mean Half-Born?"

"Yes," he said. "You are Half-Born."

She nodded. It was true. Everyone had hidden the truth from her, and it hurt. Father Joe, Mara, Miss Brown even—they'd known all along and hadn't dared to tell her. "Father Joe said there would be tests, that nothing could be proven—"

"Stuff and nonsense," Euan said. "His mother knitted his head out of wool. He's just telling you that because—" He stopped.

"Because?"

"Now I've no call to be speaking badly of a priest," Euan said, helping her up.

"Why would they hide this from me?" Corrine said. "And how is it you know? Are you Half-Born too?"

"How could I not know? My mother was Hallowed," Euan said, smiling. "As to why they're hiding it, that's easy enough. Being Half-Born carries with it tremendous power. And once you realize that, well, they can't control you very well then, can they?"

Corrine stared at him. Was that really it? Were they so afraid of her and her power that they refused to tell her about it? The rain dripped down from the edge of her bonnet, obscuring Euan in the gloom.

"Come now, I'd better get you back to Miss Brown." He pointed his chin toward the body around the corner. "There's nothing more you can do to help her now, if that's why you're here."

He led her back down the darkening alley. The knowledge that she was not entirely human—Half-Born—shivered along her veins. Back in August, in the unbearable heat of a Washington rooming house, she would have thought that anyone who had told her this was mad. And yet, she knew the difference in herself. Knew that something made her able to see things that weren't there, to call up flame or hear voices in the wind. Though she was grateful for the knowledge, though this was the third time he had saved her, Corrine remembered how Father Joe had told her not to trust anyone. Even him. And now, she thought sadly, she didn't.

They walked along in the rain until they were at the corner of the tailor's shop. Euan stopped her before she could go further.

"It's probably best if they don't see me with you. I think they're growing suspicious." He backed away toward an alley, but Corrine stopped him.

"You still don't want them to know about you?"

Euan shook his head. "I don't want to be involved in whatever they're scheming."

"Why not? People are dying—don't you want to help stop that?"

"My only role here is to protect you, Corrine," Euan said. His eyes were as green as the fire of life. "That's all."

Corrine stared.

"If you have need of me, here is a charm," he said. He came closer to her, bowed his head, and whispered in her ear, *"Gannon."* The word tickled all the way down her spine. He drew back and said, "Take the scarf I gave you, wrap it around your hands, and whisper that word," he said. "I'll hear you and come."

"Go now," he said. He backed away into the dim alley. She shook her head, wondering what he must be hiding. Everyone, it seemed, had some dreadful secret. Including her.

She turned toward the tailor's shop just as Miss Brown and the girls came out onto the street, carrying paper-wrapped packages in their arms. She saw Mara coming from across the street at the same moment and wondered if Mara had seen Euan with her. Somehow, she had the feeling that if Euan didn't wish to be seen, he could make it so.

"Corrine," Miss Brown said, as she opened her parasol against the rain, "where have you been? We were worried." The headmistress played her part perfectly, but Corrine didn't feel she could rise to the occasion.

"I found her," she said. "She's dead. And another little girl died in my arms." She gestured to the blood rusting her old dress.

Miss Brown looked around and pulled Corrine as close as she could under her flowered umbrella. "Not here," she said.

Corrine looked up at her, surprised a little by the resentment boiling in her breast. Obviously, the Council had always known that Corrine might be Half-Born. They probably even knew what that really meant for Corrine and those around her. And yet, they'd kept it from her. It had taken Euan to finally reveal it to her. Euan and the serpent-bound book she had once been able to read.

She pushed away from Miss Brown and out from under the parasol's dark shelter. Miss Brown looked at her with concern, but Corrine refused to meet her gaze and watched instead for the carriage.

On her other side, Christina suddenly gripped her hand. Corrine followed her friend's gaze across the street. Rory met her eyes for a moment before he grinned crookedly and turned the corner, pulling up his coat collar against the rain. Corrine considered alerting Miss Brown, but when she looked over at Christina, the French girl shook her head.

As the carriage dragged to a halt before them, Corrine shut out the horror of what had happened in the alley, considering instead why she'd seen the two most bewildering men she'd ever met in the same small Scottish village, only moments apart. She also wished, as she avoided Miss Brown's eyes and climbed into the carriage, that she hadn't told Miss Brown where to find the missing key.

FIFTEEN

February 10, 1866

CORRINE HAD AVOIDED EVERYONE AS MUCH AS SHE COULD since the incident in Killin. She begged permission to study magic alone, since, as Father Joe had said, they were running out of time. She didn't want to talk to any of them, not even her friends. Ilona had become more and more obsessed with fencing since Kenneth's death, and Christina seemed like a ghost of herself, drifting from room to room without seeing, gliding mechanically through her studies without engaging, chattering brightly without listening. The only person Corrine felt she could trust was Euan. And even then, something about him didn't quite add up. But she couldn't put her finger on what it might be. He was always around when she needed him, and he'd claimed it was because he was here to protect her. But was he protecting her on his own agency or at the command of someone else?

The thought, as she settled herself in the turret room, made her shiver a little. However, Siobhan had brought her the items for the spell she'd asked for, looking at her fearfully as she handed them over. The spell-box sat on her windowsill. At the next full moon, she would know the truth. For now, she decided, it was best to avoid everyone altogether.

As she had so often when she'd been fearful and alone, she turned to Angus's letters to escape. She opened the writing case and removed the letters and the copies she'd made. The ink had run a little from exposure to the damp, but all was otherwise intact. She leafed through them to the next letter to be copied.

December 1357

To my beloved Sister Brighde, Isle of Female Saints, from Angus, greetings.

My beloved—

In a fortnight's time, a man will come to you, the one the mad call the Captain. He will come to you to give you safe passage to the Prince's rath. I tell you this in hopes that you will again trust that what I do is for your benefit and the greater benefit of the child you carry. You say you have never broken faith with me, and I work daily to purge my heart of doubt. Yet I have been unable to come to you for such a long while that unless I can no longer count, I still cannot fathom how the child could be mine. But I know you and I know that you are as guileless and pure as the Lamb. I am more willing to believe in the intervention of the Holy Spirit than to believe that you would forsake me for another.

You know you must come with me now. There is no choice. You have eaten of their fruit, and if you do not come, the craving will surely kill you and the child you bear. And when the abbess discovers what you have done, I fear she will not share the faith and caring I hold for you. You will be cast out, left to wander and die in the wilds alone. (Do you truly wish that? Or do you somehow feel it would be proper expiation for our sin?)

There is another way, my love, if you would meet it fearlessly. When the Captain comes to you, heed his call and go with him to the meeting place. The Fey will greet you with open arms. They delight in human children, as they seldom have any of their own.

Whatever has come between us, whatever is God's will, I swear that the Fey will help us make it right.

All my love for all eternity,

Angus

Corrine wiped at the pen nib and set it in its holder in the case. Her cheeks were hot with embarrassment, imagining the scandal of a nun conceiving a child with a monk. What had Angus meant when he said that he wasn't sure that the child was his? Had he been locked in the raths that long? And who would have come to Brighde, if not Angus? Such a fool, she thought sadly. Angus was ever eager to do the bidding of the Unhallowed, never realizing the cost of his actions. What did he mean that Brighde had eaten of Unhallowed fruit? That the Fey could have no children? All the fairy tales about children being stolen away, about changelings, might be explained if the Unhallowed were truly childless.

The door opened. Father Joe strode in, fully dressed for the outdoors, even down to his fur cap and riding gloves.

"Get dressed and meet me and Mara at the stables in half an hour," he said. "We're going for a ride along Loch Tay."

Corrine opened her mouth to protest, but he held up his hand.

"Half an hour," he said. He closed the door. His boots clicked away down the corridor.

Mara stood back from the little mare that Euan held for her, a troubled expression on her face. Corrine was surprised that Mara seemed genuinely afraid of the horses; she'd never seen Mara afraid of anything, not even the Captain.

"Do you need help?" Corrine asked, leading her horse over to where Mara stood as far from the mare's head as possible.

Mara shook her head, gripped the edge of saddle and slowly climbed aboard, using the little step stool Euan provided.

He winked at Corrine and she smiled back.

Corrine eyed the sidesaddle on her own mount with disdain. Both girls' horses had been saddled with sidesaddles. Corrine had grown up riding astride, and she guessed Mara probably wasn't very used to sidesaddles either, if she had ridden at all. She sat straight and stiff; her posture so unyielding that Corrine feared a hard jostle might break her.

Corrine climbed up herself, a little nonplussed when a groom handed her a long crop. Though she had used a shorter one in her farm days, she wasn't sure quite sure how to handle this one. The saddle cramped her legs, but there was no help for it. She looked with envy at Euan sitting astride a gangly roan gelding.

Father Joe clucked his horse into a trot toward the Loch Tay road, and Euan and the girls followed. It was another chilly, drizzly day, but at least the wind wasn't howling as it had been for days since they'd returned from Killin. Corrine was glad of the thick, wool riding habit Miss Brown had dug out. She'd also wrapped Euan's scarf around her neck and ears under her hat. She could smell the scent of him—wild wood smoke and leather. She caught herself smiling again at the charm he'd given her. Would it really work? Had he really given her that much power over him? She had trouble believing it.

The Highlands loomed around the gray loch through the fog. She had seen their distant heights only in snatches through carriages, through the strange visions she'd had of this road. She hoped desperately that the visions would leave her be today. She didn't want to see the mouth of that cave, those girls struggling against the moth-eaten fingers of the Unhallowed.

It took two hours to travel from Fearnan to Kenmore, and thence to Taymouth. Corrine waited for something to happen, waited for that place in the road where she would feel the overpowering urge to flee up the hillside, where she would find the mouth of the cave in which the water-diamonds glittered.

But the road remained quiet, and the only unusual thing they passed was an abandoned tinker's cart mired in the mud.

They passed through Kenmore with its white houses and churches. Euan turned aside there to do business for Sir James and, Corrine imagined, sit in the tavern and talk up the old salts over a pint. He smiled that wolfish grin she'd come to know so well and waved before he clucked his horse forward.

Corrine watched him turn away, winding the scarf even more tightly around her neck, telling herself it was a longing for a cup of hot broth that made her throat tighten. Father Joe led them onto a little path that brought them to the loch's stony shore.

They all dismounted. The fog made the breadth of the loch invisible, but Corrine could sense its narrow journey through the valley, the bald head of Ben Lawers rising away to the south. The ruined island was just offshore; Corrine could see the remnants of mossy walls where the priory had once stood. Over the centuries, the water had receded enough so that it looked possible to walk across the muddy stones to the island.

Father Joe wore a carefully hooded expression as he doled food from his saddlebags. Corrine watched him, wondering what he was thinking, reminding herself that she didn't care. She still nursed a hurt over his withholding information from her. They ate in silence, each seeming to sense the other's mood. Corrine tried to hold back the visions that tripped toward her across the stones. She swallowed the lumps of hard bread and cheese, the cold, greasy sausage. *I will not see. I will not . . .*

Her back shivered as if eyes watched from all directions, and Corrine wondered if the Captain would find her again as he had in the alley. She tried not to see the dead little girl in his arms or to hear him croaking her father's pet name at her. Long ago, Angus had sent him to fetch Brighde. Was the Prince sending the Captain to her now? Though the Prince had said that she would come to him, she wasn't going to make it easy for him, not if she could help it.

Father Joe stood and walked to the loch edge. He stepped carefully out onto the stones, testing the mud at various places with his crop. He shook his head a few times as he did so, and when he returned, said, "I think it best not to risk the horses;

it will be much easier for us to cross on the stones, as long as we're careful."

He glanced at the girls' heavy riding skirts and boots dubiously as he gathered the horses' reins. Then he led the mares up the rise to a wooded copse and tied them there.

Corrine caught Mara's eye as she stared out into the fog.

"They's watching, you know," Mara said in a low voice. "Trying to see what we're gonna do."

Corrine nodded. Suddenly, she longed for some sun, some light to chase away all the mist and darkness.

"Can we make them go away?" Corrine asked.

Mara shook her head. "The best we can hope is that they'll leave us alone. I'm not sure why they haven't tried to take us yet."

"Well, Father Joe—"

Mara cut her off with a snort. "They cursed his powers long ago. He's got less power than your little finger. Why do you think we always have to do the big stuff?"

"Because we're the only other Half-Born," Corrine said. *Besides Euan*, she thought.

Mara glanced at her sidelong. "So, you finally figured it out."

Corrine felt her cheeks heating. It had slipped out without her meaning it to. She nodded. "Don't tell."

Mara stared out at the loch again, hugging herself to keep warm. "Well, I've said all along you should know. But they said as it wasn't the time, that they weren't sure . . ."

She cut her eyes again at Corrine, and Corrine shivered at how black they were, black as the waters of the fogbound loch. She saw the twisted trees again, the ghost orchids blooming around a scarlet lily cradle.

Mara half-smiled. "It'd take a true fool not to know what you are."

Corrine's reply was silenced by Father Joe's return. He carried three stout saplings he'd broken and handed two of them to Mara and Corrine. As Corrine followed him to the mudflat, she half-smiled to think that she and Mara carried a secret between them, something they could finally share.

They began the slow, difficult task of the crossing. Corrine's soles were slick, which made the crawl all the more treacherous, but the walking stick helped her keep her balance. Mara fared little better. She growled that she should "just take off my damn boots" until Father Joe glared at her. But they continued their struggle, puffing and groaning after the priest, who crept like a black-cowled crab from rock to rock.

They were halfway between the shore and the island when the hiss sang out from the shore.

"Half-Born!"

Corrine looked behind her and immediately wished she hadn't. They were there, more numerous than she could count— the Unhallowed courtiers riding mounts made of bones and fog, cloaks of bracken and thorn scraping the black stones.

The Captain stepped forward and raised his scarlet-palmed hand. A long leash trailed from under his hood, held firmly by the figure next to him. The woman pushed back her hood. Golden hair tumbled around the woman's shoulders. Amber eyes flashed like striking sunlight. *Leanan!* Corrine remembered her from her vision of Father Joe—tossing flowers down for Father Joe to catch, leaning over him like a lioness on the prowl, looking up at her from the parapets of the towers of the East.

The witch smiled. "You have unsettled my hound. He no longer obeys me."

Corrine stared. Mara whispered behind her. She couldn't hear Father Joe at all.

The Captain tried to pull forward, but the witch jerked him back. He squatted at her feet.

"But you have also unsettled the Prince. And that I cannot abide."

Unsettled the Prince? Corrine thought again of dancing with him, of the dreams in which he wept tears of blood.

"Not to mention that you outwitted my servants in the ocean, which certainly does nothing to endear you to me." Leanan smiled wryly. She lifted her hand.

"Girls," she heard Father Joe croak behind her. "Run."

Somehow his voice loosened Corrine's limbs, freed her from staring helplessly at the golden-haired witch on the shore. She turned and scrabbled across the rocks, slipping on their slick surfaces and plunging into the mud. Mara, still muttering, helped lift her and together they floundered across and up the bank of the abandoned island. They fell into a thicket, boots and hems heavy with mud.

"Josephus."

The witch stepped forward, jerking the leash so that the Captain rose and followed.

"Beloved . . ."

Mara continued muttering and Corrine saw now that the water was rising quickly. Soon the water was up to Father Joe's waist, lapping up toward the shore.

Ice. Frost crackled from Leanan's feet, freezing the water and holding Father Joe where he stood. He brought his palms down against the impenetrable ice. The witch glided forward as easily as though she still walked on the shore. The Captain followed her, slipping and sliding, clutching at the leash with both hands.

"How pleasing to find you again at last," she cooed, bending over him, her golden hair falling like light through clouds. Corrine watched the witch's pale finger trace its way from Father Joseph's temple to his lips.

"Corrine," Mara said, her teeth chattering. Corrine felt

Mara's fingers through her damp wool sleeve. "We need fire."

Fire? Of course, they were both wet and cold, but Father Joe . . .

"To free him," Mara said. "She can't cross running water. If we can melt the ice . . ."

"But he'll be burned!"

"I'll protect him. Just make the fire—the way I heard you did before."

Corrine glanced at her and was surprised to see a secret grin. Then, Mara nodded toward the frozen priest. "Hurry," she said.

Corrine drew her hands from her muddy, moss-stained gloves. She thought again of fire, of the green fire moving through the vines, being carried away by the hummingbirds and bumblebees, of the sun at high noon.

Emerald flame rolled from her hands. It licked out across the water, dying into steam where it touched ice. It parted and rolled around Father Joe, where Corrine saw the faint blue of Mara's shield protecting him from harm. The witch glanced up. Her eyes grew into twin golden moons that loomed over Corrine before a white owl flew away into the fog, carrying a black rat in its talons. The rest of the Unhallowed who had been with her disappeared.

Father Joe struggled through the water toward them and at last heaved himself up the bank.

When he could breathe properly again, he said, "Thank you." He didn't look at them.

Corrine didn't know what to say. Though she had seen many deaths now, she couldn't remember a time when she had ever saved anyone's life. Leanan would have taken Father Joe or killed him if she and Mara hadn't been there. She was surprised to feel necessary.

Father Joe put his head in his hands, his fingers shaking. Corrine had never seen him so unmoored. A slight shake of the head from Mara kept her silent.

Corrine looked around at the dripping trees, the downed stones of the old priory among the moss and debris. A young woman watched her from the shadow of a crumbling arch. From beneath her gray wimple, the novice's doelike eyes locked with Corrine's. She made a gesture that at once seemed to beckon and plead for silence at once. Brighde. A chill that had nothing to do with the day raced down Corrine's back. The stench of mud was thick as she followed the woman beyond the arch.

"Corrine." She heard Father Joe's voice behind her, then Mara's. Then, she was running, because Brighde was turning away from the arch, turning into the shadows of the fallen abbey.

They shouted after her, but she didn't heed them, tripping through the stones, heaving herself forward, despite her mud-weighted boots. It was like the day she had chased after her father's ghost at Uncle William's old house. She wanted desperately to speak to Brighde, to ask her why she had loved Angus when he had betrayed her, what had happened to her child, what their story had to do with her life. So many whys and wherefores she couldn't count.

She made the arch and looked around. Between the shadows of the crumbling nave and the spruces that had grown between the old stones, a gray habit flickered. Brighde gestured to her again. Corrine sped toward her, her ankles threatening to turn over the uneven abbey floor.

Brighde led her out of the abbey to a knoll that Corrine guessed was the center of the island. In the fog, two tall stones loomed, and as she passed between them, Corrine realized she had entered a ring—a circle of nine stones that crowned the hill. The old wound on her ankle, where the Unhallowed had placed the circlet of roses in her dreams, itched.

An old altar tilted to the ground to her left. Something was wedged under it; Corrine would have thought it was a rusting iron trunk, despite the improbability of it. Brighde stood near the altar where it slid legless into the earth.

"We can speak here, though time is short," the ghost said. There was a lilt to her words that made Corrine think Brighde spoke another language, a language that somehow in this place she could comprehend.

She drew closer. Brighde looked as though she was only about sixteen or seventeen, not much older than Corrine herself.

"Brighde?" Corrine said.

The novice tilted her head slightly. "The Hallowed have spoken to you," she said.

Corrine nodded.

"You know what you must do," the nun said.

"They said I should——"

"Find Hallowmere before the Unhallowed do," Brighde finished.

"But I don't know——"

"Yes, you do. I have sent you visions."

"You sent?" Corrine stared at her. "Those come from you?"

The novice gave a clipped nod. "I am near you always; sometimes you see what I wish, though you do not always understand." She half-smiled, as if she'd told a joke that Corrine would never fathom.

"I don't understand now either."

Brighde gazed beyond the stones into the rolling mist. "He comes for me."

Corrine stared at her, perplexed. All her questions seemed useless. "Who?"

Brighde looked at her again. "You know him. The Prince. The time is coming." She sighed. "You must take back the rathstones you gave him, especially the one he uses as his heart. It has made him very powerful. Without it, he will be little more than a shadow again, skirting the edges of mortal dreams."

"I don't know if I can," Corrine began.

"You must. Only you can do this."

"Me?" Corrine fidgeted. "But I'm not—"

"Only the Half-Born can kill the Prince," Brighde said.

"Then why me? Why not Mara, or . . . or . . . Father Joe?"

Brighde stared at her. "You don't know, do you?"

The ghost's measuring stare discomfited Corrine. She put her hands in the scarf at her throat, rearranging its folds to try to warm her freezing ears. She smelled him again—wood smoke, leather . . .

The novice's eyes narrowed. "What is that?"

Corrine looked around.

"Around your neck."

Corrine took the scarf and uncoiled it from around her throat. "Just a scarf," she said.

Brighde looked at it as though Corrine held out a spider.

"Oh, you wretched fool," the ghost said. And without another word, she was gone.

"Corrine!" Father Joe shouted.

His voice dragged her through an invisible wall back into the real world. She stared at the spot where Brighde had stood, the ghost's last words ringing in her ears.

"Corrine!"

Father Joe and Mara entered the standing stones behind her, puffing with the effort of topping the knoll.

She turned.

"Corrine, where have you been? We were searching everywhere!" Father Joe said.

Corrine debated hiding the truth, but didn't see how she really could. "I saw Brighde," she said finally. "She spoke with me."

"Brighde?" That stopped Father Joe cold. He looked around, as if he expected the ghost to suddenly leap from behind one of the standing stones.

"Yes." Corrine said. *Oh, you wretched fool . . .*

"What did she say?"

"What we already knew," Corrine said. "That I must get the rathstones back to help save the Hallowed." She couldn't speak of killing the Prince. The very idea of killing any living creature was too reprehensible to say aloud.

"Did you ask about the key?"

Corrine shook her head.

"You didn't ask about it." Father Joe took off his spectacles and rubbed at his eyes with his other hand.

"There wasn't time. She told me I had to get the stones back, then she called me a fool, and left."

Father Joe looked up. "Brighde called you a fool?"

Mara snickered. Corrine nodded, a bit hurt by Mara's laughter.

A whimper near the altar made her look up. Father Joe and Mara had heard it too and were looking around the circle. A thumping noise was followed by a hiccupping sob.

Corrine looked at the altar again. She remembered what the pixie had said. *They have locked my cousin in an iron box.* "The iron box." The pain of touching it was muted by her gloves. Weak vibrations came from within the box, as though something was beating on it with tiny fists.

She looked up at Father Joe and Mara as they bent near. "Help me," she said.

Together, the three of them managed to pull the box from under the altar. They stood back, flexing their fingers at the shadows of pain.

"We need to open the box," Corrine said.

"You sure 'bout that?" Mara said. Corrine noticed she no longer called her "Miss Corrine" and was glad of it.

"I think maybe Brighde led me here for this reason."

"You think the key is inside?" Father Joe said.

Corrine nodded. "The pixie said so. How do we open it?" Corrine said.

Father Joe inspected it without touching it. There was no way to force the lock, but a great rust spot bloomed where water must have dripped off the altar for centuries. Father Joe thumped at it with his walking stick. The cries within ceased.

Father Joe stood over the box and pounded the staff down into the iron. It gave somewhat on the first try, splintering the staff in the process. He pounded until the hole gave way. He gritted his teeth and reached for the rusted metal lip, straining to tear the trunk in half.

"How they bear to touch this stuff is beyond me," he grunted.

At last the trunk fell apart, the lock rolling useless in the grass.

Inside was a being like none Corrine had ever seen. He was slender and small, though larger than his cousin, the pixie who had died in her hands in the forest. The edges of his eyes canted upward. His ears and heels were similarly pointed. His skin was gray and covered with red blisters, his lips cracked and shiny with that strange substance that Corrine recognized now as Hallowed blood. He tried to look at them, to speak, but all that came out was a groaning croak.

"A pillywiggin," Father Joe said. He scooped the creature in his arms. "Come, we must get him to his spring."

He carried the pillywiggin out of the standing stones, searching for some long-forgotten spring. Corrine and Mara followed slowly, and Corrine tried not to see the fragile, wilted limbs drooping past Father Joe's black frame.

At last, Father Joe found the spring, a stream of clear water issuing from under a bramble-tangled stone.

He laid the pillywiggin as much in the stream as he could. Corrine watched, hoping that for however long the pillywiggin had been so cruelly locked away, they were not too late.

The sprite lay in the water unmoving for many more breaths than Corrine could count. She was beginning to fear that he too was dead.

As the cold, clear water ran over him, Corrine waited with a growing sadness. Sleet pelted the back of her neck between her scarf and hair. She glanced at the closing fog, the trees that grew through the old ruins, and drew her scarf closer.

Something exhaled, and then chuckled. The pillywiggin floated in the air before her. He leaped and skipped around the stream, the tumbled rocks, and brambles like a dragonfly, then floated lazily before Corrine's face. He tilted his head, his hair standing straight up like milkweed floss. His grin was as slanted as his eyes.

"So, what you want?" he said. He leaped around a bit more, in flashes of white light before floating again near Corrine's shoulder.

"Want?" Corrine asked. He tugged her bonnet down over her eyes before he bounded off again.

"Pillywiggin," said Father Joe, while Corrine readjusted her bonnet. "We need you to help us find something."

"Find a something?" the pillywiggin said, when he came to rest again. "That be hard to do. Something could be anything."

"We need," Father Joe began, his voice rising in exasperation as the pillywiggin galloped around the clearing, then danced briefly on Father Joe's head. Father Joe cleared his throat, and the pillywiggin grinned and pirouetted before leaping down into the grass. "We need a key. The key to the Council chamber at Fearnan. You are holding it here, yes?"

The pillywiggin zoomed around the stones, dipping above the stream momentarily. Then he disappeared.

"Pillywiggin?" Father Joe said.

But the sprite was gone.

They all looked around. Mara looked particularly unimpressed, hunching in her muddy riding habit. The sleet came down harder and Corrine shivered.

"Won't be too long before they come back," Mara said.

"I know," Father Joe said, the irritation evident in his tone. "And I know you're both tired and cold. I've no idea how we'll get back to the horses without swimming the loch."

Corrine thought Leanan had had a good idea with the ice bridge, but decided it would be best not to say so. She thought how nice it would be if someone turned up with a boat. The image of Euan rowing a dory across the loch slipped into her mind, remembering how he had looked in the ocean, his head bent over the oars, his hazel eyes seeking the shore. She lifted the scarf to her mouth. "Gannon," she whispered. A strange vibration echoed through the fog.

Mara and Father Joe looked around. "What was that?" Father Joe said.

But at that moment, the pillywiggin appeared again, darting around the clearing with something in his hands, his hair like a candle in the sleeting fog.

He drew a tarnished key from the air and laid it at her feet. *For this little thing, the cuideag had nearly killed me*, she thought. And still might, she knew. He looked up at her and shook his finger, as though he knew she'd used Euan's charm.

"Naughty girl," he said, so low only Corrine could hear it.

"Very naughty indeed."

He zigged and zagged around the clearing again one more time before floating to a stop in front of Father Joe's nose. "On another day, you get another favor. But not today," he said. "Not today." He zoomed around and stopped again in front of Father Joe. He pointed a long finger in Corrine's direction. "Watch that one," he said, grinning.

He ran up through the fog as though bounding up stairs, then dove straight down into the tiny spring and vanished.

The day felt colder and dimmer, if that were possible. Corrine leaned down and picked up the key, feeling strange that she hadn't had a moment to say thank you. Why did everyone on this island seem to think she was naughty or foolish? She still smarted at what Brighde had said.

"Well, then," said Father Joe, "best to go before we have more unpleasant surprises."

As she followed the others, Corrine slipped the key into her jacket pocket and wondered if Euan would truly come.

At the edge of the island, they all stared down the steep embankment at the sleet falling into the dark water. Much of the farther shore had been drowned by the rise in water, practically up to the wooded copse where Corrine hoped the horses still waited. Just as she was steeling herself to swim, Corrine heard the scraping of oars against oarlocks. A familiar figure sculled around the edge of the island. Corrine smiled into her scarf as Euan came closer.

"Euan!" Father Joe shouted, his voice dulled by the fog.

Euan looked up, resting his oars.

"What brings you here?" Father Joe said.

"I was suddenly taken with the urge to do a little fishing," Euan said, his eyes searching out Corrine's.

"Good thing too, I'd reckon." Euan said. He brought the dory as close as he could, gesturing for the girls to climb down.

"Indeed," Father Joe said.

As Euan took Corrine's hand and helped her step in, the unsteadiness of the boat rocked her against him. His wood smoke scent overwhelmed the reek of mud from her shoes and riding habit. His eyes searched hers, and she sensed more things than she could track—disappointment, irony, and something else she couldn't name. His hold on her hand reminded her strangely of dancing with the Prince. She heard the witch's words echo again in her head. *You have unsettled the Prince.*

He helped her seat herself, then turned to aid Father Joe.

"This loch isn't tidal," he said, looking puzzled.

Father Joe seated himself. Staring out into the fog, he said, "Today it was."

Euan rowed the rest of the short way in silence, Corrine feeling the heat of his gaze on her back. Her cheeks warmed with nervousness. As they made the new shore, they heard the horses rustling around uncomfortably up in the thicket.

Euan helped them step out of the boat. Corrine was last. He held her hand a little longer than was necessary as she righted herself on the shore.

"Next time," he said under his breath, "be more cautious."

"I'm sorry," she said, feeling less guilty than she supposed she should have.

"Magic is not to be used lightly," he said.

She looked down at the dark water reaching for her mud-stained boots.

"I will meet you back at Fearnan," he said to them, "if you'll be well without me. I've got to return this dory and retrieve my horse being shoed over in Kenmore."

Father Joe nodded. "I'll give you a push," he said. He waded a little way out into the water, enough to help Euan push off.

Father Joe shook his head as he watched the gillie disappear into the fog. "That was not an accident."

He looked at Corrine, who hid her smile behind the scarf.

"Be careful of him, Corrine," Father Joe said. "There's always been something strange about Euan. He's saved us many times, but his propensity to be around at the least sign of danger is somewhat alarming."

Corrine nodded. But all she could think about as she went to her horse, and climbed into the saddle was that she had called him. And he came. *He came.*

When they made Fearnan, it was almost dark. There was never a more welcome sight than the gaslit stairs of the Fearnan estate, in Corrine's opinion. She let the reins fall from her cold-stiffened hands and uncurled herself from the saddle. She leaned against the mare for a moment, touching its neck apologetically.

"Rest well," she murmured before the groom led the mare away. She followed Father Joe and Mara into the hall.

Miss Brown met them in the foyer, almost before they'd given their hats and gloves to Mrs. Guthrie. Corrine nearly forgot to retrieve the key from her coat pocket before Mrs. Guthrie took it. When the maid reached for her scarf, Corrine shook her head, winding it around the key instead.

The worried look on Miss Brown's face grew when she saw the damp, mud-stained boots and skirts. "Leave what you can here," she said. "I'm sure in this case Mrs. Guthrie prefers cleanliness over propriety."

Father Joe seemed to catch her mood. "Thea?"

She shook her head, then said, "Well . . . I suppose there's no harm in telling you what you'll all know soon enough."

Corrine looked up from where she was wrestling with her

frozen bootlaces. Miss Brown's eyes were a little red and puffy at the edges.

"I'm afraid Christina's fallen ill," Miss Brown said at last.

"Christina?" Corrine said.

"She's always been such a delicate creature," Miss Brown said. "I suppose I just mistook this for one of her fainting spells."

Corrine remembered how Christina had trailed up the stairs dreamily, her lips red and swollen as though she'd eaten some kind of fiery, forbidden fruit.

"May I see her?" she asked.

Miss Brown considered for a moment. "It might be better to wait," she said. "The doctor has been sent for and should be here in the morning. If Christina has the fever . . ."

Corrine nodded. They would be afraid to risk her catching the disease, as she had been so weakened by the swamp fever before coming to Falston. Though she was not certain Christina's illness was caused by anything so natural.

"Come get warm," Miss Brown said. "Siobhan has laid a fire, and I'll see to it that someone brings tea and food. You're like to catch your death of cold, as it is!"

Mara said her usual terse farewell, but her eyes glinted knowingly as she glanced at Corrine before she went away down the hall. After enduring such an ordeal together, Corrine wished that Mara was walking upstairs with them to a cozy bed and lit hearth and a maid of her own to bring her tea and warm bread.

"May I have the key, Corrine?" Father Joe said in a low voice. "Perhaps I shall search the chamber tonight."

Corrine nodded and handed the key over to him. The cuideag hadn't been seen since that first night. She supposed Father Joe would have to take his chances. Or, she wondered sourly, would she have to aid them in this too because she was something they refused to name? Even for a wretched fool, she still seemed quite indispensable.

She followed Miss Brown up the stairs, her stockinged feet chilled against the marble stairs. All was as Miss Brown had said, including the clean nightgown and dressing gown beside it. She also noticed a great brass tub by the fire, and sighed with relief.

"I'll tell them to bring the hot water when I leave," Miss Brown said.

"Thank you," Corrine said.

Miss Brown fretted with her shawl and said, "Of course, I want to know about your journey, but perhaps it's best to wait until the morning." She looked toward the door. "And I must get back to Christina."

Corrine nodded.

"Tomorrow, then," Miss Brown said.

She went toward the door, and opened it. "I'm glad you're back safely," she said in the doorway before she left.

Corrine went to the table by the fire. Tea and toast with jam had already been laid out for her. She dipped a bit of toast in the jam and nibbled, too tired to bother spreading it with the silver jam spoon provided.

A manservant and Siobhan came not long after Miss Brown left, bearing pitchers of hot water. They filled the tub, settled the bath things on the tray over the tub, and departed, Siobhan as always refusing to meet Corrine's gaze. After the space of a few heartbeats, Corrine tore out of her stinking riding habit, and stepped shivering into the near-scalding water. She sighed with relief as she hunched down into the tub and let the water close almost over her shoulders. She straightened just enough to pull the pins from her hair, throwing them into the tray with the soap. She wet her hair and scrubbed the soap through it first, and then scrubbed herself. She lifted her leg out of the water to look at her ankle—the band of reddened skin had faded somewhat and didn't itch as often as it once had. But it was still there, a reminder of old dreams, a mystery she couldn't quite fathom.

She thought of Brighde, of Euan, of Leanan winging away as a white owl in the afternoon. She sensed that something was coming, but it was something too dim to see. Something was turning. The Unhallowed were moving. There was but one thing left. The rathstones. She didn't relish the part she would have to play in their return. She swallowed and stood, reaching for the towel. The cooling water seemed suddenly much less inviting.

She changed into her nightgown and sat with her tea by the fire, thinking of the warnings of both Brighde and the pillywiggin. Maybe there was something even more fearsome about her beyond being Half-Born?

She crawled between the icy sheets, realizing Siobhan had forgotten to ready the bed warmer. She drew her knees to her chest and wrapped her gown around her feet, shivering until she fell asleep.

He was waiting for her on the other side of her dreams.

You do not come to me as you once did, *he said. She waited for him to weep tears of blood, but his face, what she could see of it, was cold.*

I know what you do, *she said.*

They sat in a cave, looking at each other across a fire. His features shifted, colors and shapes fleeing through his eyes like clouds.

I do what I must.

They were silent a long time. She heard the music emanating from his heart, not so much a drumming as a soft, high singing that made her long for sky and birds.

Show me your face, *she said.*

You could not bear it.

I can, *she said.* The Half-Born can see what others fear.

He laughed, as though delighted by her admission. You are mortal yet, whatever else you may claim.

She was about to protest, but he held up a flame-shadowed hand.

When you come to me, then you will see my face.

Sixteen

February 11, 1866

A CLATTERING SOUND WOKE CORRINE. AT THE SAME moment she realized the lateness of the hour, she had a dim fear that someone was trying to climb into her room. She sat bolt upright. Her eye, which was now mostly healed, was gritty with sleep. The window was up and the shutters were clacking against the casement. There was nothing in the room.

Corrine climbed out of bed and was nearly to the window before she saw the scattered contents of the spell-box on the stone floor. The moon was not yet full. She didn't miss the potential omen, but she gathered up the spilled herbs and took them to the hearth. She couldn't help but think of the juniper sprig again, and how her lack of trust had brought her to this pass. The fire ate the spell components greedily, and Corrine wrinkled her nose at the smell of burned feathers. Maybe some magic was better left undone. She knew she could trust Euan; he had proven his worth.

In the afternoon, Corrine met Father Joe in the turret study. His face was pale and wrinkled as though he hadn't slept, but he was smiling, nonetheless. In his hands, he held curiously bound books and a few scrolls.

"I was able to get in last night," he said. "The cuideag was gone. I spent almost all night there. By Elaphe, I was on tenterhooks all night at the thought of being locked in that chamber with one of those monsters showing up outside."

Corrine had to smile at his enthusiasm, even though she still resented his hiding knowledge from her. She loved books too and the thought of a secret chamber full of them was a wonderful lure. She would have liked to explore the chamber herself, but it was hard to believe the cuideag wouldn't come again, though she knew she had no reason to disbelieve what Euan had said.

"I think I've found the charm we need for the astral domains," he said. "It's here." He unrolled one of the scrolls.

"When may I see Christina?" she asked.

He paused in his paper rattling. "When the doctor has determined it is safe for you to do so. We're not certain what sort of illness this is, but we can't risk any of you." He set the scroll down on the table, trying to smooth its edges.

"Can Mara make a root?" He didn't seem bothered by Christina's illness at all.

"Possibly," Father Joe said. "But we aren't sure that it will work. Precious little she's tried has worked since we've been here. In fact, it seems that only your magic has been working since we arrived."

She dropped her gaze, feeling guilty without knowing why.

"But it's too wild," he said. "Before we send you into the domain of water, we must help you get some control."

She thought about the fire she had thrown across the loch yesterday. He seemed to be saying it was too much. How was she supposed to control it if she barely knew how she did it?

"But, Christina—" she began.

He set a candle on the desk in front of her.

"Worry about her later. There is work to be done. You cannot pass into the domain of water until you've learned to control fire. Right now, you're very good at sending a scorching inferno at anything you see, but that will tire you out quickly and leave you open to attack. You need control over your gifts."

She frowned.

"Go stand in the corner," he said.

She obeyed reluctantly.

"Now, try to light this from that distance. Just light the candle. Try not to throw the flame. Also try not to burn the room down."

Corrine wasn't quite as amused as he was. What he was asking for felt impossible. When she called the fire of life, it was a torrent. She didn't know how to make it otherwise.

She stood for long moments, looking between the candle wick and the priest.

"Go on," he said. "Just the faintest puff of flame. That's all you need."

She frowned. She tried to imagine it, the smallest spark, the wick lighting itself, the puff of smoke.

Green flame roared from her toward the desk; her hair and skin crackled in the enclosed space.

"STOP!" Father Joe's shout frightened her enough that the flames ceased before they engulfed the desk. The room was as hot as an oven and smelled of singed carpet. A long burn mark stopped just before the desk.

"Perhaps we should have done this outside," he said weakly, mopping sweat from his brow with his arm. "Let us just study charms today."

Corrine nodded. Her lack of control was disappointing, but not surprising. When fire filled her, it was like someone opening a steam valve inside. All that pressure had to go somewhere.

Father Joe opened a book called *Curses, Lucks, and Talismans* and invited her to come to the desk. When she saw the opened page, she hesitated and looked up at him. The charm was an eavesdropping spell, used especially to unmask deceptive people.

"Why this one?" she asked.

"Because, as I told you, you cannot trust anyone," he said. "It's best if you can find out the truth about them."

She thought of this morning's botched spell. She already knew she could trust Euan; she could trust him with her life. "But . . ."

"Euan, for instance. This charm would work well on him; you could perhaps find some insight into who or what he truly is."

She gaped—if only because she herself had been guilty of trying such a thing, and also because she'd already made up her mind. There was no reason to use magic on Euan.

"You must learn appropriate use of magic, as well as the magic itself," Father Joe said.

Magic must not be used lightly, she heard Euan say again.

Long ago at Falston, Miss Brown and Father Joe had both chided her for eavesdropping, discovering only part of a larger story that they believed she should not hear. Corrine had eventually learned that she had aligned herself with the Unhallowed, all because everyone withheld the truth from her. It was the eavesdropping that had ultimately caused her to take the Falston stone to the Prince. And now, it seemed, Father Joe had reversed the edict.

"Corrine, you must learn who to trust. You have already seen the cost of making mistakes."

She stared at him. He had never once accused her of being at fault for giving the stones to the Prince. He had seemed to understand that she had been deeply misled and had admitted his own part in her actions. Now, he seemed to be aligning himself with Sir James and Uncle William, blaming her for things she couldn't possibly have known. For all she knew, he might still be withholding information that would help her, information even more important than the fact that she was Half-Born.

"Let me put it this way," Father Joe said. "We need to know if Euan is aligned with the Unhallowed. Sir James doesn't believe it, of course. He has been Sir James's gillie for many years, though no one knows where he came from or how he learned his trade."

Corrine couldn't say anything.

Father Joe continued, "We need you to find out who Euan is, who he serves. He may be responsible for many of our difficulties. For these deaths, the loss of the serpent-bound book—so many things could point back to him. He could even be the cuideag."

Corrine shook her head violently. "No," she said. "I'm sure he's not the cuideag. I'm sure of it. And you're a priest! How can you possibly—"

"I am also a Council member," he said. There was no hint of nervousness about him, no anxiety. He was firmly set on this path. "And it is in the best interests of the Council to discover where Euan's loyalties lie. We made a great mistake with Rory. We'll not do it again."

Corrine shook her head, but he didn't seem to notice.

"I want to know where he was when Kenneth and Cecily were murdered. I want to know what he was doing in that boat yesterday, how it was that he showed up at just the time we needed him."

"I summoned him," Corrine said.

Father Joe stopped.

She wished desperately for Christina's talent with charming people.

"You did what?"

"I summoned him. I . . . I taught myself a charm and I called him. That's why he was there," she said, trying to sound confident.

"Corrine, are you certain? You wouldn't tell me an untruth, would you? Because there are ways . . ."

She saw Leanan again, leaning over him, trailing her finger across his lips. *Beloved*, she had said.

"I just thought we should be ready to have help if we needed it. And he knows the woods and how to fight. So—" She shrugged. She didn't know if he would be convinced, but she would protect Euan if she could. He had protected her so often in the past. He had told her the truth about herself when no one else would.

"Corrine, this is what I mean about appropriate uses of magic. Calling someone to aid you, someone who may or may not be your ally—it's very dangerous."

"And spying isn't?" Corrine snapped.

"Corrine—"

"At Falston, you told me that eavesdropping was a very bad thing. Now you're telling me that I should do it because it suits the Council?"

Father Joe shook his head. "No, no. I'm not. Sometimes the rules are . . ." He stopped, exasperated. Corrine imagined that he wondered how he'd ever gotten involved with a school of young girls and their magical problems.

Just as Corrine was about to retort, a knock came and the door opened. Miss Brown entered. She clasped her shawl about her as if it were her last bit of support; her normally clear gaze was cloudy and unfocused.

"Christina is asking for you, Corrine," she said.

"But the fever. It might it be best—" Father Joe began.

Miss Brown silenced him with a look.

Corrine went with her without looking back. She heard Father Joe slam the charm book shut as Miss Brown closed the door.

Miss Brown put her hand on her shoulder and said, "This may be difficult, Corrine. I've written Christina's parents."

Corrine looked at her. "She's not . . ."

Miss Brown shook her head. "I don't know, but I've never seen her this ill before. And the doctor doesn't know what to do."

"Is the illness magical?" Corrine asked. The last time she had seen Christina, her friend had been going up the stairs after eavesdropping on the Council meeting. But had she really been eavesdropping? Had she been somewhere else? Where?

Ilona was already in Christina's room, sitting by the bed and clutching one of Christina's hands. Ilona had cut all her hair off when her friend Jeanette disappeared from Falston. What would she do if Christina died?

The starched pillowcase looked almost dirty next to Christina's porcelain skin. Her bones stuck out at strange angles. Her mouth was very red, as though she'd recently drunk burgundy wine. *Or blood*, Corrine thought and shivered.

"Corrine," Christina said. She tried to smile, but it was the grin of a death's-head. Christina reached for her with her free hand. Corrine took it, surprised at how dry and light it was.

A shock, like a tiny bolt of lightning, zipped up her arm from the contact.

She saw a familiar crooked grin, a glint of blue eyes as Rory turned back to help her through wet bracken. It was so much like the visions she'd had at Falston about Jeanette that she almost shuddered herself out of it. But, this time, she knew she was looking through Christina's eyes. *Rory led her by the hand through the dark forest, holding a shuttered lantern ahead of him. He came to what looked like little more than a mound of leaves.*

There was grinning and whispering and even perhaps some kissing before he said a single word. The mound opened and pale light spilled across the lovers' feet . . .

The creaking of Miss Brown's chair as she sat snapped Corrine's vision back to Christina's face.

"What have you done?" Corrine said, letting go of her hand.

"Corrine," Ilona murmured.

Christina looked at her helplessly.

"What have you done?" As she said it again, echoes of her mother's voice returned to her. Her mother's ghost had asked her the same thing in a dream. *Oh, what have you done?*

"I couldn't help it, Corrine," Christina said. "He said we could be together."

"And you believed him?" Corrine sighed. Anger beat inside her like a bird in a glass cage.

Corrine turned away before Christina could answer, even as her wasted hand fell across the sheets in a vain attempt to reach her.

Corrine went to where Miss Brown stared into the fire.

"I know what caused this," she said, agitation as sharp as nettles in her voice.

Miss Brown looked up at her dully.

"I know what happened," Corrine said. "It's Rory." It was still hard to say his name, even after all this time.

"Rory?" Miss Brown snapped awake. "Rory did this to her?"

Corrine took a breath. Of course they knew that she had visions, but no one really knew their true nature. No one knew how vivid they were. "I think he took her into an Unhallowed rath somehow. Maybe she ate the food there."

"Into an Unhallowed rath?" Miss Brown said, rising from her chair and arranging her shawl.

"If she did, no doctor can help her," Corrine said. She thought of what Angus had said to Brighde. *You must come now, or else die of longing for want of that one elusive fruit.* Corrine suspected this was what was happening now.

"I'll fetch Father Joe," Miss Brown said.

"And Mara," Corrine said, looking back toward the bed. Christina's fevered eyes watched her.

Corrine came to stand at the foot of the bed.

"Corrine," Christina pleaded. "Do not be angry with me."

Corrine couldn't think of anything to say to her. She turned to Ilona instead. "Have you known about this? How long?"

Ilona didn't hang her head or release Christina's hand. There was no guilt on her face. "We couldn't tell you, Corrine."

"You knew about this? And you didn't tell me?"

"Corrine—" Ilona said. Her voice was low, almost dangerous. She reminded Corrine of a mother wolf protecting a sick pup.

"How could I tell you?" Christina said. "It was Rory!"

Corrine gritted her teeth. "And he did awful things! He—"

Christina shook her head until she was forced to cough. She struggled to clear her throat. "He did not mean—"

"Didn't mean to what? Steal the stones? Allow the Unhallowed to destroy the school? Steal Jeanette and Penelope? Deceive me?" Corrine's voice went shrill.

"Corrine, I love him," Christina said, shrinking back toward Ilona, who reached down to stroke her limp curls with her free hand.

Corrine opened her mouth. She had the odd knowledge that if she called fire at this moment it would burn the entire estate to the ground.

"No more," Ilona said, shushing her before she could speak. "It's done. Now we must try to set it right."

Corrine turned away and went to the fireplace. She stood there with her back to Christina and Ilona, her mind reeling from the insanity of it all, until Miss Brown returned with Father Joe and Mara.

"Corrine," Father Joe said, coming to stand next to her. "Miss Brown says that you think this is Rory's fault?"

Corrine looked at him, her eyes dazzled by the fire. When her vision cleared, she saw that all traces of his former anger were gone.

"I saw it," she said. "Brighde told me that she has been sending me the visions. She just sent another."

"Brighde?" Father Joe glanced over at Christina. "You don't think . . ."

Corrine tried to keep her voice low. "She said it was easy to send me visions because she was always near. She said the Prince was looking for her. I think I'm beginning to understand what she meant."

"Then that must mean—"

"He's trying to draw her back into his rath, to use her for some purpose," Corrine said.

"Or to torment Brighde's spirit further. The Unhallowed delight in such games," Father Joe said.

Mara, who had been examining Christina, came to stand with them.

"Whatever's gotten her's riding her hard again," Mara said. "We need to cast it out."

Corrine looked at Father Joe. "Should we really do that?" she asked. It might be better to keep Brighde near. She remembered the first day she'd ever seen Christina so possessed back at Falston. She had scrawled Latin prayers on the board, begging for protection. Even then, apparently, the nun had been trying to speak through her to Corrine.

Father Joe shook his head. "Not if it's truly Brighde's spirit that's possessing her."

"Rory took her to a mound. She may have eaten Unhallowed food," Corrine said to Mara. "Can we call him here? Make him answer for what he's done?"

"I've tried," Mara said.

"I think you must try again," Father Joe said. "Only Rory can tell us what we need to know."

"Can I help?" Corrine asked. "What do you need?"

"Power," said Mara. "I'll do the rest."

"Meanwhile, I'll search the Council chamber again and see if any cure is mentioned."

"When should I lay the root?" Mara asked. "The moon's new tonight. Better for banishing than summoning," she said.

"Tonight," Father Joe said." We have no choice."

SEVENTEEN

February 11, 1866

THAT EVENING, MARA, CORRINE, FATHER JOE, AND MISS Brown returned to Christina's room. Christina's glittering eyes darted between them, though Corrine wasn't sure she truly saw anymore. She wished for a moment that she could hunt down Rory herself and keep him from slipping through her grasp with magic. He was worse than a weasel, that one.

They positioned themselves at the points of the compass around Christina's bed, except for Mara who went and knelt at the hearth, summoning the spirits with scotch and cakes thrown into the fire. The fire blazed high and blue for a moment, and Mara bowed her head.

"They've accepted the offering," she said as she took her place in the circle.

Mara had instructed each of them in the proper verses prior to the ritual. After Father Joe said his part, he crossed himself. Mara looked askance at him.

Corrine was given the south, the element of fire. When she spoke, she felt the green fire within her, ready to be unleashed if she asked. She thought again of Father Joe asking her to delicately light a candle flame. She could no more do that, she thought, than forget her anger at Rory's betrayal.

When Mara spoke, Corrine felt the energy rising between the two of them. Miss Brown and Father Joe were just conduits; neither of them could call or control the energy the way Mara could, the way Corrine hoped to do in time. Corrine imagined, though, what might happen if Father Joe's powers were completely unbound. She guessed he was very powerful.

Mara tossed leaves at Christina's head—whether tobacco or something else Corrine wasn't sure. Next, she flung water and salt. Corrine gasped when the salt caught fire in green sparks as it fell. She could feel the drawing down of the energy, as Mara wove a summoning to find Christina's betrayer.

A loud crack rippled through the room, sending a needling wave through Corrine's body that pushed her out of the circle. She saw Mara fall to her knees, while Miss Brown and Father Joe stumbled back, as though against a great gale. Christina's head fell slack on the pillow, her eyes closed and her fingers open against the sheets.

"Christina!" Corrine rushed to the bedside. She shook the girl and called her name over and over again. But she didn't wake up.

Miss Brown almost pushed Corrine out of the way.

"Dear Lord!" she said. "Is she alive?" She felt Christina's cheek, touched her throat to find a heartbeat.

"Yes, I think so. I hope so," Corrine said.

Father Joe brought a small silver hand mirror and placed it near Christina's lips. Tiny puffs of breath frosted the glass.

Mara came to the bedside. She was angry—her black eyes flashed, her face was stiff as a tree trunk. "There's a bad root on me," she said. "And I'll find it one way or another." She left then, her bag slung across her shoulder like a dead animal.

"What shall we do now?" Miss Brown said.

They all looked at one another, speechless. There was nothing anyone could say.

February 20, 1866

Over a week passed and there was no sign of Rory. Christina remained the same, locked like a fairy-tale princess in her deep slumber. Father Joe had searched the chamber again and found that Corrine's suspicions were correct. Unhallowed food was needed and a charm from the Hallowed to alter the food's poisonous effects. Father Joe had also searched for the Fearnan rathstone, which had long been kept in the chamber as the estate's means of protection.

"Sadly," he told Miss Brown, Ilona, and Corrine as they sat at Christina's bedside, "the stone is nowhere to be found."

That makes three, Corrine thought.

She looked at Christina's dark lips, her wasted hand upon the coverlet. Before Miss Brown or Ilona could stop her, she ran from the room.

She went downstairs, heedless of where she was headed. She took her newly cleaned coat and scarf, bundling into them as she flew out of the door.

She didn't go to the woods this time, but entered the labyrinth hedge. Something about its tall, green walls soothed her as she walked and thought.

There was nothing else to do, she knew. Someone would have to go into the rath and bring the fruit back for Christina. Someone would have to find the rathstones. Only she or Mara could do it, and Mara was still obsessed with finding the root that had warped her powers. Or the person. Corrine shuddered to think what Mara would do when she found whoever was responsible. So that left only her. And possibly, she realized, Euan.

She thought of calling him again, and her fingers twitched across the scarf at her throat. But then she remembered how he had looked at her when she called him onto the loch to row them to shore. Though what she asked was no feat of vanity, she wondered if she had already asked too much.

At last, after many wrong turns and retracing of steps, the labyrinth opened in a broad circle at the center of which the marble gazebo rose on its little mound. She stepped up into the gazebo and surveyed the lines of the labyrinth around her. A single raven squawked and flew low over the boxwoods, making her flinch a little at the memory of the raven attack, which now seemed so long ago.

Yes, she would have to go into the rath. But how could she do so without a rathstone?

Boots crunched on gravel. She half-expected the Captain as she turned, but was surprised to see Euan instead. He wore his hunting cap and jacket and a brace of coneys dangled over his shoulder.

"I see I'm not the only one who comes here to find some peace," he said. He dropped the rabbits on the marble floor, and she shrank a little at the blood that dripped from one rabbit's mouth.

She nodded and turned back to look at the trees looming beyond the hedge. "Did they send you after me again?" she asked, a little more coldly than she meant.

"No," he said. "I came on a whim. I expected only silence, but I've found much more."

She tried to draw herself up taller. "Well," she said, "I'll leave you to it." She moved to leave the gazebo, careful of the dead rabbits near the entrance.

"Wait." He put out a hand to stop her. "That wasn't what I meant. I meant that the sight of you is an unexpected pleasure." He searched her face. He seemed completely unbothered by her strange eye or the fading scratches on her cheek.

She nodded and tried to pull her arm from his grip.

"Corrine, what has happened?" he said. "Why are you angry?"

"You already know what's happened," she snapped. "Christina is dying."

He nodded sadly.

"And the one person who could help her," Corrine continued, "the man who caused all this, won't come. We're all in terrible danger, and I can't do anything to stop it!" The tears overflowed almost before she realized they were there. "Do you know what that's like, Euan? To watch everyone around you die without being able to stop it?"

"Yes," he said. He took a breath and released her arm. "Yes, I do know."

"I don't know what I'm supposed to do," she said. "I don't know how to fix this."

He was silent for many long moments.

"You cannot 'fix this,' as you say. And you should not have to."

"But I'm the only one—"

He stopped her with his fingertips on the forearm of her coat. "Not the only one, remember?"

"What can you do?" she asked. "Do you have a rathstone? Do you have a spell to remove the curse of Unhallowed food?"

"I have friends," he said.

She dashed at her eyes, trying to wipe away the last of the tears. "Who?"

He shook his head, as if disappointed that she'd digressed with such a question. "I cannot answer that."

"Why would they help?"

"Because I ask," he said. He played with a loose thread at her cuff. "It's what friends do, Corrine. They trust each other, help each other, without questions or expectations."

Corrine thought of the rules of the Society, the secret group she had been part of at Falston along with Christina and Ilona. She found herself nodding in agreement.

"Will you help me?" she said.

"As long as you continue to believe in me," he said. "There are times when you have been sorely tested, but what I do is for your good. I will try to bring you the things to make your friend Christina better, so long as I may one day ask a favor of you in return."

Goosebumps raced across the back of Corrine's neck. She thought of how Rory had once promised her to get rid of the Falston witches if she'd only bring him the rathstone. She had believed him and had landed herself squarely in this mess. But what choice did she really have? Euan had never once betrayed her. He had always protected her and she knew that he was like her, constantly forced to hide what he really was, constantly harried by forces most people would never understand.

He coughed slightly and she looked at him in concern.

"A touch of the damp," he said.

"If I did consent to your help, what would you ask of me in return?" she said. *Oh, you wretched fool,* she heard Brighde sigh.

"Must a gentleman reveal all his secrets?" Euan smiled. His fingers moved from her cuff to the bit of skin between her sleeve and glove. The touch sent shivers up her arm.

"I'm tired of secrets," Corrine said.

Euan let go her wrist. She pulled her gloves up tighter, trying to cover the sudden absence of his touch.

"Honestly, I don't quite know. Perhaps one day, when you have control of your magic, I will ask a favor of you. Perhaps one day I will need rescuing, as you seem to so often. Who knows?" He tilted his head and his eyes seemed to draw in the deep green of the boxwoods.

It occurred to Corrine that she wouldn't be in Scotland forever. How could he call in a favor when she was back across the Atlantic? *And yet,* she thought, *he might at that.*

Twilight was coming. She knew she should return to the house. Christina's emaciated hands and dark lips swam up in her sight. What did any of it matter if another girl died? If she truly trusted him, then she would do this thing. What he asked seemed so small in comparison to what he offered.

She inhaled and nodded. "All right, then."

He smiled, but there was also a sadness in his eyes that unnerved her. "I will leave the things here for you in the morning. Unhallowed food and a charm of the Hallowed."

"Yes," she said.

He put his hands on her shoulders. She thought for a moment he might kiss her, but he just gazed into her eyes, drinking in the sight of her. "Christina will be well again," he said. "Have faith. Soon, all of this will be over."

"I hope so," she said.

"Let's go back to the house," he said. He swung the brace of coneys up onto his shoulder again and led her out of the gazebo. She felt her promise lingering there, like a thread of fog in the empty air.

When she returned to her room after supper, someone was in her room. She hitched up against the door when she saw the shadow near the bed.

But it was Siobhan, sliding the bedwarmer into the foot of Corrine's bed.

"Miss Corrine," Siobhan said. "I was wondering . . . that is to say . . ."

She peered more closely at Corrine as she came forward. "You've been with them, haven't you?" she whispered. Her sad, accusatory tone reminded Corrine of Brighde's.

"No," Corrine said. "I've been with Euan."

"They always have their way," Siobhan muttered, "Always . . ."

"Siobhan, you know that Christina's deathly ill?"

Avoiding Corrine's gaze, Siobhan turned down the bedcovers.

"Siobhan—"

"Yes. Mara told me she'd eaten *their* food, that Mr. Rory had—" The maid shook her head.

"Yes. And we're all doing what we can to save her."

Siobhan nodded. She opened her mouth to say something, then licked her lips, and just shook her head.

Corrine wished again for the serpent-bound book, wondering if there were perhaps some easier way to help Christina or something that would keep her alive longer. Surely the Unhallowed had ways of keeping their "mortal locusts" alive as long as they needed them?

"Siobhan, do you know—have you seen a book somewhere with serpents on the cover? The cover is a kind of golden leather."

Siobhan's gaze shifted away for just a second. Then, she looked at Corrine. "I haven't seen that in a while, Miss Corrine."

"Well," Corrine said, her voice falsely light, "if you do see it, would you tell me? It might save Christina faster than anything else. I'm sure of it."

Siobhan nodded. She arranged the bedclothes one last time. "Will you be wanting tea or anything, Miss Corrine?"

"No thank you," Corrine said, holding Siobhan's gaze. In that moment, she felt Siobhan's will as something malleable, a thing she could shape like clay to her own design. Corrine could have reached, but she didn't. She broke the gaze and said simply, "Good night, Siobhan."

Siobhan cast her a watery, frightened glance before scuttling out of the room.

Corrine changed into her nightgown and crawled into the

bed. She listened for a long time to the dying fire, the wind, the throbbing of her own heart against the pillow before she fell into jittery sleep.

~ Eighteen ~

February 21, 1866

*Y*OU LOVE ANOTHER, *THE PRINCE SAID, AS HE TURNED HER through the intricate steps of the dance.*

She looked beyond him to the empty throne that sat beside his. She'd never noticed it before. It was carved of white wood, smooth and hard as polished bone. It was padded with living green moss and a robe of shining fur was draped over its carved arms.

No, she said.

I have felt your heart move toward him, *the Prince said.*

Something peeped out from behind the new throne. A face. Unveiled. A face so terrible that Corrine felt herself slowly turning to stone in the Prince's arms.

The woman lifted her finger to her lips.

Shhhhhhh . . .

She sat up in bed. All her limbs tingled painfully, as though she'd lost circulation.

Mara knocked on the door and came in with an armful of clothes.

"Your new dress is finally ready," Mara said. "I suppose now I'll have to be dressing you every morning."

Corrine crawled out of bed.

Mara stared at her. "Breakfast's on," she said. "We should hurry."

Mara followed her behind the dressing screen.

As Corrine shivered out of her nightgown and into the new chemise, she asked, "Have you heard anything about Christina today?"

"No, not a thing." Mara helped her into the corset, which intimidated Corrine with its terrible lacing. She grunted and held to the edge of the screen as Mara pulled the cords tight. Whether this made her look more grown-up or not, Corrine already longed for days when she could still breathe while clothed.

"Can you tell them I'll be there in just a bit?" Corrine panted. She lifted her arms for the crinoline and then for the skirt.

"What are you on to?" Mara said suspiciously.

"Nothing . . . At least, not yet."

Mara shook her head as she fastened the buttons of the skirt, and then the blouse.

Corrine pulled on her jacket as Mara went toward the fireplace. "Better not be up to no good. Father Joe'll have your hide." She knelt and picked up the ash bucket and broom and began to sweep away the ashes of last night's fire.

"I'm not. Really and truly."

Mara stood when she was finished and went toward the door with the bucket. "Good. Then best get to breakfast."

Corrine nodded. She wrapped herself in a shawl that Miss Brown had left her, pulled on her boots, and crept outdoors into the dawn.

She tried to hurry, but the corset made it almost impossible to breathe and itched terribly in odd places—the small of her back, on the left side of her ribcage. Everything rustled when she walked as though she carried a pile of crackling leaves in her dress. The chill soaked into her such that by the time she reached the gazebo, her teeth chattered and her fingers shook.

Her boots echoed on the aged marble as she stepped up into the empty gazebo. Looking around, Corrine tried to deny her disappointment. She'd been half-hoping he would be waiting for her there. She spied a damp paper sack tucked in one of the darker corners. She scooped it up, unwrapping the top to look at its contents. A black apple squatted beside a pure gold feather. The proximity of the two things made Corrine faintly nauseated. It felt wrong for two such opposite things to touch each other. She bit her lip as she closed the sack and walked as quickly as she could back through the labyrinth.

All through breakfast, she kept the sack concealed under her shawl. Sir James was unusually quiet and didn't acknowledge anyone for the duration of the meal. Ilona ate her meals upstairs as she watched over Christina. Father Joe barely touched his food before he left. Corrine tried to eat in as measured a pace as she could, but the porridge tasted like glue, the toast like sodden paper. At last, she was permitted to excuse herself and returned upstairs, holding the sack against her side.

She crept to Christina's room and opened the door.

"Where have you been?" Ilona said, her eyes dull.

Corrine put a finger to her lips, smiling.

She drew the sack from beneath her shawl and unwrapped the apple and feather. Ilona's gaze went to them, and then to Corrine's face.

Corrine was surprised at the revulsion that crept across Ilona's normally stoic features.

"What did you do?"

Corrine stopped where she stood.

"Did you go to the Unhallowed?" Ilona said.

Corrine was shocked at Ilona's accusatory tone. "I never . . . I didn't . . . No!"

"Then who?" Ilona said. "Where does this magic apple come from, if not them?"

Corrine didn't want to give him away, but after a long silence, she didn't know what else to tell Ilona. "Euan," she said finally.

"Euan?" Ilona said. "My fencing master?"

"Yes. Euan. The fencing master. The gamekeeper. And Half-Born. Like me."

Ilona stared at her in bewilderment.

Corrine realized she hadn't told them about herself because she'd been afraid of what Ilona or Christina would say, that they would shun her again as they had at the school.

"Half-Born?" Ilona said.

She stood, crossing her arms defensively across her chest. Visions of Ilona in armor and with a shield still clashed with her long dress, the shawl she drew about her for warmth.

"Some of us are part-Fey," Corrine began.

"Hallowed or Un-?" Ilona said.

"Ilona—"

"Which is it, Corrine? Good or bad? You told us the Hallowed were good and the Unhallowed were bad. Which do you come from?" Ilona said.

"I don't know." The apple was growing heavy in her hand, the feather duller. She would almost have said they were somehow losing their properties, becoming less magical.

"Or you will not tell?"

"I don't know!" Corrine said. She moved toward the bed where Christina lay like a living statue. Ilona blocked her way.

"Ilona, it's hard to believe, I know. But trust me. Trust Euan. He wants to help. I think he can help where the rest of us can't."

The thought briefly entered her mind that she could force Ilona to do her will. But even if Ilona never remembered being so manipulated, Corrine would never forgive herself.

Ilona stared at her for a long moment, towering, her eyes so dark and terrible that Corrine had difficulty holding her gaze. Then, Ilona's visage cracked. The tears she had been holding came. "Corrine, she's dying. I just can't bear it."

Corrine embraced her. Ilona's chin was hard against her skull. She murmured against Ilona's collarbone, "But if we can save her and we don't try, could you bear it any better?"

Ilona sighed and Corrine thought a tear fell on her scalp.

"No," Ilona said, releasing her at last. "No. You are right." She patted Corrine's arm awkwardly, then stepped back.

Corrine went to the bedside. The apple was gaining gravity, losing its magic. Its skin no longer gleamed, and it was matte black like new cast iron. The feather was the dull gold of beech leaves.

She touched the feather to the apple, and the feather transformed to a golden knife in her hand. She sliced the apple quickly, and it wept juice like sticky, black blood, though its flesh was white. Quickly, she slid the slice between Christina's lips. She bent to the shell of Christina's ear. "Eat it," she whispered. "It will make you well."

At first, there was nothing, no movement, the bit of apple skin bleeding obscenely on Christina's blistered lips. Then, the apple disappeared. Christina took a deep breath, and it was as though the sun bloomed under her skin. The familiar roses spread across her porcelain cheeks; the pallor fled. She sighed again and opened her eyes.

Before she could speak, Corrine shoved the apple at her. "Here, eat the rest." The feather-knife dissolved in her hand.

Christina lifted her hand shakily to take the apple from Corrine and began eating. Corrine's glance flicked to Ilona, who watched as she clutched the folds of her skirt, unsure whether she witnessed a celebration or a mockery.

Corrine wiped her mouth with her fingers, and she tasted the juice on her fingertips. As she watched Christina consume the black apple, her craving was terrible. The smell of the apple was sweeter than every spring in every apple orchard she had ever walked through as a child. Slowly she lowered her hand from her face, slowly closed her eyes against Christina devouring it.

But at last Christina was done. She was still weak. But she was awake and alive. Ilona hugged her and she opened her eyes.

"Thank you, Corrine," Christina said. "I do not know what you did or how you did it, but thank you."

Corrine nodded, unable to speak. A bitter taste set in, eclipsing the wild sweetness of the apple forever. She thought she might cry.

"I'm sorry," Ilona said, as she released her.

Father Joe and Miss Brown entered then, each rushing to Christina's bedside when they saw the girl was awake. Miss Brown took her hand and maternally pushed a stray curl from Christina's brow. Father Joe's smile lit his face in a way Corrine hadn't seen since she'd known him.

The apple core on Christina's bedside table shimmered and disappeared before anyone else saw it.

"What happened, Christina?" Miss Brown said.

Christina's eyes went to Corrine's. Corrine put her hand to her lips in a shushing gesture. The smell of the apple was completely gone.

"I woke up when Corrine came in the room," Christina said. "And I felt better."

A look passed between Father Joe and Miss Brown. "Corrine must be gifted with healing," Miss Brown said, smiling and straightening the covers around Christina. "I suppose I shall have to write to your parents again and let them know you'll recover fully. They might fear the worst when my other letter arrives."

Christina smiled, but Corrine could see no true emotion behind it. She wondered again what Christina had done to be sent to Falston and what lay in the chasm between Christina and her parents. She doubted that she would ever know, though she was unsure how Christina's secret could be any more terrible than her experiences with the Unhallowed.

"We'll let you rest," Father Joe said. "Come, ladies."

They were all filing to the door, when a knock came and Mr. Turnbull entered. His hair was pressed flat over his forehead and his sallow skin made Corrine wonder if he ever left the manor house.

"Sir James requests the Council members to join him in the study at once," the man said, nodding his head sharply.

They followed Mr. Turnbull out of Christina's room and into the corridor. Corrine stopped with Ilona at her door while Father Joe and Miss Brown went on ahead. The butler vanished down the stairs.

Ilona laid her hand on Corrine's forearm. "Thank you," she said.

Corrine smiled. She could feel the trust in Ilona's grip and was glad of it. "I will go now to practice with Euan," Ilona said. "Should I thank him too?"

Corrine shook her head. "He asked me to keep it a secret. I'd rather he thought I did."

Ilona winked and entered her room.

Corrine hurried on toward the landing; Miss Brown and Father Joe were probably already downstairs waiting on her. She dropped briefly into her room to divest herself of the shawl; it made her feel uncomfortably like a widow. Or one of the three veiled ladies. She shivered at the dream of them hiding behind the throne last night. At the same time her stomach rumbled, a flash of gold from the bed caught her eye.

The Book of the Unhallowed.

She drew a swift, painful breath. A scrap of paper lay across it that read in painstaking, uncertain letters: *I foond yer booke. —S*

S? She looked at the tidy bed, the swept hearth, and understood. S. Siobhan.

But how had she mysteriously just found it? As she picked it up Corrine felt the serpents slide across the cover. She thought of Kenneth. She was certain he had died because he had returned the book to her from Sir James's study. If Sir James had finally taken it and hidden it from her, Corrine's life would have been in danger. But if Siobhan had taken it, that would explain why Sir James was still angry and suspicious of her. If, in fact, he was angry and suspicious. Father Joe still seemed to think Sir James was blameless.

She lifted the book and opened it at random, wondering if the book would finally reveal itself to her.

Letters swam up as she squinted, realizing she should hurry. The Council waited.

To force truth from mortals . . . To bind Hallowed power . . . To tame . . .

She shut the book and slid it into her petticoat pocket, then dashed down the stairs, trying to push away her dread.

Father Joe and Sir James were in the middle of an animated conversation when Corrine entered the room.

"Corrine, we were wondering where you'd gotten to again," Miss Brown said. "I sent Mara for some toast and now it's gone cold."

Miss Brown gestured at a chair around the table and Corrine slid into it, avoiding the silent glares from the opposite side of the table.

"What happened now?" Father Joe wanted to know. "Were you called to rescue another damsel in distress?"

Corrine kept her eyes on her toast as she ladled marmalade across it, hungry as she had not been at breakfast. "No, Father," she said. She glanced up for a moment and considered telling them about the return of the book, but thought better of it. Sir James was still after it. She would tell Father Joe in private.

Miss Brown said, "Another body was found, drained of all blood in the forest."

"Another?" Corrine said.

"One of the dog handlers," Miss Brown said behind her hand.

Corrine held her toast halfway to her mouth in shock. Marmalade dripped from the edge and splattered onto her plate.

"Who found him?" she managed to ask.

"The lead handler," Miss Brown said.

Corrine wondered if that was why Euan hadn't been waiting with the paper sack in the gazebo this morning.

"Came upon the dead handler this morning when he was working the dogs. They went right to him," Sir James said.

"Do you know anything about this, Corrine?" Father Joe asked.

She stared at them, aghast. Mara entered with a tea service, the china cups tinkling gently as she walked.

"No," Corrine said. "I don't have any idea."

Mara set out the cups and poured tea. Corrine reached for hers to chase away the chill in her hands.

She was about to take a sip when Sir James asked, "You're certain?" He looked at her just as he had when he'd accused her of being responsible in some way for the other deaths.

"No, sir," she said. She glanced at Father Joe. "You don't think I—"

"No, no," Father Joe said. "Nothing like that. Just . . . if you have any idea why the Unhallowed might have struck last night."

If it had just been Father Joe, Miss Brown, and Mara, she might have been able to admit she'd gone seeking help. But with Sir James sitting there, glaring at her from under his bushy brows, she found she couldn't.

"Corrine," Miss Brown prodded gently.

"No," she said at last, her voice hoarse with fear. She cleared her throat. "No, I don't know."

"Has the Prince come to you? Or tried to contact you in any way?" She thought of the dream last night. *You have given your love to another.*

"No," she said. "I haven't seen him again since the ball." She didn't want to reveal the dream in front of Sir James and face more possible accusations from him.

"And yet, this morning," Sir James said, "Christina is mysteriously well."

She felt the noose of their questioning tightening, and she wondered why every Council meeting always seemed to end this way. Much as she disliked the lies, they came easier than ever. "We worked on charms for healing yesterday. I tried one last night. Maybe it worked."

Glances flew around the room.

"Maybe," Sir James said. He signaled Mara to pour more tea.

Mara looked very much like she would like to pour it on his hand instead of into his teacup as she lifted the pot.

"And maybe," Sir James continued, "there is something darker at work here."

"Sir James," Miss Brown said.

"Quiet, woman," he said.

Miss Brown stared at him. Few men spoke to her so perfunctorily. Though many women endured such treatment, Miss Brown had always demanded respect simply in her demeanor. She was a far cry from the ornamental adornment that many women strove to become. Corrine could see a sharp answer building in the headmistress.

Father Joe spoke before Miss Brown could. "Sir James, you know how much we appreciate your generosity, and how much, as fellow members of the Council, we hope for your continued good will, but—"

Sir James spoke as though Father Joe had not said anything. "What I'm telling you is that since you have come to Fearnan, there has been nothing but trouble. I've seen the reports from Falston. Trouble started there when this girl showed up."

"Sir James, that is not entirely true—" Miss Brown began.

"Quiet, I said!" He slammed his fist down and the teacups danced. Corrine shrank from the table.

"I have seen the reports! The Unhallowed were able to enter Falston only after Corrine arrived. And the same is true here!" Sir James shouted. He leaned over the table at Corrine. "William has long been a friend to me, but I believe he took a serpent into his bosom when he took you in, girl. How we are all paying for it now!"

If this had happened a few months ago, she might have cried. As it was, she slipped her hand into her pocket, letting the serpents glide beneath her fingers. She observed Sir James as she might a strange animal. Her detachment only infuriated him more.

"Well!" he shouted. "What have you to say for yourself?"

Father Joe and Miss Brown tried to speak simultaneously, but Mara's words rang out first.

"That's enough, Mr. James," she said.

"How dare—" he began.

Mara pulled something from the pocket of her apron and threw it across the table. It rolled, scattering mud and bits of black cord. A few rusting pins fell out of it and hit Sir James's saucer with a *tink*.

"You think I don't know what this is? Or who laid it?"

Sir James looked to Miss Brown and Father Joe, as if it were beneath him to quell this impetuous servant. When neither of them spoke, he said, "I don't know what you mean."

"You know damn well what I mean."

"Mara!" Miss Brown said.

Mara's anger gave her height; her black eyes flashed and Corrine saw again the tall, mossy trees leaning over a scarlet cradle, a ripple of alligator eyes rising above the black water.

"I'm not above having you taken out of here and horse-whipped, young lady," Sir James said. "So, by all means, enjoy your accusations while you have time to make them."

"Mara," Father Joe said in a low voice, "have a care."

"That man who died last night—he was a conjure-man. I knowed it not long after I met him in the servant's mess. You had him set the root on me, but for the longest time I couldn't find it; I was just too weak. Then, when I dug the root up out of the stable last night, you had him killed so he couldn't talk. It wasn't no Unhallowed killed him. He had a drain hole in his back, not in his throat. No one drank him."

Sir James's laugh was forced. "My, what a storyteller you are. But you can't prove anything. I should have you jailed for slander. In an iron box. You'd like that, wouldn't you?"

A malicious, spidery gleam flitted across his features as he leaned forward and grasped the wax doll. He threw it into the fire. The pungence of burning hair and dust filled the room.

"My patience is at an end," Sir James said. His edges started to go grainy and cloudy. He pushed away from the table and stood. His body altered and warped. Corrine saw something dark and many-headed look out at her as though from a mirror. "I have waited long enough on all of you. And now, I will wait no more."

Mara snarled. Just as the cuideag shed the skin of Sir James, Mara's skin rippled into fur, her fingers into claws. As she leaped, Father Joe tried to stop her, but the power of her momentum sent him sprawling. The black panther cleared the table, scattering teacups and biscuits everywhere. The cuideag's heads screamed. The many-barbed tail poised to strike.

Father Joe got up and pushed Miss Brown and Corrine back.

Mara pounced on the scorpion-like beast, sending it skittering into the fire.

Corrine imagined the cleansing fire of life sweeping in and consuming the creature, shriveling its horror into chitinous ash. Green flame surged from her, consuming part of the table, the chairs, bursting the delicate porcelain cups with its heat. It caught the tail of the creature as Mara stalked around it, trying to find an entry point. The little heads screamed as the flames wrung them into shadow.

Then there was silence and the smell of singed carpet and burned hair.

Mara stood in panther shape where the cuideag had been, her shoulders heaving.

"Mara," Father Joe said. *"Mara!"*

There was still some power left in him, even if it appeared he could only use it in short bursts. The panther shifted back into the girl, who leaned on the broken table for support. Corrine gaped. The cuideag and Sir James were gone.

Miss Brown helped Mara to sit. Corrine, feeling useless, began picking blasted porcelain up from the floor and laying it in the one undamaged saucer. Mara tried to rise when she saw Corrine cleaning up, but Miss Brown pressed her back into her seat, saying, "No, Mara, I'll do it. Sit for a while."

Father Joe looked at Corrine. "You were right, as usual," he said. "I didn't want to believe it, but you were right."

Corrine nodded. For once, she was not pleased to have been proven correct.

Miss Brown looked up from where she helped Corrine with the china. "But does that mean that Sir James is dead?"

"It might," Father Joe sighed.

"Then what should we do? Should we hold a funeral?" the teacher asked.

Father Joe shook his head. "Let's wait a while. I'll tell the household that Sir James has gone to visit a friend somewhere, Pitlochry maybe. Perhaps the Unhallowed are keeping him prisoner. Though, I, like you, fear the worst."

There was a long silence in which the fire crackled and Corrine could hardly bear to breathe for the heaviness in the room.

"We must get the rathstones back as soon as possible," Father Joe said. "Somehow, we must open that rath and get them back."

"But we don't know where the rath opens," Miss Brown said. "We've been searching, but it's still unclear. And with the Prince on the loose, exploring the forest more closely isn't very wise."

Corrine thought of the magic charm that would summon Euan, but she resisted that idea again.

Where are you? she thought at the Prince. She realized with a chill that if she volunteered to go, she would indeed fulfill his prophecy that she would come to him. But she was also certain that she alone would find the entrance and that she alone would be admitted.

"I'll go," she said.

Everyone looked at her.

"Corrine," Miss Brown said.

Father Joe held up his hand, his gaze locking with Corrine's.

"No. I think Corrine feels responsible. And it's likely that the Prince will believe she is coming to him of her own accord. She is valuable to him; he won't harm her."

Corrine heard echoes of Brighde's charge. *Only you can kill the Prince . . .*

"This is very dangerous, Corrine," Miss Brown said. "You do understand, don't you?" Her blue gaze was gentle as velvet. Corrine saw hints of the woman her uncle must have fallen in love with, the woman he loved still.

"I do," she said.

"The pillywiggin still owes us another favor," Father Joe said. "Perhaps he can help us open the rath and go along for protection. He can help disguise you, if needs be."

Corrine slid the serpent-bound book from her pocket and placed it on the table.

"I also have this," she said.

Before anyone could speak, Corrine said, "I don't know who had it. It was returned to me this morning with a note saying that it had been found. I'm just going to be glad that whoever saw fit to return it did so."

She would not incriminate Siobhan. She felt tender for the girl who hated the Unhallowed so much that she wouldn't use the gifts buried inside her. Corrine guessed that Siobhan might have Half-Born blood—it would account for her Sight—but Siobhan would never use it, never consider it anything other than devilry. And for that, Corrine felt a deep pity.

"This is good," Father Joe said. "I will summon the pillywiggin."

Corrine nodded. The book might help, but she was sure the best way to find the Prince wasn't between its pages.

Conversation ensued about summoning the pillywiggin and readying Corrine magically for her venture, while attempting to anticipate any contingency. Corrine fidgeted in her seat and listened with only half her attention. Now that it had been decided, she simply wanted to be away. She wished briefly that she had Ilona's skill with weapons or in battle or, not for the first time, Christina's skills with charm.

At last, the deliberations were over. Father Joe and Mara adjourned to summon the pillywiggin, while Miss Brown went to see to Christina. Corrine picked up the serpent-bound book. She clasped it to her chest as she left, thinking of how she would soon have to kill a man with a heart of stone.

~ NINETEEN ~

February 23, 1866

EVENING CAME. SUPPER WAS SUBDUED AND TENSE. Corrine's fingers shook so hard she could barely hold her soup-spoon. She had begged a black-handled kitchen knife off of Mara, who had said only, "Whatever you do to him will hurt you too. Remember that." Corrine had nodded and bound the knife in a scrap of leather she'd found in the stables. She'd stayed away from Ilona's fencing practice in the afternoon, unwilling to be distracted with thoughts of Euan and the favor he had done all of them by helping save Christina. She needed to concentrate, and concentration was no longer possible in his presence.

Everyone went out onto the patio after dinner. The peak of the gazebo rose through the fog. Mara whispered softly, her call echoing out across the winter garden.

There was nothing for a long time. Then he came like a torch, zipping this way and that, stopping only long enough for Corrine to lose him again in the fog. His hair was like witch-light dipping between mist, boxwoods, and naked trees.

At last, he stopped in front of Corrine. "You want to go to him now, eh? Had enough of here?"

Corrine shook her head, confused.

The pillywiggin's eyes widened then. "Ah," he said, giggling,

"But you can't go to a murder dressed like that."

Corrine blushed.

The pillywiggin assessed her, sculling around on a stream of air around her head. Then he snapped his fingers and sprinted up through the fog.

There was darkness and silence. He was gone. Again.

Then a shower of light exploded above Corrine's head. She cringed as the sparks drifted down around her, but they were as soft and glittering as snow. They wove around her in a net and where they touched, she changed. Her skin turned black, blacker than Mara's, but with a slick, blue sheen that caught and held the magical light raining down on her. Her hair fell blue and coarse past her waist. Her ears grew into the sides of her head and nearly disappeared. Her nose flattened, her mouth widened, and her eyes tilted and narrowed. Gill slits opened along either side of her throat. She gasped at how the air burned and she cupped her neck with slightly webbed hands. Soon enough, her body seemed to realize she was in air and stabilized.

She looked down at herself and cringed, much as she had when she'd worn the pirate queen costume. The dress was made of some dark, fine material like silken shadows, embroidered and edged with what looked like shimmering cobwebs. Next to her skin, the dark fabric made it look as though she wore only cobwebs, though in truth there were layers of fabric between her and the growing night. A hooded cloak of the same material, embroidered with thousands of tiny, spider-silk stars came to rest over her head and shoulders, making her feel at least slightly more modest.

The rain of sparks stopped and the pillywiggin appeared before her, wagging a long fingertip at her. "Nixes were never known for modesty. You'll give it away if you act human. Which you aren't." He grinned.

She tried to stand a little straighter. The air felt liquid and alive in a way she'd never before experienced. She thought about holes and dark places where water sprung from the earth. About wells and ways to lure humans to come drown in them . . . She shook her head.

Witch-light erupted from the pillywiggin's fingertips. He juggled the little fires, often letting them hang frozen in midair before tossing them about again. Green dots coruscated the fog. "Remember, this is no glamour. Until this night ends, you *are* a nix." He tilted his head on the side like a bird. "Unless something else happens."

His body dissolved into the dancing green fires, then swam under her hood. Turning like a cat, he tickled her about the head and ears until he finally settled in a band around her head. She put a hand to her forehead and felt a garland of flowers.

The pillywiggin's whisper tickled her ear. "I'll ride like this," he said. "Then I can tell you what to do. If you listen." He giggled. Corrine wondered how he would manage to stay in one position for such a long time.

"Now, go to the heart of the labyrinth," he said. "The gate is there at that old temple."

"Old temple?" Corrine said.

"Not so loud," the pillywiggin said. "At the center of the labyrinth—the little white building."

"The gazebo?" Corrine whispered.

"Yes. That."

Corrine burst out, "But that would mean . . ."

"Shhhh," the pillywiggin said.

Corrine noticed that everyone was looking at her.

"He says the entrance to the rath is in the labyrinth under the gazebo."

"My word," Father Joe said. "No one wonder the Prince got into the ball so easily!"

271

"And why he sent his raven to stop you from seeing it," Miss Brown said.

I don't think that was really him, Corrine thought. But she didn't want to speak about the three veiled women. She didn't want to invoke them accidentally.

"We should go now," the pillywiggin said in her ear.

Corrine looked at everyone, their faces were lost in the dusk. An odd, unsettling hunger for them made her step back from Ilona when she would have hugged her.

"Best not," she said under her breath.

Ilona nodded. "Christina wishes you well," she said. Their friend was still abed, but nearly strong enough to resume her studies.

"Corrine," Miss Brown said. "I wish I had something to give you to help you, but I have little more than advice. Keep your wits about you, and know that we believe in you."

"Return safely to us," Father Joe said.

Mara didn't say anything, just nodded slightly.

"Time to go now," the pillywiggin said, tightening himself uncomfortably about her brow.

She took a deep, burning breath and walked down the stairs and into the labyrinth.

The dark columns of the gazebo pushed through the fog. Corrine felt ridiculous as she went to the side of the mound, bent, and knocked on the grass.

A figure stepped out into the night, a tall, cloaked person she knew all too well. She choked and backed up a few steps.

"Steady," the pillywiggin hissed. "He's the Prince's envoy; he greets all the Prince's guests."

He's also the witch's hound, she thought. She remembered his face and shuddered.

The Captain pointed. And just as it had always been in her dreams, a hole opened in the earth. Witch-light streamed from it, bathing her in light that somehow didn't hurt her eyes as much as fire or the sun would have. She peered down into the hole and saw the broken city, glistening with the same lurid light. A faint singing from somewhere in the city's heart lured her.

The Captain gestured for her to hurry. He didn't know her. Apparently, all he saw was a nix holding up the beginning of his lord's celebration. She stepped inside.

She was walking along a road with many other Unhallowed beings. For the first time, she saw them whole rather than as flashes of frightening eyes, thorny smiles, or branching fingers. She them all—phooka and ellydan, nereid and nix—all in glimmering fins and trailing finery, bearing gifts for their lord on this full moon night. She panicked, thinking that she had no gift and would, thus, somehow come under suspicion. But the pillywiggin whispered to her, as she looked wildly around, that she could pretend that the book was the gift she gave, that she could say she'd tricked one of the human servants at Fearnan into dropping it into her well.

"Calm," whispered the pillywiggin. "A nix is never hurried or agitated. You are still as deep water. You lay in wait until the right moment."

She only hoped that when that moment came, she could play the proper part.

None of the other supplicants spoke to her as they all made their way toward the city center. Hobgoblin guards stood watch over the palace gates with cruelly curved halberds. Corrine kept her eyes lowered as she entered.

The singing was so loud now that she could barely hear the pillywiggin when he whispered to her. It was a double-voiced harmony. One voice called from her right, down a dark corridor; the other called from directly ahead, where most of the other Unhallowed were headed. She paused to adjust her hood and cape.

"What should I do?" she asked, turning her head aside so no one could hear.

"Follow the singing down the corridor," the pillywiggin advised. "The other we can take last." And she knew all too well what that taking would entail.

She slid deeper into the shadows, an uncommonly easy thing with her pitch-black skin. Then she crept down the hall, hoping her webbed feet didn't slap too loudly on the wormy wood.

She had no difficulty finding the chamber; the singing was deafening. "Can no one else hear this?" she muttered to the pillywiggin.

"What you hear is the rathstones we seek. The Unhallowed cannot hear or feel the stones. It is part of their curse. And why they need Half-Born like you, who can walk between raths and the mortal world to find them."

"They don't hear this?" Corrine said.

"Quiet," the pillywiggin said. "They can't hear the rathstone, but they can hear *you!*"

Corrine stood before the door, uncertain as to how she would enter. There was no lock or handle.

She put her hand on the door, trying to determine its sturdiness or feel for cracks she might not see in the dimly lit hall. Suddenly, blunt teeth gnawed at her hand. She drew back, so shocked that she felt the gills on her throat gasp open in pain.

"Bah . . . nix," a snarling, wizened face in the door said, spitting as if it had tasted something awful. Its bulbous chin and broken teeth reminded Corrine of a troll.

"It's a riddle lock," the pillywiggin whispered.

The face regarded her with watery, mud-colored eyes. "Riddle," it said. Its voice reminded her of her old teacher, Miss de Mornay, who had died in the Unhallowed destruction of Falston—somewhere between a hiss and the slide of a dull blade against stone.

"Riddle?" she said.

The lock sighed and rolled its eyes. "I tell a riddle. If you guess it, you tell me one. If I can't guess it, then I let you in."

"And if you do?"

"Surely a nix knows better. The Prince will know someone tried to enter his treasury."

"That hardly seems fair," Corrine said.

The lock stared at her.

Corrine's fingers twitched. She had loved riddle games as a child, but it had been long since she'd played them and the stakes had never been so high.

She closed her eyes. "All right," she heard herself say.

The door recited its riddle, its eyes bulging out with pleasure:

> "Alive as you but without breath,
> As cold in my life as in my death;
> Never a thirst though I always drink,
> Dressed in a mail but never a clink."

Corrine thought a moment. "Fish," she said. She had been baited as easily as that selfsame creature too. Now she would have to think of something to stump the lock, something that would not cause it to call the whole city down upon her.

The pillywiggin was silent. If the lock knew she had help, the game would instantly be forfeit.

There had been one her mother had told her many ages ago, one that had tormented her for several days. How had it gone?

> "The beginning of eternity
> The end of time and space
> The beginning of every end,
> And the end of every place."

If the riddle lock had had arms or fingers, she guessed it would have scratched its head. It hemmed and hawed, opening its mouth to speak and then closing it when it couldn't produce an answer.

At last, the lock rolled its eyes. The door slid up.

Corrine went inside the room, which was little more than a hollowed-out cavern. The singing was so deafening that she had to force herself to keep her hands at her sides. Roots hung from the ceiling and protruded from the dirt walls. Cobwebs festooned the roots while little glowing worms moved through the dirt.

"What was it?" the pillywiggin shouted into her ear.

"What?" Corrine whispered, not daring to shout.

"The solution to the riddle!"

Corrine smiled. "The letter 'e'," she said.

"Hmmph." If the pillywiggin had been floating before her, he would have crossed his arms across his chest in consternation.

Corrine surveyed the hoard. There were many things she'd hardly count as treasures—broken goblets, bits of bone, old, faded portraits.

One of them caught her eye in the dim witch-light. It leaned against a wall, half-shadowed, but she thought she'd glimpsed a familiar feline smile . . . She knelt and grasped the rotting frame.

"Mary Rose," she breathed. This was a different portrait than the one that had haunted her since the time she'd seen it in her mother's trunk. It was a full-length portrait, and Mary Rose was dressed all in white, a splendid ermine stole clasped around her neck. The iron cross was gone, but the smile was still there. The eyes seemed to come alive and hold her gaze.

"Corrine," the pillywiggin prodded. "The door will not be open forever."

She nodded and released the portrait, standing. The singing was all around her, such that she barely knew where to turn to look for the stone.

"There," the pillywiggin said. She felt a tiny hand pull at her hair to direct her eyes to the spot.

It reminded her very much of the time she had taken the stone from Mara's wardrobe. Objects surrounded it, obviously spells and charms set against its theft. She wondered how the Prince, who couldn't bear to touch the stone and certainly couldn't feel it as she could, had been able to set such wards. And how she would get through them. It was only as she got closer, and the dim light revealed the objects that she stopped.

Many of the things were bits and pieces of her childhood, things lost that she had never expected to see again. There was a tiny portrait of her and her mother that had been lost just after her father went to war. There was a sketchbook of hers that had gone missing when she was eight. A rag doll Nora had made for her that she had cried oceans over when it had been lost by the Elk River. A little wooden horse her father had carved. And, hanging above the place where the stone glimmered in the wall, a little golden book on a golden chain—her locket.

A sob tore out of her.

The pillywiggin unwound from her head and zipped to life in front of her, blocking her view.

"This won't do," he said, putting his hands on his waist. He looked much denser and heavier here, as though he were made of lead. "This is part of how he made you do his bidding. Why are you surprised?"

Corrine shook her head. It was as though someone had stolen her heart, dissected it in secret, and hung its pitiful corpse on a wall. She had no idea why it hurt so much or how to stop it from hurting.

"No, no, no," the pillywiggin said, growing duller and more exasperated by the moment. He stomped the air.

She dashed at her eyes with her hands and glimpsed white

flesh. Her tears were causing the pillywiggin's spell over her to dissolve.

"Control yourself or we fail," the pillywiggin said.

Corrine gritted her teeth, took a breath, and nodded. Night-black inked her hands again.

The pillywiggin taught her the words to say, the words that would allow her to break the warding spell and take the stone from its place in the wall. The first time she tried, nothing happened. The invisible wards held. The pillywiggin wouldn't even allow her to test them.

"Have faith," he said. "Unless you want to call all the Unhallowed down on us."

She tried again, pushing the hurt out of her heart, clearing space to allow her to work. It was more delicate than anything she'd ever tried to do and she wished briefly that Mara did this instead. She understood now why Father Joe had insisted she try to control the flames. Without control, there was no way to direct the power.

She breathed, imagining herself floating across the surface of the water, beyond the towers of the East and into the garden of the Sun. There in the garden, she watched the sparks of life drift through her bower, and there in the jeweled net they made, she saw the opening. She reached toward it, chanting softly, "Return that which has been taken. Release that which must be free."

She reached in, brushing a buzz of invisible power that sent chills down her arm. She closed her fingers around the stone.

She backed away and faced the door. But the locket drew her back. Without thinking, she turned and plunged her hand through the slicing cold of the wards, tearing the locket down from where it hung on a root above the stone.

An eldritch shriek trembled throughout the treasury, rising until the entire city reverberated with it. The pillywiggin moaned and disappeared. Corrine heard the harsh grinding of stone against stone and turned to see the door closing. She ran to the door, but it was down before she could get under it or figure out how to keep it from closing.

Then, the lights went out, and she was alone in the shrieking dark.

~ TWENTY ~

February 24, 1866

CORRINE DIDN'T KNOW HOW LONG SHE'D SAT IN THE DARK. The shrieking eventually stopped and there was stillness. She wished she had learned the trick of lighting a candle as Father Joe had tried to show her, but even if she could have, she had no idea where a candle might be. It was deadly dark, but her eyes slowly adjusted. The worms' faint glow was just bright enough to allow her to find a hiding place. She crawled across the floor and hid behind a tilted stack of portraits.

"Pillywiggin?" she whispered. "Pillywiggin!" But he was nowhere to be found.

She clutched the locket, silently praying that if her mother and father could hear her, they'd show her the way out.

And then she heard the footsteps.

The lock spoke to someone beyond the door, little more than murmurs. The door slid up and the light rose. Corrine squeezed herself as far behind the portraits as she could.

Two sets of feet patrolled the room, one cloven-hoofed, the other on all-fours—a giant rat by the looks of the feet and the tail hissing behind.

"Find the nix," the satyr guard said, and before she knew it, a great moldy pink nose pushed in behind the portraits and bared yellowed rat-teeth at her. A huge, rough hand pushed the portraits aside and Corrine cowered as they clattered away from her.

"Come on, then," the satyr said. Corrine looked up at his sharp features, his hairy, heavily muscled shoulders. She briefly thought of setting fire to him and everything in this room, but she stood instead and let him take her dark arm, leading her out of the treasury. Fire wouldn't bring the rathstone back to the Council.

The satyr didn't speak to her the entire way, but it kept a firm grasp on her upper arm. She didn't dare try anything. She heard the Prince's voice again, *Next time, you will come to me.* How right he had been after all.

The satyr gave over his rat-hound to the guard at the door of the ballroom and dragged her inside. Courtiers parted before her, smelling of mold and nightshade and the places in the earth where humans feared to venture—the deep oil pits and coal shafts, the eternal night of the seafloor. As she was pulled forward, she glimpsed twisted root columns, hangings of woven moss, pale death orchids blooming from the walls. A steady rain of gold sparkled down from the ceiling, dusting everyone in a fine, glittering sheen. A faint clicking noise drew her gaze upward to the ceiling. It moved like a glittering jet, and she realized that the ceiling was, in fact, alive—a horde of beetles eternally fanning their ebony wings. It was from them that the gold came, frass raining eternally down from their endless enterprise.

The satyr pushed her to the floor before the Prince's dais. The guard knelt behind her. She had only glimpsed the Prince—standing in profile, speaking to a hob through a mask he held to his face. Then he turned and she looked up.

Euan stared down at her, his hazel eyes curious, almost amused. The shock of it made Corrine slip from the nix like a peach peeled from its skin.

"Corrine," he said. And now she knew his voice for true. She bowed her head.

The room went still, except for the beetles' clicking and chewing, which echoed softly in the silence.

"You have come to fulfill our bargain," he said, half-smiling. Before she could speak, he continued. "But you have a strange way of doing so. I never took you for a thief, Corrine, whatever else you may be."

Dark blood stained his shirt—his blood pressed out by the jarring magic of the rathstone that was now his heart.

"I came only to take what you stole," she said.

"As I recall, you gave the stones to us. I did nothing." He smiled again.

"You tricked me!"

He came down off the dais to stand before her. "How did I trick you? When you required it, I gave you health. When you and your friends would have been boiled alive or drowned on board that iron monstrosity, I saved all of you, despite the cost to my domain. When you desired to know your true nature, it was I who told you the truth. I even came to you at great risk to my person simply to dance a waltz with you on your birthday. And now you would come as a thief in the night to steal my rightful possessions?"

"You didn't tell me the truth! You said you were like me—you said you were Half-Born! You made me believe you!" She clenched her fists against the tears that threatened.

"Did I say I was Half-Born? Think again. I told you that my mother was Hallowed, which is quite true. Never once have I lied to you Corrine. I doubt you can say as much of the members of your 'Council'!"

What he said was so true that she didn't know what to say. An aching sob built in her chest, and she struggled to breathe against it.

Brighde had called her a fool; the pillywiggin had disappeared again and left her in the dark. All that was left was this. Through everything, the Prince had been constant in both his aims and his affections. But what about all the girls who had disappeared or died? Jeanette, Penelope, Cecily, the nameless little girl in Killin, even Melanie, who had been tricked and corrupted in the hope of having her dead Confederate lover restored to her.

"You killed all those girls," she said, her voice ragged with sorrow. "And when you didn't kill them, you twisted them to do your will."

"I am a creature of necessity, Corrine," the Prince said. "Mortal blood is my food, just as the creatures of the earth are yours. Do you hear the complaints of the ewe when her lamb is slain for your table?"

"It's not the same."

"Did you not also come here with murder in your heart?" He lifted a hand and her cloak untied itself and slid to the floor. The black-handled knife was revealed at her side.

He unfastened his shirt to the waist and pulled it away from his heart. Horror filled her as she looked at the seeping wound where the rathstone drummed in his chest. Her eyes rose to his face—Euan's face and yet not. The changeable eyes held hers.

"Do it," he said. "For I would rather be slain by your hand than be maligned in your thoughts."

Corrine's fingers found the knife, but it was too heavy to pull from its makeshift sheath. She stared at him in hopeless defeat. She glimpsed his wolfish smile as she bowed her head.

He closed his shirt. She felt the roses encircle her ankle, the thorns needling her skin. "Guard!" he said.

Corrine saw the white flicker first through the golden rain. It spun and cavorted, floated and sang. The pillywiggin sliced through the hall like a clean wind, cutting down tapestries, ripping through dresses, tearing delicate masks. He set all the musicians' instruments to dancing, then hung their strings around their ears. He cut through the canopy over the Prince's dais; it crashed to the floor in a great cacophony.

The Prince gritted his teeth. "A pillywiggin?" he said.

The guard, who had been about to take Corrine, stood watching the pillywiggin dance through the air in awe.

"Take him!" the Prince shouted. The pillywiggin lit upon the Prince's head, kicking witch-light down onto his brow.

Corrine gaped.

"Run, foolish girl," the pillywiggin whispered in her ear before he was off again, breaking pitchers and smearing banquet food on Unhallowed faces.

The Prince was so distracted that he'd completely forgotten her. Corrine edged slowly back into the fray, then turned and slid and stumbled her way to the ballroom doors. The doors were unguarded; the satyrs were frantically running about the grand hall, trying to catch the pillywiggin as he whizzed and zoomed over their heads. A horde of bat-winged spriggins took to the air and pursued the pillywiggin through the twisted columns while everyone else screamed and fought against their imaginary assailant.

The Prince looked back then and saw her at the door. "STAY!" he shouted. The word reverberated through the city. Corrine's ankle was heavy as lead, but she dragged it down the hall for many agonizing minutes until she made it to the unprotected castle gates and headed out into the deserted, broken streets.

Corrine wasn't sure where she was going or how to get out of the city. She realized she had never really thought about getting out on her own; she'd expected the pillywiggin to be there throughout the entire ordeal, guiding her. But she also had a rathstone now. There must be some way to use it to leave this rath and reenter the mortal world.

At that moment, she fetched up short, trying to decide which way to go next. Her breath caught when she saw a man far down the narrow street in front of her. It was so like the dreams of her father that she pulled herself after him without really thinking of the consequences. Was her father here? Had the Unhallowed trapped him? Had he been trying to come to her along?

"Father!" she called. The echoes flew away through the buildings like frightened bats.

The man stopped. She came to him and realized that the darkness of his clothes were simply from stains. His hair was white; his body looked as though it had once carried much weight but now his clothes sagged from his frame. He turned.

"Sir James!" she said. Disappointment bloomed, but the joy of finding him so unexpectedly eclipsed it.

He frowned when he looked at her. "Do I know you, young woman?"

"Yes! I mean, no, not really. But I'm William McPhee's niece, and I'm trying to get back to your estate."

"William McPhee—" He pondered, his white brows furrowing over his sunken eyes.

Then his face lit. "Ah! McPhee! The Council!"

"Come on," she said. And she dragged him along as the sounds of pursuit grew behind them, even though she had no idea where she was going.

They stopped to rest in the shadow of a dilapidated market building. Corrine dared not think about the Prince; it would bring her to tears. Taking the rathstone from her pocket, Corrine looked at it in the eternal twilight. This was the one that she had given to the Unhallowed at Uncle William's; she was sure of it. It had those strange, carved stairs that curled around it. It nestled in her hand like a kitten, full of magical potential that she didn't know how to tap.

"Do you know how to use this?" she asked Sir James.

For answer, he took it from her hand and threw it at the ground.

"What are you—" she began. Stone stairs unfurled toward a decrepit door on a balcony above them that glimmered now with uncertain light. Corrine pushed Sir James ahead of her and watched him disappear through the wavering door. She was about to set foot on the bottom step when a tremor went through her knees. Filled with dread, she turned. The Captain stepped from the twilight. He lunged toward her, and she shrieked, scooping up the stone and pushing herself up the stairs toward the door.

But dragging her ankle was like trying to pull a steamship anchor up with her slight weight. She turned on her back, sobbing as he loomed over her.

"Possum," the Captain croaked. She was grateful she couldn't see his face. But it almost sounded like he was crying too.

"Please, please," she said, "don't take me back there. Please don't—"

He reached for her. She closed her eyes.

His hand clamped around her ankle. Corrine remembered how he had carried the dead girl from the alley and she shuddered to think of him carrying her back to the Prince like a dead doe for his master's table.

And then she felt the thorns retract. Burned roses softened the dusty air and the weight fell from her leg. She opened her eyes and saw wilted petals on the stairs, the Captain kneeling before her.

He didn't touch her again or say anything further. She glanced back toward the door—the light was dying.

"Thank you," she whispered. "Thank you so very much."

Then she pulled herself up the stairs and through the door, tumbling at last onto the dawn-frosted grass at Fearnan.

~ TWENTY-ONE ~

February 24, 1866

CORRINE SAT AT THE TABLE IN SIR JAMES'S STUDY, BLEARY-eyed and exhausted, the sound of the rathstone's song still ringing in her ears. A cup of tea sat cooling before her and most of a slice of soggy toast. Nothing had tasted the same to her since the juice of the apple she had given Christina, and she found she wanted food even less now. Sir James had told his tale, how he had been kidnapped around Samhain, "replaced, I take it, by that monstrous thing," and trying to escape ever since.

"I wandered the streets of the rath for ages, looking for something, though I had no idea what. I'd almost forgotten my own name by the time Corrine found me," Sir James said. "I'm not sure why they kept me alive."

"Probably to keep feeding the glamour on that monster," Mara said.

Father Joe nodded.

Sir James leaned forward in his chair to pick up his teacup. He gasped as though in pain and dug into his waistcoat pocket, frowning.

"Something poked me in the ribs . . . ." He fished the thing out of his pocket and held it out to examine it. His face turned the color of a ripe cherry. "Well, I say."

Between his thumb and forefinger was a sharp bit of flint that hummed as the light reflected off its milky planes. Corrine was too tired to smile, but was glad the ringing in her ears wasn't an echo, but the song of a rathstone returned to its proper place.

"The Fearnan rathstone," Father Joe said.

"I had it with me all along," Sir James said, staring at it. "All that time I wandered . . ." He was so consternated by this that he called for Mr. Turnbull and Mrs. Guthrie to help him to his bed. He left the rathstone on the table near Father Joe. "See you put this back in the chamber where it belongs," Sir James said.

Father Joe nodded, hiding his smile as Sir James departed.

"So, you returned with two rathstones instead of one," Father Joe said to Corrine.

She nodded. She had explained everything that had happened in the rath. When it came to speaking of the Prince and her attempt to wrest the rathstone from him, she had said only, "The knife was taken from me." And that was true. The knife hadn't returned from the rath with her. She couldn't bear to admit that she couldn't bring herself to kill him. She needed time to understand why.

"A pity you couldn't get the Falston stone," he said. "Though I'm glad you brought back what you did, including Sir James."

"What about the pillywiggin?" Miss Brown asked.

Corrine shook her head. "He saved me, but . . . I don't know what became of him."

"And you said it was actually the Captain that let you go?" Father Joe said.

"Yes." She frowned a little, unsure why she had to tell this again. "He released the anklet. It was too heavy for me to lift my leg otherwise."

"Some kind of holding spell," Miss Brown murmured.

"A Mark," Mara said. "To be able to find her too, if needs be."

Miss Brown nodded.

Siobhan burst into the room. "Father Joe, Miss Brown . . ." She gestured frantically. Everyone rushed out into the corridor, tea and toast forgotten. Corrine followed last.

Siobhan led them to where morning light streamed through the front door. Something was huddled on the front steps, an ashen heap that quivered and raised its head as they approached. Corrine pushed through the others, going down on her knees before the pillywiggin. His normally glowing skin was gray and crusted with sores and burns, much as he had been when Father Joe had freed him from the iron box. As he looked at Corrine, she saw that one eye was gone; only a blackened socket remained. She gasped and reached for him, but stopped when she saw him tremble.

"Pillywiggin," she said.

"I came for the last favor," he said. His voice rasped as though his vocal chords had been singed.

"No, no. We need to help you. We'll take you back to your spring."

The pillywiggin shook his head. "No. Only Hallowmere would save me now. And that is closed to all." He shuddered. "I just came to say he is coming for you. The Prince has taken the Iron Oath."

"I don't know what that means," Corrine said. She looked up at the others and saw a strange look in Father Joe's eyes. He knew what this oath meant.

"It means," the pillywiggin gasped, "that he has sworn to take vengeance upon his enemies for the theft of his property himself. If he does not do so, his people may lock him in iron and bury him deep in the root of the world, there to suffer forever—"

"As you suffered," Corrine said.

The pillywiggin shook his head. "That was just malice," he gasped. He twitched and fell forward, his little hands clutching at nothing. He rolled and looked at Corrine with his one good eye. "And now," he said, his voice fading, "that malice is done."

The sunlight set him to shimmering, and in a moment, he was nothing but a clear, shining pool upon the steps. Before Corrine could put her hands out in protest, even that was gone.

Corrine felt Father Joe pull her up from her knees as she wept. He held her to his chest, as he murmured, "This is not done, Corrine. In this, as in so much else, the Unhallowed will pay."

And, as Corrine struggled against her grief for breath, she knew she couldn't agree more.

AFTERWORD

This book could very easily also be subtitled "The Steamship That Ate My Life." In the writing of this book, I became absolutely fascinated with the history of the *Great Eastern* and her designer, Isambard Kingdom Brunel. Obviously, I've taken a great liberty by including the ship in this book; historically at this time, she was laying some of the first telegraph cables across the Atlantic, her grandeur as a passenger ship all but forgotten. Still, with such a history of ghosts and curses, how could I resist?

There are many fascinating references about Brunel and his "great babe." An out-of-print book, *The Big Ship* by Patrick Beaver, provided a great deal of inspiration. Likewise, much information can be found about the lovely countryside surrounding Loch Tay in Scotland. Its history, particularly that of the Isle of Female Saints, drew me. I hope readers feel the same.

ACKNOWLEDGEMENTS

Huge thanks to the Mirrorstone team for all their energy and enthusiasm for this series. Thanks to the usual suspects (you know who you are) for putting up with me through this writing/teaching full-time thing. Special thanks to Jeaniene Frost and Melissa Marr for being wonderful writing friends. Appreciation also goes to the YALSA team and Benito Juarez High School (especially their awesome librarian, Sheryl Osborne) for hosting me in Chicago for Support Teen Literature Day. And, of course, eternal thanks to the husband for putting up with more than everyone else put together.

Will Corrine make a deal with the dark Fey Prince?
Find out in

Between Golden Jaws

CORRINE AND HER FRIENDS RACE TO LONDON IN THE hopes of finding a rathstone that will help them end this terrible war with the Fey. The girls search the Victorian city only to find that their plan has led to more danger than ever before.

With the girls' lives on the line, the Fey Prince offers Corrine a deal: become his consort and her friends can go in peace. Will Corrine fall into the Fey Prince's arms to save her friends? Or can she find another way?